Thin Girls Dont Eat Cake

Lindy Dale

Copyright © 2014

Secret Creek Press

All rights reserved.

ISBN:1502462575
ISBN-13: 978-1502462572

ACKNOWLEDGMENTS

As always there are so many people that have to be acknowledged for their assistance and support in getting a book ready for print. This time it's certainly no different. A huge hug to my beta readers — Anna, Leanne & Julie, my fabulous cover designer, Scarlett and my proof-reader — Caroline, who came to the rescue at the last minute! I'd have never been able to do this without you and I thank you for all of your help (some of it unpaid!). And to my fabulous husband, G, who has listened to so many new plot twists with this book his ears must be bleeding — mwah!

Chapter 1

"Are you serious?"

"'Fraid so."

Looking across the counter at Connor, I swallowed my shock, trying to take control of the hurt raging inside.

"You're breaking up with me?"

"Sorry..."

I stared into Connor's round dark eyes, framed by thin wire glasses and filled with a look that had nothing to do with being sorry. There wasn't a hint of guilt or sorrow, rather a type of grimace that indicated he couldn't understand why he'd gone out with me in the first place. My mind began to whirl. The blood began to boil in my veins as I tried to make sense of the bombshell he'd just dropped.

How could this have happened? I hadn't mentioned the 'L' word. I hadn't been needy or clingy. I'd followed every guideline in that *Cosmopolitan* dating article. Everything had been going so well.

Or it was on my end, anyway.

Connor's and mine had been a whirlwind romance beginning the moment our eyes met over the organic bananas at the supermarket. We'd gone on six dates in the past three weeks. Connor was the perfect gentleman, in fact, so much of a gentleman I was beginning to get a little concerned he hadn't put the hard word on me. Connor told me he loved my hair. He liked the fact I had my own business. He complimented me on my sense of humour and whispered some rather dirty sweet nothings in my ear. We'd even had a romantic picnic under the willow tree at Apex Park with a bottle of *Moet*.

I repeat, *Moet*.

Nobody in Merrifield drank Moet unless they were at a wedding, and even then, the instances of such extravagance were few and far between.

I tilted my head, feeling my brow crinkle in confusion. Okay, not confusion. I was crinkling it purposely so I wouldn't begin to cry because I certainly wasn't giving Connor *that* satisfaction.

"Does this have anything to do with last night?" I asked.

"No, no. I don't think it's going to work between us, that's all."

The shuffling of Connor's feet and the uncomfortable shifting of his body — like he'd suddenly become infested with worms or the victim of a disastrous rash — told another story. What did he take me for?

Last night was the first time Connor and I had done the deed. Being so convinced that he was the one, I hadn't wanted to have sex until the moment was right and him cooking dinner for me at his place seemed like the appropriate time. I'd even bought a matching set of lingerie in preparation. Yes, the knickers were a tad on the snug side when I'd put them on and my boobs were sort of exploding from the bra but Connor loves red. And boobs. Or so he said.

Yet, despite the fact I hadn't eaten all day to ensure my stomach remained as flat as possible and had plucked and shaved my body until it practically begged me to desist, I sensed a certain hesitance on Connor's part after he'd stripped me of my clothes. It was as if his whole demeanour changed when he discovered I wasn't the kind of girl who looked hot in see-through undies.

"Did I suck or something?"

"Of course not."

I gave myself a silent pat on the back. I knew I hadn't. I had certain skills that had been described as 'bloody marvellous' and 'fucking awesome' in the past. Unfortunately, they didn't appear to be enough of a lure for Connor.

"Then, why?"

Connor let out a great big sigh. Clearly, he wasn't expecting the break up to be so difficult. He placed his hands squarely on the counter and looked into my eyes. A muscle twitched at the edge of his jaw.

"Look. I just don't find you that attractive with your clothes off, if you want to know."

My eyes opened so wide they began to smart. They really hurt. "Pardon?"

"You have cellulite, Livvy. Your bum looks like an unpeeled orange. You don't look good naked. In fact, you're way fatter than you led me to believe."

I didn't know whether to be mad or upset or both. How was it possible to be fatter than one looked in real life? So, I wore slimming jeans and a push-up bra. Heaps of girls did. They didn't change the shape of you that much. It was marketing hype to get you to buy stuff.

The hideous truth of the previous night began to sink in. "Is that why we had to have the light off?"

"Partly."

"What's the rest?" I figured I might as well get the full story while he was in a truth-telling mood.

"I thought you were a natural blonde. When the bush doesn't match the garden, well, it's a real turn off."

I could feel my mouth opening and closing involuntarily. The cheek. Nobody was a natural blonde at our age. "So, let me get this straight, you don't want to go out with me anymore because you feel you've been... uh... misled?"

"Something like that. Look, I'm sorry."

"For what? Calling me fat or for the fact that you're a complete arsehole? Tell me, was that wining and dining merely to get me in the sack?"

"Of course not."

Which totally meant it was.

"How many other girls have you picked up in the banana aisle?"

Connor looked sheepish. "Only a couple. But listen, you're a nice girl. I like you — as a person — and I'd be willing to go out with you again after you drop ten or so kilos."

Oh. My. God.

"Get out, Connor. Get out now." Moving from behind the counter, I shoved Connor towards the door and down the two steps that lead to the footpath. I was so tempted to kick his bum on the way out my foot began to rise of its own accord. "Oh, and Connor?"

He turned.

"I might be able to lose a few kilos but you're never going to hide that bald spot by combing hair over it. It's way bigger than it was a week ago."

Slamming the door after him, I leant my forehead against the glass, stopping to take a few deep, calming breaths. My entire body was trembling. My lungs felt as if the air had been sucked from them. A vein had begun to pound on the side of my head. Then, from somewhere inside, a twisted sort of chuckle formed and I started to laugh-cry all in one go.

I might have been dumped but at least I'd given him something to think about. Not that I felt any better for it. The sense of gratification was instantly gone.

Rummaging in my pocket for my keys, I flipped the shop sign to 'Back in 5 minutes', checked that Connor wasn't watching from behind a car or something — because I wouldn't have put it past him to be happy to see me suffer — and bolted down the street to the Maggie's Bakery.

Yes, I was well aware that it was two o'clock in the afternoon and the lunch trade had probably cleaned out the shelves, but if Maggie didn't have any peppermint slices left there was going to be hell to pay.

Chapter 2

My foot tapped impatiently as I watched Maggie slide the glass door of the cake cabinet along. Dark chocolaty stripes of icing beckoned me as she lifted the slice from the tray. The sweet scent of peppermint filled my nostrils as she tonged it into a white paper bag. I was salivating in anticipation.

Okay, not outwardly salivating because that would have made me look like a dog or a deranged person in need of medication, but on the inside I was definitely drooling. I needed a fix. Badly. I wished she'd hurry.

I'd bought three slices to add to the ruse that I was buying for other shop owners along the street, but I could tell from the look on Maggie's face she wasn't having any of it. You wouldn't need to be a rocket scientist to figure out I was going straight back to Doggie Divas to eat the lot myself.

"You okay, love?" Maggie folded the top of the bag and gave it a neat crease. Her eyes fell to my hands clenching and unclenching at my sides.

"Yeah, Maggie, I'm fine."

"Man trouble again?"

The peppermint slice was a dead give away. On happy days, I preferred one of Maggie's monster slabs of mud cake or a creamy chocolate éclair, thick with icing. My favourite though, was the giant cupcakes Maggie made with faces in the icing crafted from lollies. They were like a double sugar hit.

"Connor broke up with me. He didn't like the fact I wasn't a natural blonde. Oh, and he thought he was getting a Lindt chocolate but ended up with a lumpy Picnic bar when he took off the wrapping. Not to worry though, he said he'd take me back if I dropped a few kilos."

"He said you were fat? He's not exactly George Clooney."

I knew Maggie was trying to make me feel better but it wasn't working. "I know."

"Little bugger. You're well shot of him, love. He always was a terrible flirt, even when he was seven. Last week, I caught him chatting up Shannon over the organic bananas in I.G.A. Terrible things he was saying to make her blush, poor child."

"You mean Shannon-down-from-Perth, Shannon?"

It was funny how everyone called her that. Shannon had lived in Merrifield for over three years now. Been here as long as I'd been back from the city.

"The very same. I thought she was going to have a seizure when he asked if she'd squeeze his banana to see if it was too firm."

I felt the blood drain from my face. Connor had used that exact line on me. Which wasn't that bad if you ignored the fact that Shannon-down-from-Perth looked like Ten Tonne Tessie. Not that I meant to think such rude thoughts — Shannon was a lovely girl — but she looked so much like an over-ripe mango, I dreamt of smoothies every time we crossed paths.

So what the hell was Connor's deal? Did he chat up every woman he met in the fresh produce aisle? Had there been nothing special about me at all?

"I don't think he's ever had a girlfriend for more than a week," Maggie added. "So you may have broken a record."

I snorted and took a twenty-dollar note from my wallet, thumping it onto the glass top display case. "That's not the only thing of Connor Bishop's I'd like to break."

*****

By the time I got back to Doggie Divas, I'd eaten two of the peppermint slices and the rush of endorphins had been usurped by the angry pang of guilt at my own weakness. I yanked my key from my pocket and turned it in the lock. Then, I kicked the door open with my toe, shut it with my heel and headed straight for the counter where I dumped the nearly empty bag on the counter. I stared at it for a long while, forcing myself not to eat but it didn't make me feel any better. In fact, all it did was clarify in my mind a fact I'd known for ages but was refusing to admit.

I was a relationship loser. And I was possibly destined to be that way for the rest of my life.

Connor wasn't the only man to dump me in recent history, you see. In fact, I'd been the victim of quite a few ugly dumping episodes over the last two years. It began with Jacob — I'd found him in bed with a girl who looked like me but had far perkier breasts (obviously fake). Then there was Nigel. He seemed so right until he asked if I minded whether he wore some of my underwear under his work clothes. I drew the line at that. The worst was Michael. I'd had a bit of a crush on him at University and jumped at the chance to offer him a place to stay after his return from an extended overseas trip. I didn't mind at all. He bought me flowers and wondered how it was that we'd never found each other sooner. He cooked and cleaned. Plus, he looked absolutely adorable in an apron. Unfortunately, I came home from work to find dinner was not the only thing he'd been cooking. My house was in the process of being raided by a team of black-clad special operations police. Turned out Michael's overseas trip had, in fact, been a stint in jail for possession of a trafficable quantity and he was on the run from the Mafia or a bikie gang or something.

Since then, I'd understandably become a little gun-shy. It was easier to have no man than to risk involving myself with another player.

Until Connor, that was. I'd thought he was different. How wrong could a girl be?

Undoing the bag, I picked at a corner of the last slice and popped it in my mouth. The sweet taste overtook my tongue and I felt the stress begin to melt away. With the chocolate base and icing sending happy hormones rushing to my brain, I blinked away a stubborn tear.

Why was I rendered instantly stupid when a man flirted with me? How come the only men I seemed to attract were either utter weirdos, players or so totally up themselves they couldn't see daylight. Did they see me as some sort of easy target? Surely, that couldn't be the case?

I pulled the slice from the bag and took a bigger bite. Bugger Connor. This binge was his fault. I'd been having such a lovely week and now I was reduced to downing slices in order to overcome my problems. Again.

As I swallowed, the door of the shop opened and Mum bounced in. Her hair newly-coiffed, she bounded up to the counter to give me a kiss. My mother was a rather energetic person. I couldn't remember a time when she'd ever walked.

"Hello, possum." As observant as ever, Mum's eyes dropped to the paper bag on the counter. "Man trouble?"

It was annoying that my mother knew me so well.

"Something like that."

"Dear, dear. Not that lovely boy you were seeing?"

"He turned out to be not so lovely."

A look of sympathy spread over Mum's face. "And how many pieces have you had?"

"One."

Eyebrows rose in disbelief.

"All right, two and a bit. But in my defence, I needed the sugar. I'm very tired. I was up most of the night."

And if I'd known what the result of that would be, I'd never have wasted the sleep time.

Mum reached into her gym bag and pulled out a hanky. Spitting onto the corner, she proceeded to wipe a few stray crumbs from the side of my chin, clucking like a mother hen.

I swiped her hand away. "Mum, please."

My day had been pretty ordinary so far, without her trying to improve the way I looked with a soggy hanky.

"You'll never get a man looking like a washerwoman, you know."

"And I won't get one with my mother treating me like a two year old, either. Can you leave it, please?"

"I was only trying to help."

"Thank you, but it's not the sort of help I need."

"There's no need to get snippy. People will think you're having your period. Or taking drugs."

I groaned. On most occasions, it was pointless attempting to have a sensible conversation with my mother. She had the ability to go off on a tangent that even a person on LSD wouldn't be able to follow.

"So what're you up to today?" I asked, not that I needed to. Mum's outfit of purple Lycra leggings, a fluorescent pink ballet wrap and an Olivia Newton John — circa 1981 — headband spoke volumes. Teamed with her new 80's retro haircut, she looked like an extra in a *Flashdance* remake.

"I've just finished the Advanced Tums & Bums class. That Alice certainly knows how to make me sweat. I thought my bottom was going to drop off." She turned, giving her bottom, which was indeed looking quite pert for a woman her age, a wiggle. "You could do with a little Tums & Bums. Sitting around is making you frumpy."

"Gee, thanks, Mum. I'll keep that in mind. Is there anything else or did you only come in to tell me that?"

"No. Nothing else. Have you seen that new shop going in over the road?"

I had indeed. I'd spent many an hour, when I should have been getting my tax in order, imagining what was behind the rough hessian covering and scaffolding that hid the façade.

"Whatever it is, they're putting an awful lot of work into it. Maybe it's a boutique," I said.

"Speaking of clothes, I bought these for you from the home shopping channel. With all that talk of exercise, I completely forgot." Mum bent and pulled a shiny red carrier from her gym bag, handing it to me. "They were having a clearance."

My hand delved into the bag. I felt a pile of soft fabric. I peered inside, afraid of what I was going to find because...

Well, let's just say Mum's taste in clothes and mine don't exactly see eye to eye. "Are these Spanx, Mum?"

Having never seen a pair in real life, I could only surmise.

"Yes. Every girl of a certain age needs a little help in the support department. They're wonderful for smoothing lumps and bumps."

"Do you wear them?"

"No. I pay eight hundred dollars a year to have my body toned at the gym. I don't need to wear them. But I've heard they're very good."

"So why do I need to wear them?" I took the underwear from the bag, eyeing it in dismay. "Do you think I'm fat?"

"I'm not saying that. I'm merely saying the Spanx could help enhance the look of what God gave you. Tonnes of celebs wear them. You're going to need every scrap of help you can get if you want to nab a husband now that you've exhausted the supply of under forties in town."

My mother was nothing if not honest. Sometimes to the detriment of others' feelings.

"There's no need to remind me."

Shoving the underwear back into the bag, I hid it behind the counter. The way I felt was beyond description. I was twenty-seven years old. A push-up bra and some tummy toning jeans were one thing but I wasn't about to start wearing some suck-me-in-pull-me-up business to impress a man. It wouldn't work anyway. Connor was living proof of that.

Mum gathered the rest of her things. "So, what happened? You know, with the young man?"

"He said my bum look like orange peel. Apparently, he doesn't like girls who look normal."

"Oh well, those undies will come in handy sooner than you think then." With a kiss and a wave, she opened the door to leave. "Toodle-oo. See you later in the week."

"Aren't we having dinner tonight?"

"Um, ah...no. I've uh, double booked myself. I must learn how to use that calendar thingy on my smartphone."

"Where are you going?"

"Go-Karting. So exhilarating."

Exhilarating and driving little cars around a track were not concepts I'd use in the same sentence but Mum seemed to be into anything and everything lately. Last week it had been naked hang gliding from Mount Seymour, the big hill that overlooked Merrifield. "Well, have fun."

"I fully intend to. I bought this great new racing suit to wear. It's pink with a lavender stripe. I'm thinking it might be good for the charity calendar shoot at the end of the year. It could be quite a sexy look if I was leaning over the bonnet of a car, don't you think?"

Oh Lord.

Glumly, I watched my mother leave. I kicked the bag of Spanx further under the counter. I felt like crying again. She hadn't said it in so many words but it was fairly clear that even she thought I was fat. Fat and single.

My life sucked.

*****

My fit of depression growing, I finished off the last of the peppermint slice before heading into the grooming room to tidy up for the day. Usually, I liked to sweep up between clients and give the hydro bath a bit of a whizz over with disinfectant, but the morning had been such a disaster I'd let it slide in favour of feeling sorry for myself.

As I tidied and swept, I considered how my life was shaping up. Not well, by all accounts. Buying Doggie Divas three years earlier was the one bright spot. It had been a godsend at a time when I'd found myself directionless.

I'd graduated from university with a Masters Degree in Journalism five years previously and thrown myself into my job as weather girl at Channel Seven News, buying TV appropriate outfits and getting highlights that cost more than the rent on my tiny flat. I was skinny back then. Having finally sprouted into my body after years of teenage gawkiness, I could wear whatever I wanted. I didn't have to think about exercising or eating rabbit food, I was confident I looked good — but not overconfident, you've only got to share the makeup room with some stunning model to have that knocked out of you pretty quickly.

Still, it was such a stark contrast after being teased every day at school because I wore glasses and had the body shape of a gangly giraffe.

The first twelve months of working life sped past in a blur. I was happy, challenged and fulfilled. The producers noticed me and were talking about promoting me to 'feel good' segments on *The Breakfast Show*, starting after Christmas. I'd also scored a lovely boyfriend in journalist and news anchor Richard Abbott. We'd been set to buy matching Boxer puppies and a townhouse in Mount Lawley when my world came crashing down.

Right, in fact, between having the side of my lovely little Fiat defaced by a woman who turned out to be Richard's disgruntled wife and a dose of something nasty. Of the things I got from Richard, that last one was the one I least expected.

Richard had neglected to tell me about the wife who spent her winters in the north of Western Australia. She appeared on a plane from Broome one Wednesday afternoon and popped by his office to announce her arrival for *Telethon* — she came every year — which in hindsight must have made me look like a bit of a simpleton. How had I *not* known this? Richard was the most well known journalist in Western Australia. Everyone — well, except me — knew he was married.

The worst part, though, was when she discovered Richard and I enjoying an afternoon delight on the couch under the window in his office. Richard had a thing about sex in public places, and being young and foolish, I was keen to try anything as long as the door was locked.

This time it hadn't been.

All hell had broken loose and because Richard held far more professional clout than me, I found myself shoved unceremoniously out the double glass doors of the station the next afternoon. My name in the journalism world was mud. I didn't even get a leaving present. I arrived back in Merrifield unemployed, single and feeling like a failure. Yes, I had my family and friends but my life hadn't exactly been fun city over the past couple of years.

Dragged away from my thoughts by the sound of the bell out in the shop, I left the back room to find a cute little West Highland Terrier with a pink diamante studded collar walking towards me, tugging a girl I'd never seen before along behind. The girl was slim and pretty. Her hair — long, straight and chestnut — was held back by a pair of expensive looking sunglasses and her clothes hung just so. The dog, though in need of a good clip, suited her to a tee. She was cute and cuddly and very intelligent looking. They looked as if they belong on a TV commercial for up-market dog food.

"Hi." The girl picked up the dog, cuddling it to her. "I was wondering if you'd be able to groom Lulu today? I've been so busy, I haven't had time to scratch myself, let alone see to her. She's been swimming in the dam and looks an utter nightmare."

I reached over, tickling Lulu under the chin. "Sure. Do you want a traditional West Highland cut and a bath and blow dry?"

"Trim her head to toe and take about a couple of centimetres off her feathers. I don't think they were designed for foot long grass out in the paddock. Do you put bows in dogs' hair?"

"Sure do." I pointed to a selection of ribbons behind the counter. "I also have a doggie massage built into the service. The dogs love it. And if you'd like any of the add-ons, I'd have time for those too."

The girl looked up at the menu style board above offering fur dying, nail painting, bowls of gourmet doggie treats to consume while pampered pooches waited for their owners, as well as custom-made doggie coats.

"Could you paint her nails pink?" The girl asked, picking out a pink spotted ribbon that matched Lulu's collar.

"Of course." I took the spool of ribbon and placed it on the counter to remind myself. Then I opened a new file on the computer and took down Lulu's particulars. "That ribbon will look adorable with her collar."

The girl nodded in agreement. "Oh, I'm Adelaide, by the way. Adelaide Anderson."

I reached over and shook her hand. "Olivia Merrifield. It's nice to meet you, Adelaide. Hopefully, we'll see each other around town."

"Merrifield? Wow. You've got a whole town named after you."

I guessed that was one way of looking at it.

"My family were founders of the town. It has its good points and bad points."

"I can imagine. Listen, I can't thank you enough for doing this at short notice. I want her looking nice for the photo shoot tomorrow and you have to wait for, like, six weeks for an appointment in Perth."

"Is Lulu a doggy model?"

"No. It's family photos. And she's a part of the family. You know how it is."

Walking around the counter, I took the lead from Adelaide and stepped back as Lulu leapt into my arms. Friendly as well as cute.

"Come back around five. We should be done by then."

Chapter 3

It was amazing how fast I could run when I tried. Rounding the corner into the alcove of the Post Office and preparing to pound on the door to be let in, I stopped to catch my breath and glanced up at the clock on the wall above the post boxes. It hadn't gone a minute past five but Anne, the woman who ran the shop, was a stickler for time keeping and rules. And somehow, I always seemed to be on the wrong side of the law.

I put my hand over my eyes and peered through the glass of the door. Then, as I raised my knuckles to knock, Anne — who was straightening the display of CDs — turned. God, it was like the woman had some sixth sense. Or supersonic hearing. She shook her head and tapped the face of her watch. Her mouth pursed, making every wrinkle around it more prominent. A grey hair in her chin that was usually invisible suddenly became visible. I bet she didn't know that. I mean, it wasn't exactly a face you pulled in the mirror to check out how you looked, was it?

I gave her my best impersonation of a sad puppy.

"It's five-oh-three, Olivia," Anne mouthed slowly, from the other side of the glass.

Well, it was now. I upped the sad face to extremely forlorn.

"I know, Anne. I know. And I'm super sorry but I had a client till five and I legged it here as fast as I could."

"Hmph." With a furtive look to make sure no one else was hiding around the corner waiting to rush the door, Anne unsnipped the lock allowing me entry. Then she re-locked it and stomped to the counter. She clasped her hands on the laminate top. It was hard to ignore the massive number of rings she wore on every available finger. They nearly reached her knuckles, a complete contrast to the minimalist shirt that was buttoned up so far it obscured most of her neck.

"And it's a package you're after, I suppose?"

Because unless I was getting my driver's license renewed, there was no other reason why I'd ever set foot inside the Post Office. I had absolutely no need for DVD box sets from the 90's. Or pens in the shape of fluffy emus.

"Yes. A pair of jeans."

The expected parcel, ordered a week previous, contained a new pair of jeans from Not Your Daughter's Jeans — sleek, dark, skinny denim — that I'd planned to wear to on my next date with Connor. The jeans had this bum lifting and tummy tucking technology woven into the denim. I don't know how they do it, but they manage to make your bum look amazing, even if isn't. Though given the way Connor felt about being misled by a pair of jeans, I was unsure as to how they'd be received at Shannon-down-from-Perth's birthday party in a few weeks time which was where I was now planning on wearing them.

Unless Patrick Dempsey stopped by to asked me on a date first, of course.

"What box number?" Anne enquired professionally.

"You already know my post box number, Annie." I flashed my nicest 'pretty-please' smile, which was quickly countered by a roll of the eye from Anne.

"Three. Three. Zero. Seven."

Anne swivelled, disappearing out the door to the post boxes.

Having received the bulky yet squishy package, I set off down Harold Street towards home. I couldn't wait to get my new jeans on and try a few tops with them. I was determined to look my best when Connor and I met again. I wanted him to see what he was missing. Not that I'd ever take him back but I wanted him to see, all the same. It was a matter of pride. Or was it principle?

I walked down the street past the I.G.A and a few plops of rain fell on my head. Ignoring them, I smiled to myself. The mental picture was forming – the jeans, hugging my curves, a pair of heels like the girl, Adelaide, had been wearing earlier on and that nice sparkly top I'd picked up on a trip to Perth. That'd make a few heads turn. I reached the front door as the rain began to pelt. Giving the parcel a quick shake to rid it of rain, I flipped the hall light on before walking to the bedroom, biting the plastic satchel of the parcel open as I went. I was going to show everyone you didn't have to be a size eight to look good. Once I got those jeans on, they'd eat their words. Because I was not fat. Curves were womanly. Sexy.

Stepping out of the canvas trousers I wore at work, I tossed them towards the washing basket and shook the new jeans from their tissue paper wrapping.

Oh, the smell of new denim, it was like getting a new car but better. Not that I'd ever had a new, new car but I'd smelled that scent you spray at the car wash tonnes of times.

I slid open the second drawer of the chest and rifled amongst the 'going out' tops until I found the silver one I'd been thinking of. I tossed it on the bed, next to the jeans. Then, on hands and knees, I pulled a few pairs of shoes from under the bed. Holding two different heels aloft, I cast a critical eye over each. Clearly, updating my shoe collection hadn't been high on the priority list since moving home. These shoes were about as fashionable as the ones grandma had worn before she met her untimely death at the nineteenth hole of the Merrifield golf course. When had I turned into such a fashion disaster? I'd been prancing around town in these, completely oblivious to their absolute hideousness.

Disgusted, I stood up and took the silver top from the bed, slipping it over my head. I turned to look in the mirror admiring the drape and the way the fabric fell in soft folds around my torso. I hadn't let myself go, had I? If I went to the party wearing this top, I wasn't going to be the laughing stock of the town, was I?

I turned to the other side. No, it looked nice. I looked nice.

I picked up the jeans and slid them up over my hips.

Okay. Maybe slid wasn't the most appropriate word in this instance.

As the jeans reached the centre of my thighs, they stubbornly refused to move another centimetre. It was as if they sensed the impending pain of trying to stretch across my bottom and had gone on strike.

I pulled and yanked, finally managing to get the jeans up to my hips. The button and fly might be another story though. There was an expanse of skin exposed on my stomach that even I could acknowledge would pose a problem if I was trying to button anything up. There was only one thing for it. I was going to have to get the jeans done up the way Alice and I used to do them when we were in high school.

One coat hanger hooked through the zipper, some rather uncomfortable breath-holding later and bingo, the jeans were on. The only problem was, I couldn't get off the bed. I couldn't even sit because the denim was so taut across my tummy, bending was not an option. I was so stuck I could die there, right on the bed because I couldn't get off it to use the phone or get food. People would find me days later, prone on my back and wonder what the hell had happened. It'd be like a scene from that movie *Seven* but without Brad Pitt.

Well, *that* certainly wouldn't be happening. I began to roll side to side to gain momentum. Like a sausage roll stuck on the shelf in the bakery, I rolled until I reached the edge of the bed. Then using my elbows, I hoisted myself upright and turned to face the mirror.

Wow.

I looked amazing. My stomach was so flat you could have put a tablecloth on it and used it to serve dinner. That is, if you discounted the fact that the fat from my hips and stomach had formed an enormous muffin top above the waistband. Actually, it was more like a cake shelf. There was no way the silver top would cover that, not even with neck-to-knee Spanx on.

Hands trembling, I cajoled the jeans back to my ankles and flopped to sitting on the edge of the bed. The company must have sent the wrong size. It happened frequently — well, to me at any rate. I couldn't have put on that much weight. Ignoring the red marks around my middle, I picked the jeans up and turned them inside out to reveal the label. Size 12. When I saw the promo on the shopping network, the women had definitely said you should order a size down from your usual. Thus, I ordered a 12. But these were nowhere near my size.

Diving to the wardrobe, I dug through the pile of clothes, meant for ironing. At the very bottom I retrieved my Levi's — the ones I'd shoved there because the shade of denim was wrong — or, if I was honest because they were getting a little tight. I measured them against the new jeans.

Crap.

Exactly the same. No discrepancy in size.

I knew I'd been wearing those wide leg linen pants because they were 'in' and I did wear track pants around the house more than I used to but that was only for comfort.

It wasn't because I had no other clothes that fitted me without a fight. Was it?

And in that moment of uncertainty, the craving hit me again. The longing for something sweet that would make me feel better about myself was so great I would have stabbed someone if they'd stepped between me and that sticky date pudding and double cream I had in the fridge.

As I stood at the open fridge door, stuffing my face and feeling the sadness disappear, I felt truly grateful yesterday had been a good enough day that I'd been able to save half the pudding. There was no way I was going to be reduced to begging for a biscuit over at Mum's place.

*****

When Mrs Sotheby arrived the next morning with her dog, Snuffle, I was up to my nose in fur. My first client of the day had been a particularly shaggy Old English sheepdog that looked like he hadn't seen the back end of a pair of clippers in a long while. Consequently, I resembled a snowman, only with fur. Silver, grey and white fur that clung to every part of my body and no matter what I tried it refused to budge.

I wasn't in the best of moods either. Accepting Connor may have been right about my weight was like accepting you needed help from your most hated enemy. You only did it begrudgingly and it left a very dirty aftertaste. I wasn't prepared to go down that road yet.

At the tinkle of the doorbell, I leant my broom against the wall, did another swift fur brush down and went to greet my client. Mrs Sotheby had been on an Asian Escape cruise followed by a trek around the Great Wall of China for the past three months. We hadn't seen each other in quite a while.

"Hi, Mrs Southby."

I bent down to scratch Snuffle behind the ear. The dog pushed against my hand, enjoying the attention.

"Olivia. How are you?" The elderly lady stretched, giving my forearm an affectionate rub. Mrs Sotheby was such a sweet old thing. Her hair, carefully dyed, was cut into a chic bob and held with a vintage clip at her temple. Her dress reached her knees, revealing a pair of super fine hose and buttery coloured shoes that matched her handbag. I couldn't remember a time in my life when my shoes matched my handbag. Not even when I was a minor G list TV celebrity. Most of the time, I looked like I dragged my clothes out of the ironing basket.

Okay. Most of the time I did drag them from the ironing basket. Sometimes even off the floor.

"I'm well," I said. "How about you? You look as if the holiday agreed with you."

"It was marvellous. The Great Wall is such an incredible landmark, awe-inspiring when you see it in person. It was quite a hike and sleeping in a tent on the Wall was the most indescribable experience."

"You camped on the Great Wall?" Mrs Sotheby was pushing seventy-five. *That* was awe-inspiring.

"Only for one night. The second night was spent in a boarding house." The woman paused to look me up and down. A faint hint of a crinkle formed between her pencilled brows. "And you look... well."

I knew I wasn't exactly the picture of glamour, being covered in fur and everything, but I had a feeling Mrs Sotheby wasn't talking about my actual attire. "Erm, thank you?"

"You're such a sneaky young thing."

"Pardon?"

"I can't believe you kept it under wraps this whole time," she continued, her eyes travelling towards my tummy and stopping there. "And still working, too. Well, good on you. It's the sign of the modern woman. You don't need a man to be a mother."

Then it dawned on me. The last time we'd seen each other, Mrs Sotheby had had her great granddaughter, Megan, with her. She was the cutest little thing, golden bouncing curls and big blue eyes. I couldn't keep my hands off her. I wanted to snuggle her to me and tickle her to see the dimples in her cheeks. At the time, I'd expressed my desire to have children one day. I certainly hadn't meant immediately, not even if I was 'a natural', as Mrs Sotheby had put it, and I had no intention of doing it as a single mother. For me, the child came with the man as a package deal. But Mrs Sotheby had somehow convinced herself I was having a baby.

This was the last straw.

Not to mention immensely awkward.

"How far along are you?" Mrs Sotheby said.

"I'm not pregnant."

The room was suddenly quieter than a morgue. Mrs Southby's face reddened and she began to cough quietly into a handkerchief that she'd whipped from heaven knows where.

"Oh dear, I do apologise. It's... well, you seem to have put on a bit of weight since I saw you last. I didn't mean to be rude."

"It's not your fault. It's been a stressful couple of months. I guess I have been doing a fair amount of comfort eating."

Not that I'd been that stressed until yesterday but I had been eating. And as I knew only too well, one cake led to another. Okay, probably half a dozen.

"Of course, of course. And sticking to an eating plan is so difficult when you're not feeling yourself, isn't it?" the other woman justified. "You don't look fat as such... maybe a little... er, rounder in the middle."

Which made it sound so much better.

"My sincere apologies, Olivia. I'm so embarrassed."

Deciding the conversation was going to end nowhere but in tears — probably mine — I picked up Snuffle.

"The usual?" I asked, already halfway through the door to the grooming room.

"Yes, please."

"We'll be done in about an hour and a half."

Mrs Sotheby headed for the door. "I do apologise, Olivia."

"Apology accepted."

As I was clipping Snuffle, tears of realisation welling up and threatening to plop onto his coat, I had something of an epiphany. If everyone kept telling me I was fat, then clearly the image I saw when I looked in the mirror every morning *was* wrong. Clearly, I was operating under some sort of delusion that made me think I was thinner than I was, like when people take selfies from above their heads to make their faces look thinner. I'd managed, somehow, to convince myself that my clothes were tighter because they'd shrunk or the sizes were being made smaller than they used to be. I was such a fool.

I took Snuffle to the hydrobath and turned on the taps. A warm gush of water flooded through the nozzle and I tested it to ensure it wasn't too hot before I commenced spraying it over the dog's body. Then I began to lather him with medicated shampoo.

I'd be damned if I was going to be the fat chick with the lovely personality. I wanted to be thin Olivia, the sexy girl with the lovely personality. And if drastic measures had to be taken to achieve that aim, then that's what I'd have to do. When I got home that night, I was going to research diets until I found something that would work for me.

I was going to throw out the crap in my pantry and take up jogging or something and get thin again. Maybe even a new hairdo. Basically I was going to makeover my life.

Starting tomorrow.

'Cause I should probably finish those éclairs in fridge first. And the lamingtons, too. Couldn't have them going to waste.

Chapter 4

Later in the evening, I sat at the kitchen table my fingers sliding across the screen of my iPad as I scoured page after page of diet links — in between gulps of chardonnay and bites of éclair. The number of diets in the world claiming to give amazing results in short spaces of time was absolutely astounding. I had so many tabs open it was a wonder I wasn't clogging up cyberspace, but I'd no idea what diet to choose or what was best. They sounded either too easy to possibly work, or too healthy or too quick.

Who'd pay seventy dollars for a diet plan where the only thing you ate was green things? A lot of people judging by the number of people on that Facebook page I saw. And how would you survive only by drinking lemonade with pepper in it? Not only did it sound disgusting but also I hated pepper. I wasn't going to be swayed because Beyoncé supposedly lost her baby weight on it.

As I flicked through a few more links, I came across something unusual, Virtual gastric banding. I leant closer to the page, studying the words. *Surely not.* It had to be some sort of hoax. Still, I clicked on the link to the homepage and began to read.

It didn't sound like one of those buy-these-two-pills-and-watch-fat-melt-away gimmicks. People in the UK were claiming to have lost untold amounts of weight by using the system of hypnosis described. There were testimonials and videos of people who looked so normal there was no way it could be a hoax. They'd done trials that had had a ninety-five percent success rate. And if ninety-five percent of people could be happy, then when couldn't I? I could hypnotise myself into being thin and I'd never even have to give up a thing. Because everyone on the planet knew as soon as you denied yourself something, all you wanted to do was to have it. Sometimes I even dreamt about cake if I hadn't had a piece during the day.

The more I read the more I liked the idea. I mean it wasn't as if I ate badly — apart from my obvious problems with cake — I just ate too much. This promised to cure me of both those issues. In fact, virtual gastric banding sounded like the best idea I'd had in ages, despite the fact that it was the 'easy option'. Because the whole world knew the only way to lose weight was by giving things up and exercising. It wasn't meant to be as easy as putting the weight on had been.

Picking up the phone, I dialled my friend, Alice. If anyone was guaranteed to know what sort of diet was good, it would be her. Being a personal trainer, Alice was into nutrition and fitness. She knew the latest trends.

"Hey."

"Hi. What's up?"

"I'm fat, that's what's up."

Alice let out a sigh. "When did you decide this?"

"After Connor dumped me and Mum bought me slimming underwear. I mean, who gives a person a pair of Spanx as a gift? Oh, and Mrs Sotheby thought I was pregnant. That was the nail in the coffin."

"Hmm."

Alice was being very non-committal. She was a good friend.

"Do you think I'm fat?" I continued.

"You are a little plumper than you used to be and you do eat an awful lot of cake."

"Do I?"

"Yes."

This was dreadful. I'd been walking around town with everyone knowing how fat I was looking and how much crap I was eating and none of them had said a thing — not to my face, anyway. Honestly, I'd never paid that much attention to what went into my mouth. But it was like lots of things, I suppose. It crept up on you without you realising until one day, bingo! There you were. The fat girl.

"I don't want to be the fat friend, Alice." I wailed. "I want to be hot like you, like I used to be when I was on TV. I need to go on a diet. Like now. What do you think about Jenny Craig?"

"We don't have one in town. And you have to go to the centre every week."

"Oh. I didn't read that on the website. What about the one with that man who guarantees you'll lose five kilos in the first week or you get your money back?"

"Not sustainable, but good if you want to be a body builder. It's high protein. You'll never poo again."

"Shakes? I saw some on the home shopping network. There was a special where you buy in bulk."

"They do work but you need a lifestyle change, Livvy, not a quick fix. Besides, how boring would it be drinking some yucky milkshake for weeks on end? *Eww.*"

Fair point. I loved food. A shake was an accompaniment in my book, not a meal.

"What about hypnosis?"

I couldn't bring myself to utter the words 'gastric band' out loud. People would think I really *was* obese. Or completely off my rocker. Because no matter how you dressed it up, hypnosis remained one of those alternative treatments that regular people refused to believe in.

"You're kidding, right?"

I rest my case.

"Um. No."

"For heaven's sake. You won't get thin by hypnosis. That's utterly ridiculous. You need to stop eating so much cake and take a trip to the gym every now and then, not get caught up in some fan-dangled mumbo jumbo. Next you'll be telling me you're channelling Elvis."

Imagine if you could. How awesome would that be?

I pulled myself back to the topic at hand. "It sounded very good. The success rate is high."

"Which is how those companies make their money. They make everything sound easy and good."

I groaned. "I don't know what to do. Choosing the diet is harder than being fat."

"I highly doubt that. Why don't you give Weight Watchers a go? There's a meeting in town *and* they let you eat cake."

"*Thin girls don't eat cake*, Alice. I'll have to give it up."

"Not necessarily. Have a look at the website. Find out when the next meeting is. I could come with you to the first one, if you want a bit of support."

Because Alice certainly didn't need to go on a diet or make a single lifestyle change. Even after having a baby, she had the perfect body. And the perfect life to match.

"That'd be nice. Thanks."

"Don't worry. Once you make a decision to do something, you stick to it. I've never seen you give up. You'll be back to the weight you want in no time."

I hung up the phone feeling better. Now that I'd made the commitment and voiced it to my best friend, there was no backing out. And let's face it, I couldn't reverse. My bum was so big; I'd never have room to manoeuvre.

However...

After hanging up from the conversation with Alice and finishing the rest of the lamingtons from the pantry, I began to have second thoughts. There was this niggling doubt. I don't know if it was fear of failure or that I still didn't believe I *had* to do something about my weight, but I started to second guess myself. Giving up stuff and changing lifestyles required a lot of effort and I didn't know if I was ready for that sort of commitment.

Yes, I know I'd made a decision but, seriously, I only had a few kilos to lose. If I went to Weight Watchers I'd be as out of place as a nun in a pole-dancing club. It was better to sort this out in the privacy of my own home where nobody was any the wiser.

Picking up my iPad, I clicked on the link with information about virtual gastric bands again. The reviews, mostly five star ones, said the process was easy and relatively successful. Nobody would even know I was on a diet because I'd still eat the things I loved, simply in smaller quantities.

I decided it was worth a shot. If it failed, I could always go back to my original idea. Which was, basically, starve until I got thin again.

A far more stressful option...

Finger on the 'buy now' button, I eagerly pressed and waited for the app to download. Then I went in search of my earphones.

*****

I almost skipped around the shop over the next few days. After listening to the first four sessions of the gastric band app, I'd found I couldn't eat even half my usual bowl of cereal at breakfast each morning. I felt so full; it was like I'd gorged a five-course feast in five minutes rather than a quarter full bowl of Nutrigrain. Lunch seemed to become a thing of the past too. Four bites saw me wrapping my chilli chicken roll back in the plastic and putting it in the fridge for the next day.

Unheard of.

Ever.

But it was as I attempted an apple at afternoon tea and ended up throwing most of it in the bin, that I had this fabulous idea. Things were going far better than expected. I'd been listening every morning and my clothes were feeling a little looser, so if I listened to the app three times a day, I'd have to get three times the result, right? I'd have to be more hypnotised and less susceptible to temptation.

I didn't know why I hadn't thought of it before. Not giving my mind a chance to register the possible consequences I locked the door of the shop, turned over the sign to 'back in 30 minutes' and plugged my earphones into my ears. My next appointment wasn't until two. Plenty of time.

*****

"Olivia, Olivia."

BANG. BANG-BANG.

"Olivia!"

Rubbing the sleep from my eyes, I sat up in the chair and pulled the earphones from my ears, placing them on the table next to my phone. Even though my head felt fuzzy and I was somewhat disoriented, I could have sworn someone was calling me. I sat up straighter and stretched. I glanced at my watch.

BANG. THUMP.

"OLIVIA!"

Crap.

It was 2.20pm. I'd fallen asleep listening to the app and slept straight through my afternoon appointment.

Leaping from the chair and tripping over the cord to the heater in the process, I missed landing in the hydrobath by millimetres. I didn't, however, miss the shelf filled with grooming products. In my fall, I managed to tip the thing over. Shampoo bottles rolled across the floor. Brushes and clippers went flying.

BANG, BANG. BANG.

A shatter of breaking glass... more loud thumping.

What on earth was going on out there? It sounded as if a herd of elephants had been let loose in the shop.

With a curse, I raced from the grooming room and into the shop where I stopped, took a breath and tried to adopt a face that was way more alert than I was feeling. The door was open. Shards of glass lay strewn across my new timber look floor. The shop was filled with concerned looking people — Jane from the kitchen shop, Bill, the local police constable, two ambulance officers, two men in complete fire fighting garb and Mrs Tanner, my 2pm appointment, with her dog Growler.

"Thank the Lord." Mrs Tanner exhaled.

I frowned, confused by the unnatural amount of activity in my shop. "What's going on? Why are you here and..." I looked over to the front door, which I noticed had a spectacularly large hole in the glass. "What happened to my door?"

"We thought you were ill," Mrs Tanner explained. "Growler and I arrived for our appointment and I knocked on the door. I could see you out the back there, slumped in the chair. I called out but you didn't stir."

"I was, er, um, having a nap."

The ambulance officer appeared disbelieving, as well she might but I had no intention of sharing that I'd secretly been hypnotising myself. I'd be the laughingstock of town by dinner. Especially if Mrs Tanner was involved. She could spread gossip faster than I could spread butter on my toast.

"We'll need to examine you, Olivia. Could you sit down?"

"No, I could not," I replied, suddenly feeling quite indignant at having my privacy invaded. The embarrassment factor was also beginning to grow. What on earth was I thinking, hypnotising myself during the lunch hour? Or even thinking that if I listened to the app more frequently I'd get faster results. Sometimes I even worried myself.

"But I thought you were dead." Mrs Tanner said. "You were so still."

"And when Mrs Tanner discovered she didn't have her mobile on her, she ran across the road to use my phone to call the ambulance," Jane added.

At least that explained why Jane was here.

"So how did my door get broken?"

"By the time Bill and the ambos arrived, I still couldn't rouse you, so we decided we should break the lock on the door. You were back there in the chair, love. Unconscious."

"Or dead."

"Gravely injured at the very least. Are you sure you didn't hurt yourself in the fall? I can arrange for the air ambulance to come if we need it."

Lord. There were one or two people in this room who'd benefit from a bonk on the head, and I wasn't one of them.

"I wasn't unconscious. I'm not hurt or injured. I was hypnotising myself."

A look of bemusement came over the faces of the little group. Clearly, they would have preferred if I'd fallen and knocked myself senseless on the doggy hydrobath or something.

"It's true," I went on. "I downloaded this app to hypnotise myself and I was trying it out. I didn't think it'd send me to sleep. I had it set to wake me at the end."

"So you haven't taken any illicit drugs?"

"Of course not."

"Why were you hypnotising yourself?"

I looked at the gathering. I couldn't tell them. How ridiculous would it sound to admit I was attempting to lose weight using an iPhone app? It was utter madness. They'd have me locked up before I could say 'you're so sleepy'. A little white lie was a far better option.

"I needed to, um, de-stress. Things have been a bit overwhelming of late. I thought hypnotism might help."

"Well, thank the holy father for that," Mrs Tanner said. "If you'd told me it was one of those crazy weight loss things I would have rung your mother. But you shouldn't mess around with things like that. It's dangerous."

And this, coming from the woman who'd been known to hold Friday night séances in her living room. It was well known that Mrs Tanner had tried to convince Jim the Butcher his long dead mother was telling him to get rid of his wife on more than on occasion.

"I'll remember that, Mrs Tanner. Thank you."

"And you'll let me give you a quick check over?" the ambulance girl asked. "You do look a bit peaky."

Possibly from the shock of having my front door destroyed by a fire axe.

"Sure. Go ahead." With a resigned sigh, I flopped onto the chair beside the counter. I mean, she'd practically been pleading. I had no choice. Besides, everyone knew the only time she got to hone her skills was after local drunk Bert had a few too many and stumbled into the rose bushes outside the council offices on his way up the hill. So when you thought about it, I was doing the community a favour.

*****

Later that afternoon, after three consoling cupcakes with strawberry icing, I answered a call from Mum.

"Was the shop on fire today?"

"Hello Mum."

I'd been waiting for this. In a tiny town like Merrifield you couldn't scratch your bottom without someone reporting it to your family. It was entirely possible that my mother had known I'd lost my virginity before I did, the grapevine worked so fast.

"Why were the fire department, the police and the ambulance at the shop? Elaine Tanner said they were blocking the entire road. Are you all right?"

"Of course I'm all right, I'm talking to you, aren't I?"

"Don't be facetious, Olivia. I am your mother. I'm merely ringing to enquire what happened, not to get some smart remark thrown back at me. I don't know how this happened. You had such beautiful manners as a child. Now all you do is answer back. It's no wonder you can't find a boyfriend."

God help me.

"Sorry Mum."

"Thank you. Now please explain what happened at the shop. You know Elaine's prone to exaggeration."

"I fell asleep."

"Pardon me?" Mum's voice was a mixture of bemusement and annoyance.

"I was testing out a self-hypnosis app and it made me fall asleep."

"Well, of course it did, you silly girl. That's what hypnosis is for. Sometimes I wonder where you keep your brains."

"I didn't fall asleep on purpose."

"Maybe so but the whole town's talking. Maggie was worried you had some sort of drug problem. She thought we were going to have to do an intervention."

The only problem I had right then was the busybodies in my neighbourhood.

"I think perhaps Maggie should stop watching so much TV."

"I did suggest that but she was rather convincing. She said you eat at least five peppermint slices a day. She thought you had the 'munchies'."

I stifled a giggle. Did people even call it that anymore?

"I don't have a drug problem, Mum. Mrs Tanner overreacted when I didn't answer the door, that's all. You can ask the ambulance guys if you want. They checked me over. I'm perfectly fine. Or I could pop over to the police station for a drug test if that will appease you."

"Olivia."

"I'm okay. Honestly."

"Good. Because I wanted to tell you I'm going to have to cancel dinner tonight."

Again?

"Why, what's up?"

"Nothing. I'm trying out a new course. If I sign up, it's every Thursday for ten weeks."

"But Thursday's mother-daughter bonding night."

Ever since I arrived back in Merrifield, I'd eaten dinner with Mum on a Thursday evening. We never missed unless one of us was ill, and that was rare. Now, she was cancelling two weeks in a row. It was enough to make one feel somewhat unloved.

"Yes and this is yoga," Mum clarified. "*Kama Sutra* yoga."

A hysterical splutter stuck in my mouth. "Are you serious?"

The thought of Mum bending herself into sexual positions on a yoga mat was a tad over the top. I wondered if it required a partner? The *Kama Sutra* did. At least, I supposed it did. I'd never actually read it. Or looked at the pictures.

"Perfectly. It's very good for flexibility, or so I'm told."

I let out a weary sigh. "How about tomorrow night, then? I've got nothing on."

"Lovely. The pub?"

"Sure. And be careful, Mum. I don't want you tearing muscles."

"I'm not the one who hasn't exercised this millennium, possum."

I smiled at that. It was true. Exercise and I had not been friends for a good few years now. Not since I'd come back from the city at any rate.

"Bye, Mum. Kisses."

"Kisses. And don't go hypnotising yourself again. Such a ridiculous idea."

Almost as ridiculous as eating a fourth cupcake before bed.

Chapter 5

The silver-grey four-wheel drive swung into the gravelled parking area at the front of Oak Hill House, sending pebbles flying as it came to a halt and scattering a flock of wild ducks that were making their way to the pond in the front garden. Pulling his keys from the ignition, Cole Anderson opened the door and slipped them into his pocket before heading up the path towards the house. He paused for a second to admire his surroundings. This house had been a real find — a traditional stone farmhouse with ten acres of land, French doors along the front facade, wide verandas and it was convict built. It was the type of house he'd always dreamed of owning and now he did. It was a pity such sad circumstances had been the catalyst for the purchase.

Along the drive behind him, Adelaide appeared from under the canopy of the hundred-year-old willow tree. Lulu, barking animatedly at the ducks as they landed on the lawn, ran up the gravel to greet him, her tail wagging eagerly.

"There you are," Adelaide said, her perfect white teeth revealed in a broad, friendly smile.

Wrapping an arm round her shoulder, Cole gave Adelaide a pinch right on the top of her arm. "Hey, sis."

"Ouch. Cole. That hurt."

"That's what you get for leaving me alone with the electrician. Bloody bloke almost talked my ear off. Is the photographer here yet?"

"Yes. Mum's beginning to panic. You know how she abhors tardiness."

Did he ever. Since Cole was a boy, it had been instilled into him that punctuality was the epitome of manners. Ella Anderson was never late. She'd be having kittens right about now. Cole glanced at his watch. "Let's get this thing done then. I bloody hate photos. Smiling makes my face ache."

"A time will come when it won't."

"Can't see it being in the near future."

"We don't have to do this if you feel that strongly. It was a prize. It's not like we're paying for it. We can send the photographer away."

Letting her go, Cole jogged up the path toward the house, indulging Lulu in a game of chasey as he went. "No. We can't cancel it. Phoebe would never forgive me. Besides, it's about new beginnings, isn't it? A new life, a new home and new family photos to mark the occasion."

Agreeing, Adelaide followed him up the front steps and into the house.

Ella Anderson stood as Cole and Adelaide entered the room. Smoothing her short white hair, styled especially for the day, she bustled towards them. "There you are."

"Sorry I'm late. The electrician had a harder time with the oven than we thought," Cole replied, kissing his mother's line free cheek.

She was an amazing old bird. God knows what he would have done without her after Phoebe died. She'd done everything she could to help him move on, even though it was hard on her too. And now here she was — with the help of his sister — getting him set up a new home. Cole knew full well they both had plenty of other things they could be doing. One day he'd repay them. He didn't know how, but he would.

"Do I have time for a shower?" he asked his mother. He felt as if he'd been playing in dirt the entire morning, which had been fine when he was seven but wasn't a good look for a grown man. Especially one who had to have a family portrait.

"The photographer's already running late. Give your face a wash, there's a bit of something on it. And, put this on." A crisp t-white shirt flew in Cole's direction, landing on his head.

"Gee thanks."

Cole put the shirt between his knees and pulled the dirty one he was wearing over his head, tossing it in his mother's direction. A cloud of dust from his hair flew into the air around him.

"Won't be a sec," he said, taking the stairs two at a time.

"Two minutes." Ella tutt-tutted.

"No problem. Not that you can start without me."

"It would have been far easier if we had."

Up in the bathroom, Cole took in his dishevelled appearance in the mirror as he waited for the sink to fill with warm water. A quick sniff under his armpits confirmed that he reeked and he wondered if he had time to wash his armpits too. Not that it would make any difference to the photo, of course. But it would make him feel cleaner and it'd only take a few seconds. Better to smell of soap than the stench of god knows how many years of grime.

Turning off the taps, Cole peeled the fresh t-shirt off, hanging it carefully over the towel rail. He bent into the basin and sluiced water over his face. He squirted a blob of liquid soap into his hand and lathered it up, giving his neck, face and ears a good scrub, finishing with his under arms.

That felt better. At least he could go into the shoot feeling a modicum of cleanliness.

The photo thing had been Phoebe's idea. She'd won the voucher in a competition the Christmas before last but with everything that had happened, there'd been no time or even an appropriate moment to organise it so it had been pushed aside. In fact, he'd completely forgotten about it until Adelaide mentioned it last month.

Then he remembered he'd promised Phoebe it would go ahead, even if she wasn't around. He'd also promised he'd have her Photoshopped into the background of the picture, like some ghostly apparition. He'd made a lot of promises during the last few months of her life, but that was one he wasn't sure he was going to keep — his twelve-year-old daughter flying through the family portrait dressed in a kitsch angel costume. Though he had to admit it would be a talking point when visitors came.

Drying his face and tidying his hair with his fingers, a memory of Phoebe during her last days suddenly filled the small room around him. It was like she was standing in front of him, her eyes — a carbon copy of Adelaide's — scolding him for being sad, for wanting to spend every second of her last days at the hospital, for forgetting how to have fun.

"Haven't you got something better to do, Daddy? Hospitals are so boring. And the sun is shining outside."

Cole had perched himself at the head of the bed. His hand had stroked the baby hairs that were beginning to grow on her naked scalp, left bald from the treatment. "I'd rather be here with you."

"I hope you're not going to be one of those mopey-pants parents when I'm dead," she whispered, attempting to smile. "You have to live your life. Have another daughter. Of course, I'll still be the most important one and the prettiest, but you should get another one."

"Phoebe."

She was ill but that didn't mean he couldn't chastise her.

"I mean it. Just because I'll be gone doesn't mean you get out of your promises. You have to meet a nice lady and have another baby; you have to open a cupcake shop. If you don't do it, I'll never speak to you again. Which is silly because I'll be dead, but I won't even speak to you in your dreams."

"Don't talk like that, Phoebs. You're not going to die."

Phoebe had reached across the bleached white sheet of the hospital bed. Her hand, as transparent as a dying autumn leaf, had come to rest on his knee. "It's time to face facts, Daddy. We've been pussyfooting around it for days now. I'm over it. Let's say the words. I'm going to die."

"But the new treatment?"

"It won't work. You know it won't. Besides, I'm ready. I don't mind dying. This life is too hard."

Cole had almost lost it then. His lip had wobbled like it had when he'd broken his arm as a boy but he'd held it in. She was only a kid, just a little girl, *his* little girl.

"I want you to be happy. Have a nice life, fulfil our dreams. Promise."

Cole had swallowed. "And you think cooking cupcakes for a living will make me happy?"

"Nobody in the whole wide world makes better cupcakes than you, Daddy. Open a shop. It'll be a goldmine. I know it will. Promise me you'll do it."

"I promise."

"And I want you to get the family portrait done and put me up in the sky like an angel looking over you all."

Leaning across the bed, Cole placed a tender kiss on Phoebe's pale brow. "I love you, Phoebs."

"You too, Daddy. And when I'm a star, look out for me, cause I'll be winking right at you every night."

Cole had watched as Phoebe's eyes had closed and she sank into slumber. She looked peaceful and he was reminded of those nights he'd sat by her bed when she was little, watching her sleep. Only this time, she wasn't going to wake up.

Now, nearly a year down the track, Cole was attempting to do as Phoebe had asked. The kid had always had an eye for seeing outside the square and even at twelve, she'd possessed a business brain that rivalled his own. Still, as he went down the hall to greet the photographer and sit posing for a family photo that had the most important person in the family floating in the sky like an angel, he had to concede that possibly his daughter had been mad and he was even madder for listening to her advice.

Chapter 6

Adelaide climbed off the chair and brushed down her jeans. Plaster dust from the renovations blended with fifty years of grime and a few cockroaches flew into the air causing her to expel a rather loud and very unladylike sneeze that echoed around the empty shop. Cole, who was stacking supplies in the small room he'd designated as a store, poked his head around the doorjamb.

"Everything okay?"

"It's foul up there. Did the previous owners never clean?"

"I don't think hygiene was high on their priority list. It took me most of yesterday to clean out the rubbish from the store. There was so much shit, I had to ring for a new skip bin this morning. I even found a pair of used tights. The feet were crunchy with dried up sweat."

"*Eww.* Gross. What would people leave those lying around for?"

"Maybe the last owners were partial to a quickie in the storeroom?" Cole chuckled, noting the pink creeping into Adelaide's face. She was such a prude, so proper. Always had been. It was easy to shock her into turning pink.

"Or maybe they were getting changed and forgot to pick them up. You have such a one track mind."

"Not that one track. I haven't mentioned the word 'sex' for at least a year."

"And there's no need for us to start a conversation about it now."

"I'd have thought you'd be happy I was getting back to normal."

Adelaide gave an expansive groan. Clearly, her idea of 'getting back to normal' didn't involve him discussing sex.

Putting the cleaning rag down on the chair, Adelaide rounded the counter. She bent under the counter and fishing her wallet from her handbag, made a beeline for the door. "I'm dying for a coffee. Latte?"

"Thanks. Could you get a large? And a couple of those peppermint slices from the bakery? I can feel another all-nighter coming on if we're to get this place ready for the painters tomorrow and I need a sugar hit."

Adelaide turned, her hand poised on the doorknob. "You shouldn't eat any more junk. You're diet is appalling as it is, what with the cakes you've been sampling."

"Yes, Mum."

How was he meant to know if his recipes were good if he didn't taste them? He couldn't put them out to the public without testing them and being able to give recommendations.

Though he had to admit he'd been feeling queasy from the huge amounts of icing he'd consumed over the last week. Sickly stuff if you ate it by the bowlful. Those little silver balls tended to get stuck in your teeth too.

"You should do more exercise," Adelaide added. "Get fitter. Maybe I'll look into a gym membership while I'm up the road."

Cole knew Adelaide was only saying these things out of concern; that his exercise regime had been put on the back burner with the opening of the shop, but she was the bossiest woman on the planet after his mother. Ella Anderson was the queen of bloody bossy. From the day he'd been born those two had bossed him around like he was incapable of making a decision on his own and with Phoebe in the mix, it had been three times the annoyance. Nobody would think he'd had his own successful business from the way they'd carried on. Sometimes, he'd longed for a nice quiet place with a few blokes sitting around drinking beer and watching cricket, no women allowed. And he didn't even like cricket that much.

"I jog. When it's not raining."

"You need to be more consistent. You don't want to end up a flabby old man."

"And you don't want to end up murdered."

"As if."

"Keep annoying me and it could happen."

"Whatever."

The shop door closed and Adelaide disappeared down the street, taking her grumbles with her. Cole stretched and stood for a moment to survey his handiwork. It had taken him the better part of two days to get some semblance of order in the kitchen and storeroom but he was pleased with the result. Everything was stacked in neat clear plastic containers, labelled and easily locatable. You'd have to be blind not to be able to find what you needed in there. He stepped backwards, pulling the door closed behind him, mentally ticking the job off the to-do list. Now that the storeroom was done and kitchen fit out complete, he and Adelaide could finish off the prep for the painters. He'd have to source a couple of tables and chairs too and check on the expected delivery day of the fridges and the coffee machine. He wanted to source a couple of things to decorate the walls too. He wasn't sure what yet, but he'd know it when he saw them. Cole had an eye for making something cool from nothing.

Walking out to the shop front, Cole picked up an aluminium bottle and took a long swig of water. He smiled to himself. For the first time since Phoebe had passed away, he was feeling as if life had a purpose again. He was looking forward to the opening and to the day when someone would taste the chocolate cupcake Phoebe loved so much. One smile of pleasure at the fudgy mixture, made with melted chocolate and extra cocoa and he'd know Phoebe was smiling down on him.

This was a marker for a new phase of his life. A moving forward. Not forgetting. But moving on.

Speaking of which, he'd better get a move on himself. There was a lot of tidying to be done before the painters arrived. That pile of cockroaches Adelaide had left on the floor by the wall wasn't going to sweep itself up.

*****

A while later, Adelaide pushed the door open with her hip and carrying the coffees over to the counter, put the tray down. She plonked a bag of groceries, down beside them. "Hi honey, I'm home."

"Thank God. I was about to send out the search party."

"I haven't been gone that long."

Cole eyed the grocery bag, containing what looked to be ingredients for that night's dinner. For once, Adelaide hadn't come back with trinkets or clothes from the shops up the street. She'd been known to get distracted and forget what it was she was meant to be buying in the first place.

"Anything happening in the supermarket?"

It was a sad day when the only news came from a trip to the fresh fruit section.

"Yes, as it happens. I got chatted up."

"By?"

"Some guy called Connor Bishop. He wanted me to try his nice firm bananas." Adelaide giggled.

"For real? Blokes really use that line?"

"None that I've ever met. Anyway, he gave me his number. He wants to come over to the house and see the work you've done on the garden. He said he wanted to buy the house but he couldn't afford it."

Cole picked up his cup and took a glug. He made a face as the coffee stung his tongue. Damn. "Unusual angle for seduction. I'm assuming you told him to nick off."

"Not exactly."

"Addie. How many times have I told you? You don't have to be nice to everyone in the world."

"You don't have to be rude, either. Besides, I have no need for a man. I have Lulu." She took a sip of her coffee; standing for a second with her hand perched on her hip as she took in the paint samples Cole had tacked to the walls. "This shop's going to look awesome when it's done. Phoebe would definitely approve."

Cole nodded. The black, pink and silver décor wasn't exactly the scheme he would have chosen but it was perfect for a cake shop. It was classy yet fun. And if he was going to do this he was going to do it right. It had to sparkle, like a living memory to Phoebe.

As Cole and Adelaide stood in the centre of the room, the back door to the shop squeaked open and Ella came in. As usual she was decked out from top to bottom and finished with expensive gold rings and large pearls at her ears.

"You won't believe what I've just heard."

Not so much as a 'good morning,' Cole thought. Must be interesting.

"What?"

"Apparently, your shorts are causing quiet a stir up and down the street. I was in the newsagent getting a copy of *Woman's Day* and three ladies were discussing you on the other side of the magazine stand."

Cole looked at his mother. Apart from being bossy she also had the uncanny knack of honing in on gossip of any kind. It was as if she had some sort of inner radar for it. Thank God she didn't like to spread it as well. "How do you know they were talking about me?"

"The words 'new guy, dark hair and navy shorts' were used."

"That could be anyone."

"One of them said you looked like the guy in that renovation ad that used to be on TV."

Great. Cole had specifically chosen Merrifield because he'd thought it far enough from Perth to escape that ad. He could always deny it being him but he knew wouldn't work. That ad was set to follow him to the end of his days. "I'm sure there's other people in town who've been in an ad at one time or another."

"As if..."Adelaide remarked. "I told you those shorts were only fit for the ragbag, Cole. The hole in the crotch is so revealing you'd scare the old biddies into an early grave if you bent over too far."

Cole ignored the comment. He was aware his shorts were on their last legs but they were his favourites, they fit right. Besides, what was he meant to renovate in? A three-piece suit?

Adelaide turned to Ella, clearly annoyed that Cole had ignored her. Again. "I suppose they were laughing. Great way to make a name in a new business, having the town laugh at you."

"They were gushing over Cole's 'lovely eyes'," Ella told her. "Oh and his 'muscular bottom'."

"Which I'm sure they got a full view of when he ran half naked up the street yesterday." She turned to Cole, who was trying to avoid the topic by staring at a paint chip on the wall. "We can't take you anywhere, can we?"

"Hey, I wasn't half naked. And I wasn't twerking or rubbing myself with a foam finger — though that would probably have made a bigger statement than my shorts — I was jogging. You know, keeping fit like you two keep harping on about."

"And airing your crown jewels," Ella said. "One of the women said she'd almost been run over because she'd been ogling your bottom instead of watching where she was going."

Okay, so he hadn't exactly been wearing jocks on that occasion but a guy liked to hang loose every now and then. It wasn't a freakin' crime.

"She was only saved from stepping in front of the semi-trailer by the honking of its horn. The other one said she'd walked straight into a parked car. I even saw the bruise on her knee."

Adelaide shook her head in disgust. "Give me strength. Wasn't the idea of your coming here to have a low profile?"

"Guess I've shot that one in the foot then." Despite himself, Cole chuckled. What else could he do? It was better than crying. Yes, he was trying to avoid people knowing he was the Reno King but the damage was done now. They might as well build a bridge.

"They were trying to figure out ways to meet you," Ella continued, a mischievous grin lighting up her face. "I was this close to telling them I knew where to find you. For a price, of course."

"I hope you didn't."

"But isn't it time for you to get back on the horse? It's three years since the split with Jenny and Phoebe's been gone a year. You've no reason avoid a little companionship."

"Other than the fact that I'm insanely busy starting a new business, moving to a new town and keeping the apparent hoards of lecherous locals off my back."

"Or out of your trousers." Adelaide smirked. "There must be one eligible woman here."

"And you could keep your nose out of my business too, thanks, Addie. I'll dive back into the wonderful world of women when I'm good and ready."

Though who knew when that would be; Jenny had hurt Cole more than he'd ever care to admit and with Phoebe's illness on top of it, he wasn't sure he'd ever be ready to embark on a new relationship. Most days he felt like he'd gone to the Bank of Emotions and found his account overdrawn. In fact, it might be that he'd never find it full again.

Chapter 7

Cole slipped his pass card into his pocket and carrying his water bottle like he was going to the gallows, made his way to the back of the gymnasium. An extremely perky thirty-something who'd identified herself at the door as Aimee, the instructor, made her way to the front and began chatting to a small group of women. Judging by their tasselled combat pants, bright coloured singlets and masses of wristbands with bells they were obviously regulars. Cole was not a regular. He was wearing his old track pants with a hole in the knee and a crinkled ACDC t-shirt he'd found in the bottom of the wardrobe. He longed to be a conscientious objector.

Because, if truth be told Cole would rather have chewed his own feet off than go to a Zumba class but Adelaide had surprised him earlier in the afternoon with a ten class pass that had cost her over a hundred dollars. He hadn't had the heart to tell her he wasn't that into dancing. Why he couldn't hit the real gym — the one with sweat and weights and men — he wasn't sure, but according to his mother and sister, Zumba would kill two birds with one stone. He didn't want to have anything to do with any birds. Or stones. The only things he wanted to kill at the moment were the women in his family.

After handing over his card, Cole found a spot at the back of the room and put his water bottle and towel next to the wall. He looked around, not recognising a single soul. It seemed, however, that he had been recognised. Thirty heads twisted simultaneously in his direction, staring for a few seconds longer than was comfortable. Thirty pairs of eyes roamed up and down his body. Some of the women whispered behind their hands and one woman even had the cheek to let out a very subtle wolf-whistle. Softly, mind, but he heard it. He felt like a piece of meat or a prizewinning exhibit in the Merrifield Show. This is more awkward than the first time he'd gone to the school disco at age fourteen and come out of the toilets with his fly undone. Right when the teachers had turned the lights back on.

Swallowing, he moved onto the gymnasium floor, facing the area where the music was set up. The women, though pretending not to, were still staring. If only he could take his stuff and go but he couldn't, they'd realise for sure and by tomorrow he'd be branded the guy who'd attempted to brave the Zumba den and failed. Besides, Adelaide was right. He did need a break. With the opening of the shop looming, he was spending more time thinking about it than was healthy. He was also beginning to have sugar withdrawals from the huge amounts of icing he'd been consuming. Ganache, butter cream, Vienna... If he didn't take some form of exercise, he wouldn't be able to wrap an apron round his waist by the time the opening came. And Zumba was meant to be fun, wasn't it? All those wiggling hips and butts — it had to be worth a laugh if nothing else. It'd be good for him to relax and get energised. If only those women would just stop staring.

Approaching the front of the class, Aimee donned a microphone, Madonna style. She flipped her perky curled ponytail over her shoulder and bounced onto the stage at the front of the gymnasium giving Cole a perfect view of the 'I heart Zumba' tattoo on her bicep. Jesus, her biceps were bigger than his. If that was what a couple of dance classes did for you he was definitely staying, even if he did look like a dick.

"Welcome Zumba family. I hope you're ready to boogie. We've got a couple of newbies tonight so we'll take it slow. Don't want to scare them away, do we?"

At that, the entire group turned to face him again and began to clap and whoop like they were at a rock concert. Which was even more embarrassing.

"Fabulous," said the girl standing beside him, the pink in her cheeks turning even pinker. "Like I need the whole town gawking. The idea of standing back here is to NOT attract attention."

Cole chuckled. "I wouldn't worry. Once they see me dancing, they'll forget about you."

Shit. That made him sound like he was in love with himself. Which he wasn't. Hopefully, the town gossip regarding his shorts hadn't reached her yet.

"First time as well?" she enquired, oblivious.

Phew.

"Unfortunately. I was told I need to get out of the house more. The classes were a gift, if you could call it that. I haven't danced since I was in high school and I looked like one legged version of Michael Jackson then, so I'm not expecting miracles."

"'Thriller' happens to be one of my favourite music videos. I like the zombies."

"Hopefully, I won't look quite that bad by the end of this."

"I'm fairly certain I will. Exercise and I don't have a very good relationship. I'm attempting to get fitter, and well, thinner." She fiddled with her t-shirt self-consciously before turning back to the front.

"You look pretty fit to me," he replied, instantly wishing he hadn't because it made him sound like a sleaze when he was trying to be friendly.

"Thanks."

The girl's cheek dimpled. She had long lashes. Quite pretty ones that framed two large eyes the vibrant colour of freshly cut grass. Her cheeks were plump and healthy looking. And she smiled at him like he was the only person in the room apart from her. He wished that were the case. Then he wouldn't be doing a Zumba class.

The session began.

After a demonstration of the moves — for the benefit 'of our newbies' — Aimee switched the music on and the dancing commenced.

The warm up was easy enough and the music loud and fun. Cole could see how people got addicted to Zumba. It *was* more like a dance party than an exercise class with everyone yelling and laughing. The first ten minutes went by in a spin. He was almost enjoying himself even if had crashed into the woman on the other side of him three times.

Then they began the cardio section. Suddenly the music was faster, the moves more intricate and Aimee's feet and arms accelerated towards the speed of light. In front of him a pair of sixty-year-old Zumba twins were booty shaking and milk-shaking and popping. How the they hell did they do that? They were turning themselves inside out. Cole felt like he'd been beamed into a rap video but forgotten to bring his blingy necklaces.

Up the front Aimee was squealing — the enthusiastic grin never waning — to go left, right, back, forward, shake that butt and shimmy. Before this, he'd assumed he was reasonably fit but he could now see that was not that case. The sweat was rolling down his temple, some of it had gone in his eye and it stung like crazy. Worse, he was being out-classed by a bunch of elderly ladies in combat pants.

Between the sixth and seventh song Cole gratefully raced for the security of his water bottle. As he guzzled water and tried to catch his breath he saw the girl who'd spoken to him earlier from the corner of his eye. She was panting like an overheated puppy, but she wasn't giving up. There was a look of rapt concentration on her face and the tip of her tongue was protruding from the corner of her lip as she attempted to remember and copy the steps. For some strange reason, Cole discovered it was turning him on. There was no way he could concentrate with her doing that, not when his mind had descended into the gutter and he was thinking of other things she might be able to do. It was practically pornographic, even though it wasn't.

After twenty minutes or so, Aimee announced that the group should form a circle. The regulars, who obviously knew the upcoming track well, hollered for joy and got ready for action, each one facing the person in front. Cole took his place behind his fellow novice and watched the steps as Aimee gave a quick demonstration. Then the dance began.

It was useless. He was flapping and flopping, positive his dance didn't look a thing like the one the instructor was doing. Her hips were moving double time and her arms swishing in rhythm to the beat. Her belly button had taken on a life of its own. Then, just as Cole thought he might have made a breakthrough, the instructor indicated that the class should change direction and the girl in front of him tripped over her shoelace, landing, SPLOT! Right at his feet. Engrossed as he was in not looking like a fool, he flipped right over the top of her, somersaulting and landing with a thud on her left calf. His old worn t-shirt ripped from neck to hem where the girl had tried to fend his falling body from hers. His chest and abs would have been completely exposed had they not become glued to her singlet with sweat.

At least that stopped the giggling side-glances from the twins on the other side of the circle.

"Ouch! Bugger!"

A look of pain came over the girl's face. She grabbed her ankle.

Cole sat up, untangling himself from her legs. Shit. He'd hurt her. "Are you okay?"

"My foot." A tiny tear formed in the corner of her eye as she pulled her sock away and they both stared into the space beneath where the skin had already taken on a funny bluish tinge and was beginning to swell.

Jesus, he was such a dick. "I'm sorry. I can't believe I fell on you like that. I'm really sorry."

The girl sniffed. "It's... it's okay. It was my fault. I wasn't looking where I was going."

Aimee had stopped the music. The class gathered around. "Are you all right, Olivia?"

"Can you walk?"

"Is it broken?"

"Yes. No and I don't think so," the girl replied.

"You won't be able to drive home," said one lady. "I did my ankle at karate and I couldn't put pressure on it for a week. If you give me your keys, I'll drop you home. You're only round the corner from me."

"I'm sure it'll be okay once I get an ice pack on it. I'm supposed to be going to Alice's for dinner, anyway. Could you drop me there?" The girl attempted to get up but fell back to the floor. "Arrgghh! Or maybe not."

"A trip to emergency might be a better idea. It looks nasty."

The girl was putting on a brave face but she looked as if she was going to cry. "I guess so."

Cole, who had managed to scramble to his feet by this stage, scanned the rest of the group. They may have been fit as fiddles but he had an inkling none of them could lift her and she certainly wasn't walking anywhere in a hurry.

"Here. Let me. I'll give you a ride. It's the least I can do seeing as I caused the injury. You can send someone back for your car later," he said, hitching his arms under her and hoisting her up.

Okay, so that hadn't been a clever idea. He could feel himself beginning to buckle already. Either he was more out of shape than he'd realised or the girl weighed a good sight more than he'd expected. Shifting her body so she leant against him, he instructed one of the ladies to fetch her things.

"Are you sure?" The girl had wrapped her arms around his neck and was clinging to his naked chest. "I don't want to put you out."

Cole smiled down at her. She was quite a delight.

"No problem. If it gets me out of this torture chamber, I'd carry you to Antarctica."

Well, maybe not Antarctica. She weighed a tonne. Which was odd because she don't look heavy in the least. She had lovely curves.

Out at his car, Cole deposited the girl next to the door while he unlocked it. "Are you right to get in by yourself?"

"Yes, thank you. You know, it's very kind of you to give me a lift. Beth would've done it."

"I know, but I don't think Beth could lift you." Shit. "Sorry. I didn't mean that the way it sounded."

"Its okay. It's not the first time I've been called fat."

Cole wished the ground would open up and swallow him whole. "You're not fat. Curves are good. Sexy, if you must know. Men like girls with a bit of meat on their bones."

The girl stared at him. He could see a glimmer of something like mirth in her eyes.

"I'm digging myself deeper, aren't I?"

"It might be wise to stop now."

Cole swung the door open and watched as she tossed her things onto the floor of the car, then held on to the roof and door, doing a little jump to get herself into the four wheel drive. She jiggled with the seatbelt and sat looking at him, her wide eyes blinking slowly. A stray hair had escaped from her ponytail and was falling across her face. He watched as she pushed it back, wishing his hand had done it, wishing his fingers were caressing the creamy skin along the side of her neck, his lips following their course.

God, he needed to get a grip. It was pathetic to be a slave to such thoughts when he'd only just met her.

But there was something about her, something insanely attractive, something that made him want to hold her and keep her safe. Not that that was getting them anywhere closer to the hospital. Dismissing the idea, he dashed around to the other side of the car and got in.

"Where to?"

"Hospital, please, driver," the girl joked. "I'm Olivia by the way. Olivia Merrifield."

"Cole Anderson at your service."

"Nice to meet you Cole."

Chapter 8

The hospital was cloaked in darkness by the time Cole drove into the car park. Not surprising. In a small town like Merrifield hospital services were not always needed. They'd be lucky if a doctor was even on call. The busiest time of the year was usually the day of the annual grudge match between the Merrifield Footy Club and neighbouring town, Hooper's Crossing. Every nurse in town was rostered on those days. Even Mrs Tanner came out of retirement.

After pulling the car to a stop, Cole switched off the ignition and walked around to the passenger side. Olivia already had the door open and was attempting, quite gingerly, to get out of the car. Cole wasn't surprised she was going it alone, despite the fact that her foot was the size of a watermelon. In the half an hour since he'd met her, he'd gotten the impression she was an independent sort of girl. She liked to do things herself. Which was great, if you weren't a cripple. In that case, a little help didn't go astray.

With a muffled grunt, Olivia hoisted herself out of the car, her uninjured leg taking the weight.

"You're not carrying me again," she told him. "I'd never live it down. There're people who work in there that have known me since I was born."

"Are you sure?"

"I'm pretty sure one of them delivered me."

"I meant are you sure you don't want me to carry you? It's no hassle."

Olivia reddened. "Positive." She shuffled out of the way of the car door, slamming it shut with such force the car shook. She may not have been fit but she was obviously strong.

"See? Piece of cake."

"As long as I don't mind a few displaced car parts. Please let me help."

"I'm fine. It's okay."

From the wincing Olivia was doing, Cole could see it was anything but. She could barely stand, let alone get herself into the hospital. Currently, she was wobbling precariously and gripping the bonnet of the car for safety. She was also doing a fairly bad job of masking what was obvious pain.

Deciding it was pointless to argue — he'd learnt many years ago that arguing with a stubborn woman was a waste of time — Cole took her hand, placing it on his shoulder to offer stability.

In his experience, women could be rather obstinate when trying to prove they were as strong as men. Which was crazy. Every woman he knew had the pain threshold of twenty men.

"Let's go then." He pointed the remote over his shoulder, locking the car.

They began a slow hop-limp up the path towards the hospital doors, Olivia's odd sort of walk making it very difficult to keep her upright. Once or twice she almost toppled into the hydrangeas taking him with her. Cole didn't want a repeat of that. It was what had got them into this trouble in the first place.

"Thanks again for helping me," she said. "You didn't have to."

"I know but I wanted to. I feel responsible, seeing as how it was me that fell on you."

"I told you it's not your fault. I'm the dopiest person on the planet. My head is always off somewhere it shouldn't be."

They fell silent for a minute.

"Sorry I ruined your shirt, Cole."

"It was on its last legs anyway."

"I don't think I can mend it but I hope you'll let me buy you another one."

Cole looked down at the t-shirt that was now something of a jacket. Or a cardigan. He'd had it since he had gone to an ACDC concert when he was seventeen. He loved that shirt. The first time he'd had sex with Lisa Bonner — the high school hottie — he'd been wearing that shirt. The first time he'd smoked a joint, he'd had it on. He'd been wearing it the day they'd bought Phoebe home after she was born too. It was a shirt of memories. There was no way it could ever be replaced. Maybe he could get a seamstress to fix it and have it framed?

"You don't need to do that," he replied. "It's only a shirt."

"Or a jacket, depending on how you look at it." Olivia giggled, her glance falling to his bare chest. "You could start a new fashion."

"I don't think it'd take off."

"Oh, I don't know." Her eyes twinkled naughtily in the half-light. It made him feel rather vulnerable, as if he was being assessed. It also turned him on, damn her. There seemed to be a lot of things about Olivia that were turning him on.

"So, you're new to town?" Olivia asked. "I thought I knew pretty much everyone in Merrifield, but I've never seen you before. Though your face does look remarkably familiar. I'm good with faces. Have we met before?"

Hopefully, she hadn't seen that bloody ad.

"I moved here a month or so back."

"From Perth?"

"Yeah."

"I used to live in Perth. Gosh, you look familiar."

Cole tensed a little, praying silently that the dark would be his ally.

"Where do you live now?" Olivia continued.

"Oak Hill."

She gave a dreamy sigh. "You bought it? I absolutely adore that house. I've been secretly coveting it since I used to go there as a little girl. My friend Alice and I used to play in the secret room at the top of the stairs. My grandma was friends with the lady that owned it, Mrs Caldwell. I told her I was going to live in that house when I grew up."

Cole was intrigued. "There's a secret room?"

"It's hidden in the panelling, on the right of the landing, if I remember correctly. The man who built the house had it as a panic room, I think. There was a lot of trouble with aboriginal groups back in the old days. I guess they weren't too happy about having their land invaded. I know I wouldn't be. Apparently, some of them were fairly handy with a spear, which is why there are little holes bored through the wall near the front door. The original owners used to poke a gun through them and fire. The lady of the house even chased a couple of tribesmen down the gravel drive with a rake, once, so the story goes. She was fearsome."

"I can't believe the real estate guy didn't tell me about it."

"Oh, there's nothing to worry about now. Merrifield's the safest town in Australia. I don't think anyone owns front door keys. And the few indigenous people in town are very well respected and loved."

"I meant the secret room."

"Oh." Despite her obvious pain — or was it embarrassment at showing her ditsy side twice in one conversation — Olivia gave him a broad smile. A lovely smile. "He probably didn't know. It wasn't called a secret room for nothing."

"So what's this secret room like?"

"It used to be dark wood panelled with two large casement windows. There was a big daybed and a bookcase with the most ancient books in it and a dollhouse. It was enormous. I remember that very clearly. I used to dream of getting lost in there, like it was my own personal playroom where nobody could find me and make me do homework. I used to love making up games with the porcelain figures and the teddies."

She also appeared to love to talk. Outside of Adelaide, that was the longest, most honest sounding speech a woman had ever given in front of Cole. Usually they told him what they thought he wanted to hear. Or how hot he was.

"So is your family something to do with the town?"

"My great-great-great grandfather, Elias Merrifield, was one of the first settlers. It's named after him."

"Bit of an honour."

"Bit of an annoyance, you mean. I can't scratch my bottom without the entire town knowing."

Cole knew exactly how that felt.

They reached the three steps to the front door. Olivia took hold of the rail and jumped up the first.

"Need a hand?" Cole enquired. "We could take the ramp if it's easier."

"I'm cool."

Which was obviously not the case, for as she attempted to hop to the first step, she missed it entirely and came lurching rather ingloriously in Cole's direction, her entire torso landing firmly against his still exposed chest.

Twice in one night, he thought, as his arms instinctively went around her waist to avert the fall. Some might call that lucky.

They stilled for a moment, frozen against each other. Cole could feel Olivia's heart thudding out of control in her chest or was it his? Her hands, braced against him, were suddenly searingly hot and as he shifted his hold pulling her a little closer, an overwhelming surge of desire engulfed him. God, he wanted to kiss her.

Olivia gazed up into his eyes. "Sorry."

"No problem."

"Seems I can't keep my hands off you."

"Seems that way."

Pulling away, she attempted the step again with the same outcome; only this time she added a muttered "shit" to the mix.

Cole shook his head. This was ridiculous. It'd be midnight by the time they got in the door if he didn't do something. Bending, he scooped her into his arms, like it was the most natural thing in the world to do and began walking towards the double doors of the hospital.

Olivia gave a surprised gasp but didn't ask him to put her down. She did, however, nestle into his chest and twine her arms around his neck as she smiled that smile again. That very enticing smile.

Cole hip and shouldered the door open. "Where to now?"

"There's an office around that corner. To the left." She indicated the way with her head.

A few turns left and right and with his charge safely deposited on an examination bed, Cole sat himself down in a chair opposite. Suddenly self-conscious he attempted to cover his naked chest by pulling the sides of the t-shirt around him, which had absolutely no effect because every time he moved it flapped open again. He could have tucked it into his track pants, he supposed, but he already looked like a fool. He didn't want to make himself look any worse. Surreptitiously, he tied the shirt in a knot at the bottom securing the ends, at least.

A voice came from the examination bed. "I wouldn't if I were you. You look like Peter Allen on his way to Rio."

Damn.

"Unless that's the look you were going for. In which case, I have a lovely set of maracas I could lend you to complete the ensemble."

Cole looked over to the bed where Olivia sat smirking and swiftly untied the shirt. She was a tease. And funnily enough he was finding he liked it. A girl with spirit was a good thing, a very good thing. "I might need some white trousers to make it authentic."

"And a lei."

"I guess so. It has been a while."

"I was talking about the garland type, not the sex type," she retorted, her eyes directly on his.

"Sorry, Freudian slip."

"Hmm."

Olivia shuffled on the examination bed. She'd gone quiet, whether that was because she had nothing more to say or because she was in pain, Cole wasn't sure, but judging by the pallor of her skin, he was thinking the latter. Allowing her to rest, he looked around the room — the pea green curtain, the murals on the wall designed to put children at ease. This room was like the myriad of hospitals he'd been in when Phoebe was ill. If truth were told, it was unsettling. Memories — and not good ones — were filling his head. He had no idea why he was even there. He should go home. Hadn't Olivia stressed repeatedly she could call her mother to collect her or her friend? He didn't need to wait.

Yet, despite the fact that images of tubes and machines and tiny, thin girls in hospital gowns were assaulting his brain, he found had no inclination to move. His inclination was to sit with Olivia and get to know her a little better. To make sure she was safe. It was the least he could do after he'd practically crushed her. Right?

Watching as she leant over the side of the bed, examining her ankle, Cole's mind began to wander to the moment he'd felt her leaning against him. It had been a long time since he'd had an unknown woman in his arms and the softness had felt rather nice. Like a girl should feel. So many girls were like stick figures these days. Skin and bone, they were. Never eating a thing. Olivia, however, didn't look like the kind who avoided carbs. She looked like a healthy, gorgeous woman.

And those eyes. She'd stopped analysing the bruising to her ankle and was analysing him. The way she stared, her gaze unwavering, made sensations he hadn't had for ages go racing into parts of his body he'd rather they didn't. Well, not right now, anyway. That could be awkward.

A doctor came into the room. He had a clipboard with some papers on it, which he consulted.

"Olivia Merrifield. Fancy meeting you here."

"Hey Sean. Long time, no see."

"What have you been doing to yourself?"

Olivia's eyes crinkled as she gazed up into the chiselled face of the doctor. Cole felt something like a stab of jealousy.

"Silly Zumba accident." She flicked her hand as if it were nothing.

"You've no idea how many people I see after 'silly Zumba accidents'. Dangerous pastime that."

"Since when do you do graveyard duty?" Olivia asked, changing the subject.

"Dr Jones was feeling under the weather. I offered to take his shift. Have to prove my worth as the new boy."

"I don't imagine you'll have a great deal to do. You might forget your doctoring skills if you have to be here too many nights."

"It is quiet. But Mrs Tanner bought me a thermos and some homemade biscuits."

"That'd be her. She's probably trying to set you up with Elise. Watch out or she'll be inviting you to dinner now she knows your back in town and single. I'm assuming you're still single?"

Sean gave a chuckle. "And ready to mingle."

The doctor asked Olivia some questions about her medical history. Then, rubbing his hands together to warm them gently took hold of her foot and pressed here and there. He asked her to explain the pain and its exact location. "And this is your partner?" he questioned, indicating Cole.

"Oh no, Cole's a friend. Well, not a friend. We've only just met, like half an hour ago. I mean, we were standing next to each other in the Zumba class. He helped me. After he fell on top of me and I ripped his shirt to smithereens."

Make a guy feel bad why don't you, Cole thought. He looked across to see Olivia's eyes twinkling again. He wondered if that mischievous look was for his benefit or if she was directing it at the good-looking doctor.

"I see."

The green curtain was swiftly swept across dividing Cole and Olivia and leaving him under no illusion as to his role in this affair. None.

Behind the curtain, softly spoken words were exchanged and the odd high-pitched titter floated in his direction. A niggle of annoyance invaded Cole's brain. Not that he had a right to be annoyed. Olivia was correct. They didn't know each other. But hadn't she felt the spark? He could have sworn she had.

What the devil were they talking about in there, anyway? It didn't sound like the doctor was doing too much doctoring. Cole cocked his head, leaning as far to the left as he could in order to see around the curtain or under the curtain or anything. Then...

SMACK.

The only thing he could see now were two pairs of metal feet from the chair he'd fallen from. Its upturned legs were so close to his left nostril he was almost impaled. Though he did have a spectacular view of a set of trolley wheels.

And the doctor's shoes on the other side of the curtain. Bit scruffy for a man in his job, if you asked him.

"Is everything okay out there?"

A head poked round the curtain.

"Yeah. Fine. Slipped... That's all."

Jesus, could this night be any more embarrassing?

Half an hour, one trip to the x-ray room and a pair of crutches later, Olivia emerged from behind the curtain, her ankle strapped. Her face was an unusual mixture of forlorn and excited, though how one could achieve such an expression was beyond Cole.

"Thanks Sean."

The doctor smiled. "Stay off it as much as possible."

Olivia rolled her eyes.

"I mean it," he reiterated. "You need to keep it elevated, not go jumping around at an exercise class." For some reason his gaze was directed at Cole.

"How long for?"

"Three or four weeks, I'd say. We'll review it when you come to the surgery."

"Cool."

"And take the painkillers." He reached down, handing her a box she'd left on the bed. "You're going to need them for a couple of days."

"Yes, doctor."

Cole stood, pulling the door open and gesturing for Olivia to go first. She hopped gingerly through, attempting to manoeuvre the crutches without knocking into things, specifically Cole's leg and then a chair.

"You okay?" he asked, as they walked.

"Yep. I've cracked a bone in my foot, that's all."

"No plaster?"

"It's not bad enough for that, just enough to hurt like crazy." She gave a wan smile.

"You don't need me to carry you again?"

"Definitely not. I think we've both had enough torture for tonight."

It was no hardship to Cole. As he'd already told her, he'd carry her to Antarctica and back if he had to, though why he felt this way about a girl he barely knew, he had no clue. He suspected her smile had a lot to do with it. Smiles were highly underrated in his book.

It was pitch dark outside the hospital and the walk to the car was slow, slower than when Olivia had been attempting to hobble into the hospital under her own steam. As they trudged along the path, Cole's bare legs brushed against sprigs of lavender and the scent wafted into the air around them. Up in the sky, the moon was hiding behind a large bank of clouds, which made seeing more difficult. Luckily, Cole had always had good night vision. He wouldn't want another accident.

Though having Olivia fall into his arms again wouldn't have been a complete disaster.

"So you know that doctor bloke then?"

"Intimately." Olivia glanced in Cole's direction. Was she trying to make him jealous? If so, it was working. "Sean and I grew up together," she explained. "We used to get up to all sorts."

Cole wasn't sure he wanted to know what 'all sorts' entailed.

"Right."

"Kid stuff mostly," she went on. "He's certainly changed a lot since I saw him last."

There was that stabbing feeling again. It was damn hard to hold a conversation with it assaulting his chest.

"People tend to do that when they get older."

"So I've heard."

They reached the car and Cole opened the door, settling Olivia into the car. Then, he hopped into his seat and turned the ignition on. The car purred to life.

"Thanks again for helping me, Cole. It's kind of you."

"I'd say I'll see you at Zumba but I guess you won't be there for a few weeks."

"Not unless I master the art of dancing on crutches between now and next Monday."

Chapter 9

"What on Earth have you done this time?" Mum looked down at my swollen foot, her face a mixture of horror and utter disbelief.

"I fell over at Zumba."

"Elaine Tanner said you threw yourself at some man and he had to carry you to the car. You can't go about the town behaving like that. People will think you're desperate."

It was lucky Mum was bending into her gym bag as she said it. At least she couldn't see me giving her the rude finger and rolling my eyes.

I wasn't in the mood to argue logistics that morning. My foot hurt like the clappers and even though I was sitting with it elevated as much as I could, I still had to work. Self-grooming dogs had not yet been invented. Likewise, sick pay for self-employed people. I couldn't afford to close the shop for a couple of weeks.

"I didn't throw myself at him and I'm not desperate, mother. I tripped."

"But you let him drive you to the hospital? That was a wise move."

How did I tell her it wasn't a 'move', that I wasn't in the throes of executing Operation Get Cole?

"I heard he's quite the bees-knees," Mum said.

"He is handsome."

"And how's Sean? When did he get back? Is he going to Shannon-down-from-Perth's birthday?"

"Yeah. I rang and asked him this morning. I don't think it's breaking any sort of doctor-patient thing if I do that, is it? I mean, he's like a family member."

"Of course not. You've known him since you were both in nappies. What are you going to wear?"

"My choices are limited with this big balloon on the end of my foot, so I'm thinking a dress of some sort, or maybe those loose fitting pants. You know, the black ones."

"Don't forget your Spanx. Now that you have a man on the hook, you want to be looking your best."

Oh for pity's sake. She made it sound like I was going on fifty with buckteeth and five chins.

"It's Sean, Mum. Nobody is on the hook."

Though the way Sean had grown into his body, I wouldn't have minded if he were on the hook. The man version of Sean was a far cry from the teenager who never washed his hair I used to hang out with.

"And don't forget to slap on a bit of that bronzer I bought you. You're looking so pale lately. This being indoors business can't be good for you. You need fresh air. You're probably lacking in vitamin D."

Either that or I was secretly a vampire.

I hobbled to the door, ushering Mum out with a kiss. "Right, well, I must be going. I've clients coming in a minute and I'm sure you've got heaps to do."

"Are you trying to get rid of me?"

"Yes. Now go."

Mum stopped, one foot out the door. "When do you dispense with the crutches?"

"A few weeks, I think."

"That's too bad. They're a great way to attract male attention."

A slightly desperate option I hadn't sunk to considering yet.

"Hmm."

"Which reminds me, I wanted to talk to you about rescheduling our family dinner for the minute. I've decided to sign up for the full yoga course. It was so much fun."

I had no idea what yoga had to do with attracting attention and I wasn't going to ask. "But we have a standing arrangement. I plan my week around our dinners."

"It's not like I'm moving to the other side of the world, Olivia. We see each other nearly every day. I do have a life, you know."

"You seem to be having more of a life than me."

"Yes, well maybe Sean can sort that out for you. I've always found the medical profession to be quite social."

What on earth was she on about?

"So, how about we move the dinner to Mondays?"

I didn't want to tell her Monday was *Game of Thrones* night. That *would* make me sound like I had no life. "Sure. Monday's cool."

As Mum said her goodbyes and closed the door, I hobbled to the grooming room to prepare for my next client. Mum was definitely up to something she didn't want me to know about. She'd rescheduled the mother-daughter dinner so many times now it was a wonder my calendar hadn't crashed from over-editing.

*****

Two hours later, lunch eaten and a doggy mani-pedi completed, I was leaning on the counter, chin resting in my palm. Across the road, a shiny new sign was being hoisted above the veranda of the shop that used to sell shoes. The transformation that had been occurring over the last month appeared almost complete. Shuffling to sit on the stool, I studied the goings on.

I should have been working but, at that minute, the happenings on the other side of the street were far more intriguing than dog collars and hypoallergenic pet beds.

As I watched, two men climbed joint ladders in perfect synchronisation; their bum cracks visible above their work pants. A third stood in the middle of the street moving his hands left and right, directing them to the correct positioning. I tilted my head to get a better view. The stomach of one of the men was obscuring the end of the sign and I couldn't get a good look at it but even from where I sat I could imagine what the rest of it said. Imagine and cringe.

Death By C...

By now the sign was dangling in its intended position. I could see the entire thing, complete with cupcake logo. It was a swanky sort of sign: pink, silver and glittery. Very girly. It matched the now revealed tarted-up facade perfectly, right down to the silver sprinkles over the top of the cupcakes around the door. And, if the façade hadn't caused enough of a stir amongst the locals already, the finishing touches certainly would. People would be talking about it for months. Merrifield wasn't used to such overt displays of theatricality. The theatrical society was kept well within the confines of the playhouse.

As new façade came to life, I discovered I wasn't the only one with a newfound interest in architecture. Shop owners up and down the street were coming out of their shops. Some stood in doorways, blocking customers.

Others were so blatant they went right onto the footpath to stare and two men who looked a lot like reporters were taking photos. Five minutes previous, Jim from the butcher's had been heard to say he couldn't give a pork chop about the goings on in the new shop next door to his. Jane from Your Dream Kitchen, on the other side, hadn't given two hoots either. She'd passed by that neglected space every morning without a second glance.

Not now.

Now, she and Jim, disturbed by the hammering and clattering, were standing gob-smacked in front of my window, as if they'd never seen a pink glittered shop in their lives. Which they probably hadn't.

"Who d'ya reckon owns that monstrosity?" Jim yelled at Jane, his voice hardly audible over the sound of the electric drills. His hearing wasn't the best either so he tended to yell in every circumstance.

Jane shrugged, yelling back. "Must be female. A guy would never have a pink shop."

"Probably one of those cooking shows' winners. Or maybe one of those effeminate types?" Jim glanced upwards to where the workmen were grunting under the weight of the sign. "Who else would decorate the front of a shop like that? Bloody lunatics."

With a huff he went back into his butcher shop, leaving Jane alone to ponder the fact.

By then, I had completely lost the will to work, so I slid the pricing gun across the counter out of view and hobbled to the display window for a closer look. The men were lining up the sign with a laser level. They were screwing it in securely and the silver lettering was beckoning. It was practically hypnotic.

Death By Cupcake: A Sprinkle is all it Takes.

Catchy name, I thought.

Trying to look like I wasn't spying, I hopped to the counter and gathered a couple of the new dog bowls, leads and collars in one hand, tossing them into a cardboard box which I slid towards the display with my good leg. Then, I went back to the display by the window and began to reorganise it in a colour co-ordinated design — the blue accessories together, next the pinks, then the reds. Well, that's what I told myself I was doing. Actually, I was staring out the window at the cake shop across the road and wondering how many hops on my crutches it would take me to get to the front door.

I gathered a collection of green accessories and played around until the display looked pretty. Across the road, the scaffolding was being removed and the hessian covering rolled away. A large banner advertising 'Grand Opening Deals' on twelve packs of designer cupcakes had been tied between the verandah posts and an elderly, but rather glamorous looking lady had appeared from inside. Armed with a bottle of Windex and a cloth she began to clean the windows, allowing customers a perfect view of the row upon row of delights that were soon to be lined up in glass fronted cases.

Oh God. It was bad enough having Maggie's up the road when I was fit but this shop was close enough for the smell of cake to waft across the street. This was my worst *Nightmare on Elm Street*, except Freddy Krueger was a piece of cake.

I shook my head in dismay. Clearly, the owners had no idea about the obesity rates in Australia these days. A cupcake shop was the last thing Merrifield needed. Me in particular. The only good thing was, I was so slow now I was on crutches if I did decide to partake the cakes would most likely be sold out by the time I got there.

While I stood pondering ways to keep myself from the temptation inside that shop Alice came in, pushing a red stroller weighed down with baby Ethan, three recyclable bags of groceries and the many miscellaneous bags she felt necessary to take with her when leaving the house with a small child. She was dressed up a little more than usual, wearing full makeup, a new pair of jeans and heels that were so high it was a wonder she could walk in them. She looked nice but it was a bit over the top for that time of day. Or any time of day. Alice was only known to wear heels at weddings or funerals. Trainers were more her style.

"What're you gawking at?" she asked, following my gaze across the street.

"The new shop over the way. Looks like a cake shop."

Alice bumped the door shut with her hip and put the brake on the pram before leaning across the stack of doggie treats on the SALE table to kiss my cheek.

"Geez, you reckon? A cake shop, eh? Yummy."

I glared at her and headed back to the counter.

"What?" Alice asked, her voice feigning innocence. "I love cake."

"Don't we all. That's the problem."

Alice was one of those annoying friends who managed to lose her baby weight in the first second after giving birth and come home from hospital wearing her skinny jeans. She never had to watch what she ate and had the ability to consume copious amounts of alcohol without gaining a pound. Or getting drunk. I only had to sniff vodka and I was incompetent.

"I wonder when it's opening?" she said.

"Can't be soon enough for me."

Having owned up to the fact that cake was no longer my friend, I was not giving in until my old clothes fit again. And I was certainly not returning those jeans for a bigger size. The hypnotism and Zumba may not have held the answer to my weight problem but that didn't mean I was giving up. In fact, I fully intended to go to Weight Watchers that very evening. And I was nervous as hell.

Alice unstrapped the baby from his seat, where he'd begun to fight for freedom. She bounced him on her hip. His chubby fingers wound around the string of her jacket and he grabbed and pulled at it.

"Ouch! Ethan. Not everyone in the world's cake-a-phobic. Maybe they'll have low fat cakes? Here, hold Ethan for a sec." She prised his little fingers away and handed him to me.

"Where are you going?" Though it was pointless asking, Alice was already out the door. That was another thing about my friend. You could literally blink and she'd be gone. She was faster than a whippet after a rabbit at times.

Not bothering to check for traffic, Ethan and I watched as Alice zipped across to the new shop. Her hand cupping the window, she shielded her eyes and looked into the interior of the cupcake shop. I saw her knock and wave to who I presumed were the owners. Then she stepped back and looked up to admire the sign, giving them a thumbs up. I jiggled Ethan who was still attempting to eat his fist and gurgling in satisfaction.

"What's your mummy up to then, Ethan?" I asked.

He didn't reply. Possibly because he couldn't talk. He did, however, open his mouth wider allowing a string of dribble to escape. Then he grabbed a handful of fabric from my shirt and stuffed it in his mouth, along with his fist.

"Ethan," I laughed. "You can't eat clothing. It doesn't taste good." I dug a baby rusk from his bag, handing it to him. "Here. Try this. Much yummier."

Ethan gurgled again and began to gnaw on the rusk.

A couple of minutes later, Alice was back. She took the baby, who had somehow managed to cover his cheeks with soggy rusk while she was gone.

"I can't leave you two for five minutes, can I? Look at you!" She dug in his bag, producing a Wet One to clean up the mess. "There's a sign that says the shop's opening Monday. You should see the inside, Livvy, it's *soooo* pretty. I can't wait to get in there and buy a cake."

"Hmph."

"I saw someone in there. I knocked on the window but they didn't answer. Who do you think owns it?"

"An old lady was cleaning the windows earlier. Apart from that, I haven't seen a soul come in or out." I tweaked the position of a couple of the dog cushions in the new display and stood to survey the look.

"I wonder if they'll be selling other types of cakes?"

"I don't really care."

"God, you're such a liar."

"No. It's true. As of today, I do not care about cake. I'm joining Weight Watchers. The only thing I shall care about is lettuce and grilled fish."

"You make it sound like torture."

Well, it was. For me, anyway.

After buckling Ethan in, Alice pushed the stroller back and forth with her foot. "Do you want to come for tea tonight? Jed's off out somewhere and we haven't had a catch up for days. I'll whip us up something diet conscious."

I made a face. "I can't. I have the Weight Watchers meeting and I don't know how long it will take."

Alice gave me the look, the one that always pulled me into gear. "You're doing it again."

"What?"

"Being negative about stuff before you've given it a go. Getting fit and trim isn't going to happen if you walk around like Negative Nellie. You have to embrace the new lifestyle, see the positive side."

Easy for her to say. The only thing I wanted to embrace was an enormous icing covered cupcake. Despite the fact that I'd said I didn't care about cake anymore, I'd been having cravings for one since I'd seen those fake sprinkles over the cupcake shop. Or maybe two. Or three.

"So, will you come after your meeting?"

"Okay. It's a date."

At that moment, the door of the shop opened and Cole entered, pausing just inside the doorway. He seemed somewhat taken aback to find me standing in front of him. Like he'd seen a ghost or had déjà vu or something. He wasn't as surprised as me though. He was wearing a pair of navy shorts with a rip right up the crotch.

I could see his red undies quite clearly.

"Hey Cole," I said.

My, but he had lovely shoulders.

In the kerfuffle of the other evening, I hadn't even noticed.

"Olivia. Hi. I didn't know you worked here."

"I own Doggie Divas," I said proudly, "Is there something I can help you with?"

I had no idea whether Cole owned a dog but I was positive if he did, it wouldn't be the type to go to a grooming parlour. Cole was way too manly for a dog that needed designer shampoo. His dog would be large and shorthaired, like a Rottweiler or a Pointer or something.

"Adelaide misplaced Lulu's diamante collar again. I was wondering if you had any in stock? That damned dog will be the death of me with the silly outfits she dresses it in." He shook his head, obviously confused as to why a woman felt the need to dress a puppy like a child.

"Lulu's your dog?"

"She's Adelaide's. Somehow, I get stuck with the bills every time another piece of her wardrobe goes missing. I didn't think buying her the bloody dog meant I was responsible for its upkeep too."

I limped over to the wall display that held the collars, picking up a pink bejewelled collar. "This is similar to the one Lulu had on when I clipped her."

"That's exactly what I'm looking for, though why she needs it, I don't know. What happened to the good old leather collar with a circular metal tag?"

"A dog like Lulu could never wear a collar like that. She needs to be shown off."

"Don't I know it? She's Adelaide's pride and joy." He picked up a baby pink dog coat, handing it to me. "I'll take this too. It's cold here, a lot colder than Perth. Lulu's been shivering in the mornings."

Sounded like Cole loved Lulu as much as Adelaide.

Having made our way back to the counter, Cole fished some notes from his wallet.

"So, about that secret door," he said. "You wouldn't want to pop by the house and show me where it is? If you're up to it, that is. You've got me intrigued."

I turned excitedly to Alice. "Alice, this is Cole. He owns Oak Hill. I was telling him about that room we used to play in when we were little."

A smile lit up Alice's face. "I'd totally forgotten about that. We used to have so much fun there. Do you remember the day we locked my sister out because she was being annoying and she told on us? When Mum and her came back they couldn't find the door. Mum thought she was playing a trick and smacked her."

"I think it was the only time she's gotten into trouble in her entire life."

Alice addressed Cole. "So, you're the one who bought the old house, then?"

"Yep."

"Lot of work?"

"Heaps. I've got a thing about old houses. Before I moved here I used to renovate them and sell them on."

"There are plenty of old houses in Merrifield. You should get Olivia to show you around her family home. It's similar to yours. Built in the same period. No secret rooms though."

"I'd love that. I'm looking for ideas for Oak Hill."

"And how did you two meet?" Alice enquired, looking at us both.

"At Zumba," I answered. "Cole fell over me. Then he gave me a lift. Literally."

"That's rather chivalrous."

I saw Alice's eyebrows rise slightly. I knew full well what she was thinking but decided it was better that I ignore it so I put the collar and coat into a small brown paper shopping bag and handed it to Cole. "There you go. Jewels fit for a princess."

"Thanks. I'd better get going. Tons to do. How's Saturday week for you? You know, to come up to the house? I can pick you up if you can't drive."

"Great. I've got a few clients in the morning but I'll be finished around one."

I smiled up into his friendly eyes. They were quite fetching. I hadn't noticed them the night we met, either. Which proves the point that I should have paid more attention to the goings on around me instead of whining about how big my bottom was. In my defence though, it had been dark.

As the door clicked closed behind Cole, Alice flicked me on the arm. "Okay. Spill. Where did you find that dish?"

For some strange reason I could feel a blush coming over me. It wasn't in my nature to blush yet every time I thought of Cole it seemed to be happening. "I told you. He fell on top of me."

"I wouldn't mind if he fell on me. He's yummy. Did you see his eyes? God."

"You're a married woman."

"You know what I mean. And he likes you, it was so obvious."

"Don't be silly. Didn't you hear him? He's with that girl Adelaide. And if you'd seen her, you'd know there'd be Buckley's chance he'd ever look at me even if he were single. She's like a supermodel."

"Not every bloke wants a supermodel for a girlfriend."

Not many of them wanted a girl who looked like a donut either.

Chapter 10

The lights of the community hall shone out into the car park and as I hobbled up the gravel path to the beginning of my new life, I was overcome with two feelings — one of insurmountable shame that others were going to see my weight and comment on it and the other of excitement. I'd decided on this course and, despite my hesitance, I was keen to begin. Even if it did mean stepping onto a set of scales in public.

As I walked in the door, I was greeted by a line of women longer than the queue to the Boxing Day sales. Happily chattering as they waited, they paid no attention when I got in the back of the line, which made me feel more at ease. I stood listening, slowly moving up and into the room along with the line. The general conversation seemed to be about how their weight loss efforts were coming along, the new products on offer and if it were possible to eat an entire block of Cadbury and stay within your points allocation for the day. Over to the side of the line, I spied a long trestle table that bore a blue and green smiley-faced sign saying 'new members'. Taking a deep steeling breath, I hopped out of the queue and headed in that direction.

A jolly looking woman with a huge white sticky name badge sat behind the table. She didn't look anything like someone who watched her weight. There wasn't an ounce of excess body fat on her. Well, apart from her boobs, which were gi-normous — an underestimation of their size, to put it mildly.

"Welcome."

"I'd like to join Weight Watchers, please," I said as quietly as I possibly could, even though I had no idea why I was being so secretive about it when everyone in the room was there for the same reason.

"Fabulous!"

She was bubbly, so bubbly, in fact, I thought she might almost fizz over with enthusiasm. I hoped everyone else wasn't going to be like this. I didn't know if I could stand such a degree of animation after a long day at work. The woman took my credit card details and began to put my information onto a membership card, which she handed to me, punctuated with an affirming nod. "Well, you've come to the right place."

And what exactly did that mean? That I looked like the rest of the women here? Honestly, one of them would have needed two chairs to hold her bottom if she sat down. I certainly wasn't that fat. I only had a few kilos to lose.

"I beg your pardon?"

"You obviously want to make some changes or you wouldn't be here," she clarified. "And this is the place to do that."

"Oh. Yes. Right."

And clearly, I'd arrived in the nick of time, too. I was beginning to think like one of those paranoid people who thought everyone was having a go at them.

"You need to pop in the queue now," she said, "and get your height and weight noted."

My heart palpitated at the thought. And it wasn't in a good way.

"It's okay love. Everyone's been there. The first week is the worst. After that, it's a breeze, and such a lot of fun to share your successes with the group."

"I have to talk?"

I knew this had been a bad idea, a really bad idea. Standing before a camera, when I'd been the size of a stick was one thing, but exposing myself in a room full of strangers was not on. I was there to lose weight, not get therapy. Though I'd often wondered if I might need a bit of that too.

The woman behind the desk gave me an understanding look. "Not right away. In fact, if you don't feel comfortable speaking, you can simply listen. Some people never say a word the whole time they're here."

I felt the tension leaving my body, like air from a deflating soufflé.

Following the pointed finger, I got myself into the queue of women — far smaller than twenty minutes before — and waited my turn.

éclairs at Maggie's? They were the reason I was predicament to begin with. Well that, and the fact willpower had left me the day I found out Grae been playing me for the fool. It was weaker than a that disgusting tea Mum kept plying me with when to her place and even if I did manage to employ its the odd occasion, things always went belly-up hours. There was no point fighting the cravings, made them stronger.

But that didn't mean I was giving up.

Soon, it was my turn on the scale. With a lump of the size of a tennis ball in my throat and my head floor in fear of being recognised, I handed my shi membership card to a second person recording the ins whose voice sounded way too familiar. I glan through my eyelashes.

Oh. My. God.

NO.

It was Mrs Tanner.

Overcome with shock — which seemed to be the recurring theme for the evening — I swallowed and raced towards the scales, hoping to avoid her gaze and praying she wouldn't recognise me without her glasses. It was embarrassing enough being there without people knowing I was. Which everyone would by about 9pm, if Mrs Tanner realised it was my membership card she was stamping.

"Hello, love. Fancy seeing you here."

Great.

"Uh, hi, Mrs Tanner."

"I haven't seen you for a while."

Probably because she was always on the phone spreading gossip.

"Yeah, I've been busy."

"Come to get fit and healthy, have we?"

"Something like that."

"You haven't been doing anymore of that hypnosis have you?"

"No."

"Glad to hear it."

Mrs Tanner moved from behind the table to stand next to the scales. I slipped off my thongs and using the other woman as a brace jumped onto the scale balancing on one foot.

"You won't know yourself after a couple of weeks. This Weight Watchers malarkey is for the birds."

I had no idea how to reply or what that even meant.

"Erm. Ah, yes."

Mrs Tanner fiddled with something on the scales. "I mean look at me. I used to be a heifer, no two ways about it. Now I could give that Miranda Kerr a run for her money."

I wasn't too sure about that. The new Mrs Tanner might be thinner but she was definitely on the wrong side of fifty and had wrinkles on her face the depth of arctic crevices from years of smoking. Suppressing a smile, I glanced at my weight, now winking at me from the scales.

That couldn't be true. There had to be some mistake.

Ninety. Point. Five. Kilos.

I blinked and blinked. I rubbed my hand over my eyes and squinted, hoping the blurring would change the numbers. I believe I repeated the process quite a few times before I slowly raised my eyes to Mrs Tanner. There I saw a faintly concealed look of shock, or perhaps it was disbelief, pass over her face. It couldn't be true. Any second now, Mrs Tanner was going to tell me I should hop off and on again because scales were playing up a bit tonight. Or the excess amount of fluid in my sore foot could account for a good ten kilos? That could happen, right?

But no, she simply smiled, handed back my card and remarked that the hardest part of the journey was over.

Engulfed in the mortification of actually being fat enough to register for the next season of *The Biggest Loser*, I slid sadly into my thongs and slunk to the meeting area where I sat in my seat. It wouldn't do to plonk myself down too hard. At ninety kilos I was likely to break the thing.

The meeting began. I couldn't concentrate, even though I was quite interested in tips for eating out and staying within your points. How had I let this happen? It was going to take a good deal more than a few magic points and a bit of huffing at the gym to remove that amount of blubber. No wonder Connor had complained. No wonder I couldn't fit into my jeans. I was fat.

And God, I really needed a peppermint slice.

*****

"You will not believe how humiliating that was," I moaned as I limped into Alice's kitchen an hour or so later and flopped down on a stool at the breakfast bar. "Ninety kilos, Alice. I weigh ninety kilos! Everyone was judging me. I could see them."

"I'm sure they weren't," Alice said. "There's a lot of women in town fatter than you. Shannon-down-from-Perth has whacked it on in the last month or so, poor thing. She couldn't even touch her toes at Boot Camp the other morning. I thought she was going to have a heart attack after pulling the tyres through the mud. Surely, you wouldn't tip the scales heavier than her?"

"I know you're trying to make me feel better but how fat I am in relation to the rest of the town is not the point. The point is, I don't think I can go back. Not after tonight."

"Why?" Alice headed for the pantry, where she had a bottle of red already uncorked. "Wine?"

I nodded.

"Mrs Tanner's the weigh-in lady. Everyone in Western Australia will know how fat I am by tomorrow."

"I'm sure she'll be discreet. It is Weight Watchers."

"She told the whole street about the boil Mr. Evans from the school had on his bum. I have no idea how she even knew about it and I certainly didn't want to know what they did to drain it. But she told me anyway."

"*Eww.*"

"Exactly. So can you imagine her keeping my weight to herself? Anyway, I don't think I'd be welcome."

Alice's look was quizzical. "Why?"

"I was so embarrassed after seeing Mrs Tanner, I decided to avoid all eye contact with the rest of the group. I walked straight into the table that holds the merchandise as I was leaving."

"Everyone makes mistakes." Alice picked a couple of nuts out of the bowl she'd put between us and popped them in her mouth.

"The table collapsed and the membership cards went sliding under the podium. Those bottles you put olive oil so you can use it like cooking spray smashed all over the floor. I thought Mrs Tanner was going to hit me with one of those recipe books they try to flog you.

Plus, I had to buy an entire carton of Weight Watchers cookies because they were damaged. What am I meant to do with them?"

"Eat them?" Alice didn't attempt to conceal her giggle.

I glowered at her. "You know, if I weren't feeling so sorry for myself I'd hop over the bench and pop you one. You're meant to be supporting my attempt to lose weight, not taking the piss."

"You know I support you. I think it would've looked hysterical, that's all."

I gave a weak smile. "It was pretty funny. Mrs Tanner's face went this funny shade of purple. It was like her blood was stuck inside her skull or something."

Alice placed two glasses on the island bench. "Here. Drown your sorrows."

"Bottoms up."

"Not for long. In a few weeks we won't even be able to see yours."

Taking a sip of my wine, I glanced around the room. Alice had done a fabulous job with the decorating. She had a knack of knowing how to put bits and bobs together to make them look good. When I tried to reproduce her ideas, it ended up looking, well, like bits and bobs made by people with very poor decorating skills or a garage sale that hadn't been packed away.

"When did you get the painting finished?"

"The other night while Ethan was in bed."

"It looks fab. Did Jed give you a hand?"

"He was out." Alice was facing the oven pulling a tray from middle rack, but I saw her body stiffen.

"Smells good. What're we having?"

"Baked lemon snapper. The fish was on special at the supermarket. Oh, and salad things from the veggie garden. I cooked some potatoes too."

She tipped a pile of teeny round new potatoes into a strainer and tossed them in a knob of butter, fresh parsley and ground rock salt. She served the fish and potato onto three plates, covered Jed's with reused silver foil from the drawer and put it into the turned off oven to keep warm for later. Then she hopped up opposite me and took a huge swig from her wine glass before setting about cutting her fish.

"Boy, that goes down well. I'd had a shit of a day. I think Ethan's teething. He whined the whole way to the shops and back." She refilled her wineglass before stabbing a large portion of salad and shoving it into her mouth.

"He seemed okay for the few minutes I had him."

"It's those rusks. He adores them." Her voice choked and I was positive I saw her blinking away a tear from the corner of my eye.

I put down my cutlery and swivelled to face Alice. She wasn't herself. It wasn't like her to become upset over a little thing like teething.

Alice was always so calm and collected. That was one of the things I loved about her. When I was having a meltdown over how my life was panning out, Alice always had a solution. She was the voice in my head, the pragmatic, practical one.

"Are you okay?"

"I'm fine." Refusing to meet my eyes, Alice stuffed a baby potato into her mouth and swallowed it whole while poking at her fish and swearing because she couldn't get it to stay on her fork. "How's your fish?"

I went back to my dinner. "Yummy, thanks."

"Is the salad okay?"

"Delicious."

This was the most inane conversation ever. I wished she'd tell me whatever it was. I hated to see her upset.

"Please tell me what's wrong," I said.

"It's nothing. I'm being silly. Shall we do dessert here? Or have a double dose with dessert in the lounge and McSteamy?"

Okay, so she was avoiding whatever it was. I could relate to that. Avoidance was my middle name. I decided to let it be. She'd tell me when she was ready.

"Is there a need to ask?"

We'd been watching the re-runs of *Grey's Anatomy* for months now and had reached the last season. I wasn't keen to see it end. It was our guilty pleasure, the one time we got to be two girls again, not grown women with responsibilities. And clearly, Alice was in need of forgetting her responsibilities tonight.

"I made fruit salad and there's some low fat ice cream or yogurt. Want some?"

"A little bit. Please."

"Cool." Alice picked up our plates and scraped the remains into the bin. She refilled her wine for the third time and glugged it down. Then she plonked our desserts on a tray, took another bottle of wine from the pantry, picked the lot up and stomped off in the direction of the lounge.

Geez. She was in a bad way.

By the time I'd hobbled in, Alice seemed to have pulled herself together. She was scrolling through the recorded shows to find the episode we were after so I set myself up in a corner of the couch, leaning my crutches on the arm.

"I had a dream about McSteamy the other night." She giggled, her finger poised on the play button. "It was so hot it woke me up. The things that man can do with his tongue."

I never had dreams like that. More's the pity.

"It was so real, like he was actually in the bed. I had an orgasm."

Not something I wanted to think about whilst watching TV. "Can you put the show on please? You know your sex talk is off limits when I'm not getting any."

"Jed and I don't have sex. We're married. We have a child." Alice pressed play and we turned to the screen.

"But you said..."

"I didn't say anything. Most of the time, Jed's blissfully unaware I'm even in the bed next to him. Sometimes I think he'd be happier if we had separate rooms. He's always moaning about how I wake him up when I get up to the baby. He never says he loves me anymore. I can't remember the last time he told me I was pretty. I may as well be the hired help." Alice's face looked longer than Jim the Butcher's after he'd got stuck in the Cow Face pose at yoga and the instructor had called the fire brigade to get him out.

"Is that why you've been dressing up like you're going to the theatre lately?"

"I thought it might make him notice me if I put in a bit more effort."

"Well, you got noticed all right. Those workman over at the cake shop couldn't keep their eyes off you."

"Pity I can't say the same for Jed."

I was beginning to get a little worried at the way this conversation was panning out. Alice and Jed were the perfect couple. They were *the* couple. "Is there something wrong between you two?"

"Nothing I can put my finger on. The other day, when Jed was having daddy day, I came home and there was nobody here. When I asked him where he'd been he got rather defensive. It's not the first time. He's been so crotchety with me lately."

"It's probably work stress."

"Jed doesn't have stress. He's the most laid back person in the world."

"Maybe he's feeling left out with the baby and everything. Lots of guys feel a bit put out, or so I've been told."

"I did wonder about that, so I thought I'd surprise him at the footy club, give him a lift home so he didn't have to walk; you know, show him a bit of extra love. He wasn't there. They didn't even know where he was. Marcus Price said he hadn't been at training for weeks."

I could see where this was heading. But it couldn't be true. Jed wasn't that sort of guy. "You don't think he's cheating on you?"

"I don't know what to think. I've tried to talk to him about it but he keeps telling me I'm imagining things. I'm not imagining it. I'm not stupid."

"But it's preposterous. Who on earth would he even be having an affair with?"

Alice snorted. "It'd be slim pickings. Most of the single girls in town are either young enough to be his daughter or the size of a semi-trailer. No offence."

I was offended but I forgave her silently. She was venting.

"I bet it's Beth," I joked. "They're probably going at it in the bank vault as we speak. I can see her up against the filing cabinet with her knickers round her ankles."

The whole town knew Beth had been in love with Jed since the day she'd started working at the bank. It was like watching a rabid dog, seeing her drool over him whenever he walked past her station. But with her cougar-ish ways, hair bigger than Dolly Parton and a bottom to match, Beth managed to scare more men than she attracted. And if her hair didn't frighten them away, her triple chin gave it a good shot.

I gave my sexiest moan. *"Oh Jed, give it to me. Give it to me, baby! You're sooo hot! Ooh, aaaahh'."*

A huge spurt of wine escaped from Alice's mouth and sprayed across the coffee table. Splotches of burgundy began to spread over her t-shirt.

"Oh Jed, you're so big. Give it to me again."

Now Alice was holding her stomach, laughing. "Stop, Livvy. Stop. I'm going to be sick."

"Why? Because you can't bear the thought of Jed with Beth or is it the idea of Beth's big granny pants that's worrying you?" I teased.

After a minute or two, the laughing subsided.

"Look at my t-shirt," Alice said. "I'll have to soak it straight away."

"What about my dessert?" I held up my bowl, filled with red wine sodden fruit. "I know the wine will get mixed in when it's in my stomach but you've sprayed it in my bowl. I can't eat that. It's disgusting."

I watched as Alice picked up the bowls and took them to the kitchen before disappearing down the hall to change her top. I hated to see her upset. Hopefully, I'd managed to cheer her up a bit, sacrificing my dessert in the process. But what Jed was up to? It was simply too hard to fathom that anything could be wrong in their marriage.

A few minutes later, we were back on the couch — our second attempt at TV viewing imminent. "I guess you're right," Alice admitted as she picked up the remote. "Jed would never do anything. He loves me."

"Definitely. Now, could we get on with *Grey's Anatomy*? I need to clear my head. The mental image of Beth with anyone is enough to give me nightmares for a month."

Chapter 11

The big old sandstone house was exactly how I remembered it from when I was a girl. Cole led the way up the front steps, stopping frequently to allow me to clomp along beside him. My foot had been feeling better over the past couple of days and I was looking forward to getting rid of the crutches. They might be a good way to attract attention and stop me from eating but they were a pain in the bum. Or underarm. Whichever was worse.

As we approached the door to the sitting room I noticed the French doors flung open in the afternoon sun. A slight breeze was billowing the gauzy curtains causing them to rise and fall over the furniture near the window. It was so romantic. Like that movie I'd seen recently, not that I could for the life of me remember what it was called. Cole's muscular form in front of me was doing a pretty good job with distraction. There was something about it that made me want to run my hands over his shoulders and back then down to his bum.

But back to what I was meant to be thinking about. I poked my head into what was now the beige, white and duck egg blue drawing room. "Oh Cole, its beautiful, I've always loved this house. The way you've decorated — it's breathtaking — you've brought it back to life."

And exactly how I'd imagined I would do it if I ever got the chance.

The walls were painted in light and airy shades and the timber floors had been exposed and polished along with the mantle over the fireplace. A pair of sofas and two wing back chairs was positioned around a rug in front of the fire, their soft yellow checks adding another dimension of colour to the room. It was such a stark contrast to the hideous Victorian burgundy, gold and brocade Mrs Caldwell had favoured when she was alive. Now, it was more French provincial, but country style.

"I'm pretty happy with how it's turned out."

"It used to be so dark and gloomy. Everything was formal and overstuffed, that wall had hunting trophies, such ugly stags heads. There was even a tiger." I pointed to the far wall of the room. I knew I was gushing but what else could I do? It wasn't like I was could help it, the house was gorgeous. It had been reborn into something greater than it would have been when it was first built nearly two hundred years before. I was a little envious. Blue Wren Cottage was cute and chock full of character but it paled in comparison to this. Not size wise. Obviously, Oak Hill was vast but in the way things had been put together. Either Cole or Adelaide had a knack, a very artistic eye.

"I'd give you the rest of the grand tour, but somehow, I don't think you're up to it yet," Cole replied.

"Raincheck? After I get rid of the crutches?"

"For sure. Adelaide would love to show you around. She knows more about the fabrics and paint than I do. I usually handle décor myself but I've been too busy to do this, so I gave her free reign. She knows what I like." The way he smiled at me made me feel almost as if Adelaide didn't exist. Odd. Unless I was reading him wrong. It could be that he was merely one of those men who had women friends and he wanted me to be one of them.

We walked along the hallway and stopped at the foot of the stairs where I saw a collection of family photos; Cole, Adelaide, Lulu and another older woman with her alabaster hair swept into a chignon. She looked vaguely familiar but I couldn't put a finger on it so I questioned Cole about her.

"That's my mother, Ella."

"And the little girl?" I pointed to a portrait of a skinny girl. She was laughing into the camera with her big eyes twinkling exactly like Cole's. Cole hadn't mentioned a daughter.

Cole went silent. Suddenly, he looked as if he were attempting to keep some deep emotion in check, like I'd said the wrong thing by mentioning the child. "That's Phoebe, my daughter. She died a while back. Leukaemia. It's been a tough time."

I faltered. "She's very pretty."

"A lot like her mother. But with a smarter mouth. Phoebe was twelve going on thirty. She was an unmerciful bossy boots, too. Always giving me advice on how to run my life." His mouth tilted at some unknown memory.

"You must miss her."

"Heaps."

"Do you have any other children?"

It was probably insensitive of me to ask but I wanted to know more about Cole. He seemed like a nice guy, the type of guy you could have a joke with, be friends with. As long as you didn't get carried away by his looks, of course. They could set your heart racing at fifty paces.

"No. No other children." He shuffled, turning towards the staircase. "Right. That was a bit much sharing for two people who've only recently met. How about you show me this secret room?"

My gaze travelled up the timber staircase. I might as well have been contemplating a trek up Mt. Everest because that's how insurmountable it suddenly seemed with crutches. There was no way I was going to be able to get up there. I had enough trouble navigating the two steps into the shop every morning. And if I somehow managed to get up to the landing how would I get back down? On my bottom? Over Cole's shoulder, fireman style? Absolutely not.

"It's up there, to the left. You have to press a certain part of the wall to release the catch that opens the door."

"Can you see it from here?"

"No."

"Guess there's nothing for it then." Cole took the crutches and leant them against the wall before scooping me into his arms.

"Put me down," I squealed, taken by surprise.

"Got a better idea? "

"I guess not," I said, making a feeble attempt to wriggle from his grasp because despite myself I was rather enjoying the feeling of being in his arms again. Besides, he was already half way up the staircase before I knew what had hit me. I couldn't expect that he'd put me down there.

"What if Adelaide comes down the stairs?"

"What if?"

"Won't she mind?"

"I don't think she'd be that fussed. You're not the first woman I've carried up a flight of stairs." His eyes glinted with mischief.

I frowned at him. Surely Adelaide didn't approve. Maybe they had one of those 'open' marriages? That could be the case. But even if it was I had no intention of becoming the third person in their party. I'd well and truly learnt my lesson after Graeme's wife had chased me down the corridor outside his office. "Please let me down."

Cole stopped. He released an elongated sigh. "Look, you can't jump up the stairs. The last time you tried I ended up carrying you so we might as well skip the middleman, right?"

"Well, I'm not letting you carry me down. We hardly know each other. I'll shimmy. It'll be fine."

At least that was what I was telling myself I'd do. My body, however, was telling an utterly different story. Wrapped in Cole's strong embrace, I'd begun to tingle. A warm sensation spread though me as if a big cosy blanket was enveloping me. I wanted to snuggle into his arms and never come out. It was comforting and exciting at the same time. Not to mention scary. Because it could only mean one thing.

I was severely attracted to Cole.

Which was not good at all.

Married men brought trouble. Big trouble.

The good thing, I supposed, was that I usually discovered the massive flaws of the men I liked *after* I'd been seeing them a while. I already knew Cole was married. And even if his body seemed to be sending me signals that screamed interest, I had no intention of taking that bait. Ever.

After what seemed like the longest staircase trip in history, we reached the top of the stairs. Cole deposited me gently next to the wall on the left of the landing.

Grasping the balustrade, I hopped towards the timber-panelled wall, stopping to have a breather. My good leg was throbbing from the strain of having to carry the weight of my entire body. I paused in front of the Baltic pine clad wall, pondering. It had been twenty years since I'd been here. I hoped my memory was as good as I thought it was.

"There. I think if you press there, right in the middle of that circular detail that looks like a flower, the door will open."

From his position behind me, Cole reached over pushed against the wall. It didn't budge.

"Push harder. Alice and I were probably the last people to use that door. It could well be stuck."

He tried again. Bingo! A crack appeared in the wall.

Fingers to the wood, Cole prised the door open. A tiny room flooded with light opened before us. Years of dust unsettled by the movement and flew about the room like dandelions on the breeze. Cole began to laugh. "You don't know how many times I've stood under the north elevation of the house and wondered why I couldn't locate this window. This is incredible, Olivia. Thank you."

I hobbled into the room behind him and leant against the wall. I couldn't believe it. The room was exactly as Alice and I had left it, as if we'd just stepped out of it yesterday, with a promise to return. Well, apart from the layering of years of dust. I sneezed, covering my mouth.

There were tiny wooden children's chairs with teddies seated upon them and, in the corner, the huge old dollhouse Alice and I had loved so much was waiting, its doors swung wide. Mrs Caldwell had told us once it belonged to the little girl who'd first lived in the house over a hundred years earlier. The blue velvet chaise I'd read so many books on — the ones that were lining the walls — was still under the window in its spot in the sun. The velvet had begun to fade in patches but, otherwise, it was as I remembered. And under the other window, a delicate oak writing desk stood waiting for someone to sit at it again. That was the place I'd written my first story about a princess trapped in a secret room. That desk and the view beyond it had me spellbound for hours on end every time I'd gone there. It was the beginning of my dream to be a journalist or a writer or whatever my dream had been. Somehow, I'd lost sight of that. I'd squashed it and wrapped it up, hidden it away with the hurt. I ran my fingers over the back of the chair, memories flooding back. "I wrote my first story at this desk."

"You're a writer?"

"I have a journalism degree. But I never really used it. Not for writing."

"How come?"

"I went into TV journalism. I started as a weather girl. It wasn't my dream but it was exciting and fun. While it lasted."

"What was your dream?"

"To sit at this desk and write. I'm not sure what. Maybe a novel. Or a TV series on cheating exes. I know all about those. What about you?"

"I've never had an inkling to write about cheating exes."

"Ha ha."

"I used to dream of a happy family like the one I grew up in. Sort of lost sight of that."

There were no words to describe the emotional tugging that began in my heart at that moment. And apparently, Cole was feeling it too. Next to me, I heard a sniff and glancing across, I noticed the wetness welling in Cole's eye.

"Are you okay?" Instinctively, my hand came to rest on his forearm.

Cole swiped the tear away. "It's like a little girl's paradise in here. Phoebe would have loved this."

*****

"Oh Alice, you should have seen his face. I wanted to hug him. He's in so much pain."

Alice, who was in the throes of a war between herself, Ethan and a nappy, looked up. "I thought you weren't interested in Cole. I thought he was out of bounds because he's married."

"I'm not and he is but that doesn't mean I can't feel sympathy for the guy. He was crying over his dead daughter."

"And you felt the need to comfort him in a non-sympathy sort of way?"

"Don't be so gross."

"But you did, didn't you?"

"No!" I felt my cheeks beginning to get warm. She was making me sound like a bunny-boiling tramp. I felt incredibly guilty and nothing had even happened. I'd only wanted to make him feel better.

"But you like him all the same. I knew it, I just knew it," Alice exclaimed. "You don't care that he's married. You like him." Having finally got the nappy on, she pulled Ethan into a standing position on the change table and bounced him up and down, laughing as he made happy baby noises. "Ma-ma-ma-ma."

"Okay, I'll admit the whole vulnerability thing made him more than merely physically attractive but I'd never knowingly be with a married man. You know I wouldn't. That thing with Richard wasn't my fault. I'd never be able to have an affair. I'd spend the whole time we were in bed imagining the hurt of being the one who was being cheated on. It'd be awful. I could never put anyone through such trauma deliberately and you shouldn't joke about it." I hoped I was making my point clear. I needed to make it super clear. "Cole Anderson is off limits."

Alice handed Ethan to me while she tidied up. I put him on my knee, where he proceeded to reach up and pull a handful of my hair. Carefully, I extracted his fingers and blew a raspberry on them. He giggled. I blew some more. He laughed harder.

"So, moving on. The party. Is Sean still single?" Alice asked.

"You sound like my mother but, yes. As far as I know. This is not a date, though. It's a friend thing."

And a get Connor back thing.

"Any aversions to cellulite or push up bras?"

"Unsure. You could ask him if you like."

"Good-o. And what are you wearing? Dress to impress, I say."

"It's only Sean. You know, that guy who got us grounded because we were caught drinking cider under the railway bridge?"

"Yes, but I hear he's way hotter than when we were sixteen."

Oh for Pete's sake. What was it with these people trying to fix me up with the doctor?

"In that case, you'd best give me a lift home. It's going to take me at least three hours to find something that hides this thing on my foot."

"You could hollow out a watermelon and fashion it into a shoe. It'd go with that red dress."

"Or I could bonk you on the head with it and knock a bit of sense into you." I reached over the baby and picked up my house keys, shoving them into my pocket before Ethan could use them as a teething ring. "Your mummy's a nutcase Ethan, I don't know how you put up with her."

"Ma-ma-ma-ma."

"See, Al? He agrees with me."

"Mama's the only word he can say."

"Da-da-da-da."

*****

Alice pulled into my drive a few minutes later and I hopped out of the car, promising to send her a photo of the outfit I'd decided on for her approval. First things first though, I brewed a pot of tea and limp-stepping into the bedroom, I put it on the chest of drawers. It was possible that it could take the rest of the evening before I decided what to wear. I might as well be well hydrated.

A fit of madness coming over me, I decided to try on the jeans I'd got off the Internet again, the ones that hadn't made it past my knees without the assistance of a crowbar. Tentatively, I unstrapped my foot and slipped into the jeans. One leg then the other. While still sitting, I pulled the jeans to my knees, then my thighs.

This was going remarkably well.

And it only got better when I discovered the jeans went up over my hips. Okay, so they were still very tight and I had to wriggle but there was no sign of a coat hanger during the zipping.

I looked in the mirror. There had to be a mistake. I'd only been doing Weight Watchers for two weeks and though I'd stuck to my eating plan, I'd had no time to get back to a meeting to weigh in. I swivelled from side to side, catching my profile in the mirror. I looked way better — the cake shelf was still there, but it had shrunk to more of a muffin top. Which could only mean one thing. I'd lost weight. I'd freakin' lost weight. I could almost hear the alleluia chorus from above.

Lying back on the bed, I pushed the jeans to the ground and stepped out of them. Then, I went to the bathroom and with a deep breath — and eyes firmly shut — stepped on the scales. It was strange that I felt anxious about it, even though my brain was telling me I should be excited, but that was it.

I opened my eyes.

Whoa!

I looked again. The weight stayed the same. I jiggled to make the weight re-adjust but it went straight back to where it had been before. I'd lost 6.1 kilos — crazy considering I hadn't done a scrap of exercise.

My heart began to pump in excitement, making me almost giddy. The adrenalin surged through my body. I wanted to shout with joy. This was amazing. I'd lost weight. I felt so good that suddenly the idea of an itty-bitty cake smothered in lashings of icing sounded like a great reward. It couldn't do any harm, right? Not after I'd lost six kilos. And I did have a few points left in my tally for the day, plus my 'extras'. One cake would do no harm at all. I could start my diet again tomorrow.

I stepped off the scales ready to head for the door and it was as I did, I caught sight of my reflection in the bathroom mirror. I stopped. Who was I kidding? One cake always meant five. I couldn't undo the work I'd done by shoving cake into my face. It would lead to guilt and then I'd eat more to squash that feeling. I couldn't have a cake.

But I really wanted one. I wanted one so badly, I could almost taste it.

I'd have to find another way to reward myself.

Hopping back to the bedroom, I began to pull out clothes I'd been secretly avoiding for the longest time. Jeans, t-shirts and skirts came flying out of the wardrobe until the floor was covered. I began to try things on and while a few of them were snug and some went nowhere near to doing up — I told myself that this was because these were the teeny tiny clothes I hadn't worn since I left Perth — there was a definite shift.

If I kept going, I'd be back to my old self in no time. And imagine what might happen if I exercised? God, I could be wearing booty shorts by the New Year.

Okay, so that was a bit of an exaggeration but you get the drift and the motivation was enough to make me forget my craving.

I sat down on the bed. Was this a turning point? If I were being honest, I hadn't felt good about myself for years. Everything was an effort. Even having a relationship was an effort, which might have gone a long way to explaining why I ended up with such manky boyfriends. I had no confidence, so I'd become an easy target for the worst type of men. Well, not any more. Starting tomorrow, I was going to be the new, improved Olivia — thinner, more confident and in control of every aspect of my life.

After I found a top to match those jeans, that was. Which could take all night. I probably wouldn't even have time for dinner. Woohoo!

Chapter 12

"I'm on my way from misery to happiness today... uh ha uh ha..."

The cover band, comprising Jim the Butcher and a few of his cronies, were playing up a storm by the time Cole and Adelaide opened the double doors on the party the following Saturday and stood taking in the scene before them.

This was not your typical young person's birthday. In fact, Cole reckoned he could safely say this was like no event he had ever been to in his life. He had a feeling he'd been thrown into a time-travel machine and warped back to 1972. Not that he'd been alive in the seventies but he'd seen plenty of TV shows. Along one side of the room, a large buffet table was set with plates of delicacies he'd only ever heard mention of by his mother and grandmother. Cocktail sticks spiked with cheese, gherkin and cabana sausage stood proudly poking up from an upturned watermelon half, prawns hung over the side of martini glasses filled with an orange dipping sauce and mini saveloys wrapped in pastry were piled high on a platter next to another containing marshmallows, strawberries and what he thought to be French onion dip or was it a fondue?

Jesus, he hadn't seen a fondue since he was five. Ella had gotten rid of hers after he tried to stab the cat with one of the mini forks. What he'd wanted was to see how fast Smokey could run. He hadn't been a psychopath in the making.

The room had been decorated too. At least Cole thought it had — on second glance maybe it simply hadn't been redecorated since the seventies. There was a timber veneer feature wall and some hideous yellow bubble glass in the window behind the bar. The look was completed with burnt orange laminate tables, brown floor tiles and a massive artwork that vaguely resembled Bob Marley.

As Cole and Adelaide made their way around the side of the dance floor to the bar, the space surged and ebbed like waves on the beach, every able-bodied person in Merrifield, bopping along to the music. Fist pumping, hip wiggling grannies were bobbing and dipping — quite a scary sight if you weren't prepared for it — but necessary to pass if they wanted to reach their host.

On the other side of the room, Shannon-down-from-Perth was perched on a corner of the bar — pride of place — unwrapping birthday presents. She was wearing a large pink and purple felt hat in the shape of a birthday cake. Its candles were flopping in her eyes and she kept blowing them away or flicking them with her finger. Shannon's top was so tight it was easy to see she no longer fitted into her jeans and had left the fly undone. It made Cole a little uncomfortable to be greeted by such a sight, but hey, if she was happy, who was he to argue? From what he'd heard she was a bit of a wag. She probably didn't care.

"Hello!" she called, beckoning them towards her. "You must be Cole and Adelaide. I'm so pleased you could come. I like to make new people in town welcome, like everyone welcomed me when I first arrived." She put a half opened gift on the bar beside her and leant over gathering both of them into her rather large bosom for a hug. Cole felt as if a huge, pink, feather pillow was smothering him.

"Now how about a drink? Jane!"

Jane from Your Dream Kitchen, who was moonlighting as a bar wench, bustled along the bar.

"Get these two out-of-towners a drink will you, sweets? And pick your mouth up off the carpet. We're perfectly aware how hot the man is without your drooling. Oh and PS, I just got a hug so I win the bet."

Jane blushed. "There's no need to advertise it, Shannon. You'll embarrass the man, not to mention me."

"Why on earth would he be embarrassed?" Shannon turn to Cole, who had found — for the first time in as long as he could remember — that he was, indeed, blushing. "You're not embarrassed, are you Cole? It's a compliment having half the town in love with you. We had a book running on who was going to get a hug first, so I guess I've won that. Beth will be pissed off. Her and Maggie have been planning ways to bump into you all week."

"I'm sure it's not that bad."

"Not that bad! Haven't you seen my friends?" She pointed to the dance floor where a group of girls he hadn't noticed stood giggling and waving like he was Bradley bloody Cooper or something.

Right. So maybe it was that bad.

"You're the talk of the town, honey. Maggie withdrew five hundred in cash from the ATM instead of fifty because she was so busy looking at your behind," Shannon continued. "And Lucille from the real estate office nearly got run down by a car when you bent over to tie your shoelace. You should send out a warning before you go round wearing those blue shorts." She let out a guffaw at her own joke.

"In our defence we're not exactly flooded with good looking blokes round here," Jane added, as she handed Cole and Adelaide their drinks. "Last time we saw a nice looking specimen was in 1992 when that guy from that movie drove through town. Looked a bit like Robert Redford. Now there was a hottie."

"Sam Worthington was here last year, wasn't he? You know when he was shooting that Indie film over at Margaret River?"

"Oh, he's hot. Smokin'." Jane put a finger to her bottom and made a sizzling noise.

Cole took a sip of his drink. He had no idea whether he was meant to be a part of this conversation or they were merely talking *about* him but whatever, it was clear that Ella hadn't been exaggerating when she'd told him about the newsagents. Suddenly, he wished the he could find the coatroom to hide in. The place was old enough; surely it'd have one. He was used to people talking about him because of the ad but this was ridiculous.

Adelaide, on the other hand was in fits. "You poor things. Lucky we arrived, then."

"I know, you can't imagine our delight when Cole began his daily jaunts to the coffee shop. It's not every girl who can nab a man like him, you're so lucky."

"Oh, he's not—"

Cole squeezed Adelaide's hand so hard, she almost dropped her drink. "Time to move on. There's only so much praise a man can handle before it starts going to his head."

"Yeah, right." Shannon laughed. "Help yourselves to the buffet. Maggie's made the most divine fondue."

The pair made a move towards the buffet. "I'm not hungry," Adelaide said, picking up a cocktail saveloy and inspecting it before biting the end off.

"Me neither, but it might keep the wolves at bay if we stand here for a bit."

A distinct sound of tittering could be heard over the music. A couple of fingers were pointed in his direction and a few not-so-furtive glances were cast.

"Oh Cole," one of them sing-songed. "Come and dance with us, Cole."

Cole dipped his gaze, instantly intent on choosing the perfect party pie. Why was it that everywhere he went women wanted to attack him? It would have been great if he were that sort of bloke but Jesus, he was getting over the death of his daughter. Couldn't they leave him alone?

Adelaide put her lips to his ear. "You have admirers."

"Geez, you think?"

"Maybe you should ask one of them to dance."

"Maybe you should mind your own business." Cole had no intention of going anywhere near those piranhas. Those women were behaving like they were marooned on a desert island with him the only male alive. Or he was George Clooney.

"How's it going, guys?"

"Great thanks."

Olivia had sidled up beside him, thumping him in the shin with her crutch. Thank God. At last, a normal, sensible female. Well, fairly normal. She did seem to have a bit of a problem with him touching her or saying anything that was even one step above friendly.

He wondered what her deal was. Clearly, some bloke had done the dirty on her. Even he — and he wasn't the most astute guy in the world when it came to chicks — could see she'd been wounded.

"I see you're making yourself known to the netball girls."

"Not by choice," Cole replied, tilting his head towards one of the girls who was grinding against a pillar and beckoning for him to join her. "They started that behaviour as soon as we walked in the door. I feel like a piece of meat."

"Lord knows why," Olivia joked. "It's not like you're George Clooney."

Was she reading his mind?

"My thoughts exactly," Adelaide added, joining the conversation. "Hey, thanks for the little coat for Lulu by the way. She looks adorable in it."

"I knew she would."

"So how's the foot?" Cole asked.

"On the mend. I'm trying to figure out if I can dance on crutches without doing any more damage."

"You should be careful."

"I wasn't talking about damage to me, silly. I meant the other people on the dance floor. I'm a hideous dancer when I'm *not* on crutches." She gave a delightful giggle that sent shots of electricity into his groin.

Great. That was all he needed.

"How long till you get them off?"

"A couple of days. The healing process has been a bit longer than expected but I should be good to go next week. I can't wait. It's not easy navigating life with these. I keep crashing into things."

"So you won't be Zumba-ing again?"

"I don't think it's my thing, I'm too un-co. But I'm going to start jogging again. At least that's only one foot in front of the other. Or I might try Pilates. You can't fall over if you're already on the ground."

"Sounds like a safer option."

At that moment, Sean appeared.

"I wondered where you were." He handed Olivia a drink, in to which he'd conveniently put a straw. The fact that his hand lingered on hers was not lost on Cole. Neither was the fact that the guy was bloody enormous. Cole, being a couple of inches over six feet, was usually the tallest in a crowd but this guy made him feel like Tattoo from *Fantasy Island*.

"Oh, a straw! That's so thoughtful. Thank you Sean."

Anyone could put a straw in a drink. Who did this guy think he was, Superman?

"It might make it easier, if you're standing up. You have enough to worry about with balancing on those crutches."

Next he'd be whipping a fold up stool out of his jacket for her to sit on. Tosser.

"It will. Gosh, I'm *sooo* parched." Olivia flashed a cheeky smile at the other man and gave him an affectionate nudge with her shoulder. He grinned back, eyes shining. Clearly, this was some sort of 'in' joke. Cole decided he didn't like those sort of jokes... unless he was 'in' on them too.

Olivia gestured towards Cole. "Sean, you remember my friend, Cole, don't you? He brought me to the hospital?"

The two nodded at each other, but neither smiled. Cole felt something like jealousy stabbing at his chest. Who is this guy and what right did he have to touch Olivia's hand like that? Or make jokes with her that he wasn't privy to? More to the point why did he, Cole, feel that he had any claim over her? He'd given her a lift in his car, shown her his house. There'd been nothing romantic in it. Just friends. She'd said they were friends, just then.

"So Cole, have you figured out what you're going to do with your secret room yet?" Olivia asked, breaking into his thoughts.

"Not a clue."

"You could make a bunker to hide from the netball girls. You know, like on that show where people prepare for the zombie apocalypse? What's it called, *Doomsday Preppers?*"

"Funny."

"What about a shrine to those shorts everyone's talking about?" Balancing on her crutches, Olivia paused, raised the glass to her mouth and tried to capture the straw with her upturned lips. She was so taking the piss out of him.

But Cole didn't care so much. He was too busy gazing at the cute way her mouth puckered around the straw, that rosy Cupid's bow on her upper lip that he so wanted to kiss. Jesus, his mind was beginning to go places it shouldn't again. He should not have even been looking. She was on a date with the doctor. He had no business imagining things about her lips, or any other part of her body for that matter. But Olivia was bloody hard to ignore. He took a deep breath and put his beer down on a table. "Right, time for a dance. Adelaide?"

Adelaide shoved her clutch under her arm and swallowed the last of her cocktail saveloy. "I thought you'd never ask."

*****

I looked on as Cole swung Adelaide under his arm. He was a dreadful dancer, couldn't keep in time to save himself and Adelaide wasn't much better but they were getting into the spirit of things, having fun. Cole's face was animated as he chatted and laughed. They made such a lovely couple, which is why I couldn't understand it. I'd been openly teasing Cole before. Flirting when I knew I shouldn't have been. Cole was married, or in a relationship at least. Strictly out of bounds. I should have been flirting with Sean, hot single guy; not Cole, married man. Hadn't I learnt my lesson?

I turned to Sean. "Hey, you wanna get out of here? My foot's starting to ache and Alice and Jed aren't coming so there's no reason to hang around."

Unless I wanted to stay and tease Cole some more and get myself in trouble.

Sean seemed surprised. It hadn't even gone ten. "Did you have something else in mind?"

"Nothing that will involve us getting arrested, if that's what you're asking. But I have a whole season of *Game of Thrones* I haven't watched yet, a fridge full of wine and a block of chocolate I shouldn't eat alone, if I'm on a diet."

The speed with which Sean finished his drink was incredible. "That's the best idea I've heard in ages. I've been so busy with the new job, I haven't had time to catch up on my TV viewing."

"We'd better make a quick escape, then. I can see the netball girls looking this way. You're fresh meat and you're under forty. Always a bonus."

"You could pretend I'm with you, smooch up to me, like."

"And you could get a crutch in the crotch."

"Will you kiss me better?"

"God, you're even more in love with yourself than when you had braces." I laughed. "Let's go home."

We made our way to the double doors of the club where I stopped to rifle through the pile of coats left at the entrance, looking to locate my jacket. It was then, as I was attempting to pull my arm into the first sleeve that I smelled the unmistakeable woody smell of aftershave. Once it would have made me weak at the knees. Now, it made me want to puke. Connor Bishop had come through the door. Oh yes, this night was getting better. I couldn't wait to show my 'date' off.

I shrugged myself into my jacket and turned round. I hadn't seen Connor since the split, he'd been keeping a low profile, probably because everyone knew that he'd been fooling around with Shannon and me at the same time. Not that they'd told either of us. We'd both looked like idiots over him.

"Olivia. Hello." His eyes roamed up and down my body.

Eww. It made my skin crawl.

"Connor."

"What are you doing here?"

I stood my ground. My confidence was returning since I'd begun to lose weight and if he had any intention of belittling me like last time, he could think again. "More to the point what are you doing here? Haven't you had sex with everyone present? Including the birthday girl?"

Connor at least had the decency to look sheepish. "I was, uh... I came to... um... It doesn't matter. You look nice, by the way. Have you lost weight?"

Oh, the cheek of him. I wished I could hit him with my crutch but it'd be so undignified and I'd probably fall over myself doing it. "Yes, if you must know."

"That's great. You look, um, lovely." He leant towards me out of earshot of Sean. "And quite sexy."

Was he kidding?

I stared blankly as he did that thing with his eyebrows. The thing I used to find flirty, but now looked plain silly. He was looking at me as if some long lost fire had been rekindled and he couldn't wait to strike a match from it. What had I ever seen in him? He was even more of an idiot than before, if that were possible.

"I'm on a date, Connor."

Not that I was but it didn't hurt him to think that.

"Ditch him. Come home with me."

As if.

"Why would I do that? Sean's kind, funny and he's a doctor. Three things that you definitely aren't."

Connor looked Sean over. "I bet he can't do that thing you like."

Oh for heaven's sake. Couldn't the worm just slither off into his hole?

"Right well, *we* have to get going," I said. "Things to do, places to be."

Reaching for the door handle, I was about to pull it, when the door swung open a second time, hitting me smack in the chest and knocking me into the pile of coats. I gave my head a shake and tried to right myself.

Bum.

"Are you all right? Here, let me help." Connor dashed to the pile of coats and was in the throes of sympathy before I had time to gag at how truly disgusting the idea was. He held out a hand, which I refused to take.

"Of course I'm all right. And even if I wasn't I wouldn't want your help."

Befuddled, I got to my feet to find my mother standing next to Connor, who was standing next to Sean, who looked more confused than I was. Dressed that evening in a pair of printed leggings that looked like something a nineties revival band would wear with a low cut cowl neck top and heels that eclipsed anything I'd ever owned, Mum was the vision of a made-over woman. And not in a good way.

Seriously, this new life thing was getting a bit silly. Since Dad had passed away she'd completely gone off the rails.

"Mum! You almost knocked me into next week."

Mum appeared a little flustered. She was looking from Connor to Sean and back to Connor again like her head was a revolving door. "Oh possum, I'm so sorry. I was preoccupied."

Which was nothing new lately.

She settled her gaze on Sean. A rather lewd smile spread across her face. "Oh my lord, Sean? What happened to the braces and pimples?"

Sean took her hand. "I grew up."

"You certainly did! And filled out too." Mum let out a girlish giggle that was almost a complete replica of the one I did at times.

Scary.

"It's lovely to see you again, Mrs Merrifield."

"Are you off home?"

"Olivia's foot's aching. As her doctor, it's my duty to make sure she gets home safely and puts it up."

"Well, behave yourselves. I don't want to have to bail either of you out of jail." Mum winked. She clasped the hand she'd shaken between both of hers and gazed into his eyes. "You have very nice healing hands."

Oh. My. God.

"And on that note, we'd best get going," I said, praying that Sean wouldn't judge me for my mother's absolute inappropriateness.

"Yes, of course. Toodle-oo darlings."

With a wink at Connor — *eww* again — Mum raced off to do lord knows what. I stood shaking my head. I adored my mother but it was an effort at times.

"Your Mum's still as cool as ever," Sean said.

"A little too cool if you ask me."

"Was she trying to chat me up?"

"Probably. Let's go."

"So I'll give you a call then, shall I?" Connor said, still standing expectantly beside the jumbled heap of coats.

I gave him my best withering glare. "I wouldn't bother, Connor. That'd be about as pleasant as having my eyes pecked out by magpies."

Chapter 13

Alice and I were sitting on the swings at the park the following afternoon, while Alice swung an increasingly excited-looking Ethan up and down. It was unseasonably chilly and Ethan's cheeks and nose were pink with cold. I'd shoved my hands between my knees but it didn't seem to be making a great deal of difference. My nails were going blue.

"I saw Connor at the party last night."

"What did he say? Did he notice you've lost weight?"

I rolled my eyes. "Of course he did. He'd hardly said hello before it was mentioned. Then he promptly tried to make like we were still a couple."

"He always did have a bit of a nerve. So, how was Sean?"

"Funny as ever. He's so nice."

She must have been able to sense my hesitance. "Did you kiss him?"

"I wasn't even tempted. We sat on the couch and drank wine and talked about old times. He put his arm around me at one stage and it was almost creepy, like he was my brother or something. I'm pretty sure he felt it too. When I came back from the toilet, he'd moved to the armchair. It was like he was testing the waters, like he thought he should feel something now that we were adults, but it clearly wasn't there. The only chemistry between Sean and I would be the stink bombs we made in eighth grade."

Alice pushed against the ground with her feet, propelling the swing a little faster. Ethan's arms flailed as he attempted to clap with joy. "So how did it end up then?"

"We agreed that friends is a far a better idea. That banter we had at the hospital was merely teasing like you would with an old friend. You can't make something out of nothing."

Alice nodded. "Probably for the best. At least you didn't delude yourself into thinking something would come of it. You knew it was only meant to be a friendship. But you know why this has happened, don't you?"

"Why?"

"Cole. Subliminally, you hold a glimmer of hope that you'll wake up one morning and he'll be single. Therefore, you were sending him the 'I'm not interested signals'."

I stopped my swing and bent down to retrieve my crutches. "That's ridiculous."

"No, its not."

"But I'm not attracted to Sean. How could I send out vibes if I'm not attracted?"

Alice brought her swing to a halt too and began to strap Ethan into his stroller. The baby wriggled, showing his protest at being taken away from the swing. "I don't know, I read it somewhere. That's all."

We began to walk down the road towards Alice's house. What was normally slow going with the stroller was made even more so by the clonking of crutches. We passed a few houses, side stepped a chicken out for a walk — you saw all sorts of sights in Merrifield — and stopped a couple of times for Alice to check on Ethan. She seemed very quiet. It was almost as if she didn't want to go home.

"Is there still trouble in paradise?" I asked. A fight with Jed was one of the only reasons the smile left Alice's face. And they had been arguing. Alice would have to be giving birth before she bailed on an event she'd RSVP'd to. And even then she'd give it a good go.

"Jed and I don't live in paradise anymore."

"Oh Alice."

"I'm thinking about leaving him, moving back in with Mum."

It had to be serious if she was considering that as an option. Alice's mother wasn't the easiest person to deal with. She played favourites with Alice and her siblings and Alice was always the loser.

"Did you fight last night? Is that why you didn't come to Shannon's birthday?"

"I think it was the worst fight we've ever had. I'd taken Ethan to Mum's — she was looking after him so we could go out — I'd put extra effort into my hair and makeup and cooked him a lovely dinner. Then when he got home, half an hour late, the only comment he made was to ask if he was meant to be wearing fancy dress. I completely flipped my lid and he went storming off. He didn't come home till after eleven."

"I don't understand what's up with him. Jed would never do anything to hurt you."

Alice paused. There were tears in her eyes. "I found messages on his phone. Texts from a girl called Vicki. I don't know anyone called Vicki. Do you?" Her lip began to wobble.

"No."

"I won't stand for it if he's seeing someone else. I'm not going to have Ethan subjected to arguing parents and an unhappy house. I'd rather move out now and let him have no father."

Which was totally understandable given that Alice had grown up in a similar environment. Her father had been a notorious womaniser and her mother had stayed with him 'for the sake of the children'. When the youngest of the siblings had turn eighteen, her mother had changed the locks, hired a lawyer and told her father where to go.

Literally. He'd gone to live in Albany, two hundred kilometres away.

"Shouldn't you talk to him before you make any decisions? There may be a perfectly good explanation."

"I can't. He's never home."

"You have to do something. You can't give up on your marriage like this. Not with your anniversary coming up. I know how special the day is for you."

Alice and Jed always made a big deal of celebrating the day they got together as a couple, rather than their actual marriage. This year was going to be the biggest yet — fifteen years.

"Clearly, its not that special any more." A tear slipped down Alice's cheek. She didn't bother to wipe it away. "I don't know how its come to this. What have I done? I'm not fat. I'm a good wife. I cook and clean, I don't nag. I contribute to the household income."

I gathered her in my arms, rubbing her back as she sobbed. And as I did, it dawned on me that all my silly little issues with being fat and cakes and stuff were nothing compared to what was happening to my friends. Yes, they were important to me but this was life changing. Alice's course of action now could potentially alter three lives forever.

And I'd been worrying about bloody cake. It was so ridiculous.

"Why doesn't he love me anymore?" She sniffed.

"I'm sure he does. I'm sure this is a misunderstanding."

If it wasn't, I was going to be first in line to punch Jed right in the nose. How dare he do this to my best friend? How dare he.

At last, we reached the gate of Alice and Jed's cottage. The front door was open and looking down the hallway, I could see Jed balancing on the top step of the ladder. He was installing the new light fittings Alice had bought online. Even though it was his only day off in the week. And even though he'd vocalised rather loudly before we left for the park that he had places to be other than standing on a ladder and couldn't it wait until next weekend. Still, he was up there doing it to make Alice happy.

He couldn't be having an affair, could he? Men who had affairs reeked of cheap perfume and slunk around the town looking shifty. They didn't go about doing nice things for their wives. Not unless they were feeling guilty. Gosh. Was Jed feeling guilty? From the look on Alice's face, I could tell she was thinking exactly the same thing.

"Are you still okay to babysit on Friday night? For our date night? If it's on, that is," Alice asked. She and Jed had a standing date at the pub every Friday at six. It was often only an hour but Alice didn't care. It made her feel like someone other than a mother for part of her week. She guarded the time ferociously.

"Not a problem. I'll be off my crutches by then. I'm looking forward to it."

I hugged Alice and kissed Ethan goodbye. Despite the fact that she'd offered me a ride to Mum's, I felt the need to hobble there under my own steam. It wasn't the warmest afternoon to be braving the fresh air, but Alice and Jed needed all the alone time they could get. They didn't need me taking up their time.

*****

The sun had begun to set when I finally hop-walked down Mum's front path. The garden of the big old house was in swathed in gold and tangerine, giving it a surreal type of glow. I'd grown up in that house, lived there until I went to Perth to attend university and then stayed on for my job at the TV station. I had an attachment to the creaky front door and the way the draft whistled up the hallway in a storm. Even though Mum had begged Dad to fix it a thousand times before his death, he never had. Now she refused to have it repaired. She said the creaking was Dad, reminding her he was still there watching over her.

Lord knows what Dad would think if he could see the way Mum behaved these days. All this talk of exercise only meant for twenty year olds and gushing over movie stars and travelling about the place dressed like she was teenager was too much. Even to me, and I considered myself rather open minded.

Dad had left a personal note with his will that he wanted Mum to go out and live her life if he died first, not to mourn. I don't think he meant her to live it quite as outlandishly as she was doing, though. Sometimes I felt my mother was going to the extreme to prove a point to my dead father.

After knocking on the door and receiving no answer, I dug my key out of my pocket and slid it into the lock. It was nothing for my mother not to be at home when I arrived. Often, I began dinner myself and Mum would come swanning in wearing some outrageous outfit and apologising because she'd been held up doing something or other before shooing me away from the kitchen knives. I wasn't exactly sure what it was Mum got up to now that she'd given up work at Autumn Leaves, the aged care home on the hill, and was living on the life insurance policy Dad had left. I wasn't sure I wanted to know either. In certain cases, ignorance was definitely bliss.

Clomping up the hallway, I headed towards the meditation room Mum had created from my old bedroom. Often, Mum could be found there, wearing harem pants and a singlet top and chanting a mantra of gobbledygook designed to attract goodness and light into her life. Personally, I thought it was a little silly though I never said so to Mum. Why hurt her feelings over something so harmless?

The meditation room was empty so I made my way slowly down the hall to the kitchen. It was as I was passing Mum's room that I heard the noise the first time.

I paused, my head cocked, listening. It was a muffled sort of moan, something akin to a cat being strangled. I turned and looked along the hallway. Mum's cat was nowhere in sight.

The noise occurred again. This time it was followed by a long slow painful 'ahhhh.'

Had Mum tripped and hurt herself? I'd heard horror stories of elderly parents lying on the floor waiting to be rescued for days because they'd broken a hip or a leg and couldn't move. Of course that was a silly notion. The only one who tripped in the Merrifield family was me. Besides, Mum wasn't anywhere close to elderly.

The noise grew louder, reaching a frenzied cry. It definitely wasn't the cat.

"Mum?"

Uncertain as to whether I should invade her private space — or more worryingly what I'd find if I did — I put my ear to the door. "Mum?"

The noises came to an abrupt halt. There was a certain amount of grunting and shuffling from behind the bedroom door and then out popped Mum, done up to the nines in full makeup, a red silk shortie kimono she'd bought on a recent trip to Japan and little else than a rather awkward look.

"Olivia!" She fluffed her hair.

"Is everything all right? I heard noises. Are you hurt?"

Mum's face was flushed. "No. No. Of course not. Everything's perfectly fine. Come to the kitchen and let's get a wine. I wasn't expecting you till seven but I've started on a roast beef for dinner." Her voice was louder than usual, and forced, as if she thought I'd developed hearing loss overnight. Bustling me towards the kitchen, she glanced over her shoulder at the bedroom door.

What on earth was going on? Had she had taken one too many of those cold and flu tablets again? Last time she'd gone into such a hallucination she was convinced I was Mariah Carey and had asked me for an autograph.

I looked as much like Mariah Carey as Jim the Butcher looked like Tom Jones.

"But the noise, Mum. What was that noise?"

"Ah, er, the cat. He got stuck in the wardrobe. I was trying to get him out and he wasn't being that cooperative."

Whilst naked? I doubted it.

"And you were naked why?"

Mum's cheeks coloured. "Well, obviously I was getting changed when the cat got stuck."

I didn't believe a word of it. I'd been caught in enough compromising positions in my time to know a fib when I heard one. Especially seeing that the cat had appeared through the cat flap from the backyard seconds before and was twining itself around my legs.

Once we were in the kitchen, and Mum scuttled about in the pantry, pouring glasses of wine and filling platters with pate and biscuits. The conversation was inane and followed no logical path. We were both too distracted by what was hidden behind that bedroom door.

"How long are you going to keep him in there?" I asked, at last.

"Who?"

"Whoever it is you've got hiding in your room. If it's Jim, I don't mind, Mum. He's lonely; you've got no one. It'd be nice to see you together. He's a lovely man."

The chardonnay in Mum's mouth sprayed across the bench. She began to cough so hard I had to slap her on the back. "It's not Jim."

"Then who? And why won't you introduce me? Are you ashamed?"

Mum looked like I'd asked her to 'fess up to having the Pope in her room. The rearrangement of the cheese on the platter was suddenly quite pressing. And her glass of wine had disappeared faster before I'd taken a sip of mine.

"Um, he's rather younger than me," she admitted at last.

Surely not. My mother had a toy boy?

"How *much* younger, Mrs Robinson?"

Mum shifted on her stool but offered no information.

"What's he, like, twenty? You think I won't approve?" I could accept Mum having a man of say, oh, forty-ish but if he was my age; I wasn't too sure what I'd think about that.

"I suppose I did. Especially after you broke up with that last lad. I was concerned you'd be hurt."

"I'm not hurt, Mum. I think it's nice you've got yourself a man. As long as it's not that groper Phil from the football club." I couldn't stomach if that lech was in the house after he'd had his hands on every girl's bum in town. Plus, he most likely had some dreadful disease that could only be cured by a strong dose of antibiotics.

"It's not Phil."

"Great. Can I meet him then?"

"You'll be nice? No twenty questions?"

This was a bit of a role reversal. I could remember a time when my parents used to quiz every new boy I bought home. It was so embarrassing when Dad used to ask them if they intended on taking me 'parking' at the end of the date. "You mean I can't ask him what his intentions are?" I giggled.

"Not unless you're prepared for the answer." Mum walked down the hall, opening the door to the bedroom. "You can come out. She won't bite."

A smooth tanned hand with a silver signet ring on the pinkie appeared on the doorjamb. Oh no. *It couldn't be.*

Chapter 14

"Connor."

"Hello Olivia."

"What are you doing here?"

Stupid question, seeing as how he'd come out of Mum's bedroom and not ten minutes ago I'd heard them in the throes of a rather rowdy sex session. So much for *Kama Sutra* Yoga.

Mum looked from Connor to me. And back. Quite a few times. Her brow crinkled. She even scratched her head. "You two know each other?"

"Let's just say he's seen me naked," I replied. There was no point sugar-coating the situation. Connor had been intimate with both of us. Mum needed to know what sort of a slime ball he was. "Connor's the one who dumped me because I was too fat."

The colour drained from Mum's face, an indication she may well have been about to vomit. Or it could have been the retching and holding of her mouth as she ran to the toilet that gave the game away.

I faced Connor. "You're a piece of work. First you tell me I'm fat, then you say you want me back and now I find you've been whooping it up with my mother. Was this going on while we were together? Were you bonking me, Shannon *and* my mother?"

"I'd like to know the answer to that question too." Mum had returned from the toilet and was standing in the middle of the kitchen with her hands on her hips. Her face was delineated by a scowl from ear to ear that said if Connor didn't give an answer she was satisfied with she might use the paring knife for something other than preparing vegetables.

Connor gave a nervous swallow. "I never meant to hurt anyone. And I wasn't seeing you both at the same time, Betty."

Had he called my mother Betty? Nobody called her Betty unless they wanted a dressing down that would last an hour. My mother was Bettina. Bettina Gwen Merrifield.

"Olivia and I split up at least a month before I met you. You can do the timeline yourselves if you don't believe me."

I was astounded. He sounded so... well... sincere. Who was this person and what had he done with the real Connor Bishop?

"What game are you playing exactly?" I asked, determined not to let him fool me again.

"Were you thinking this to be a little bit on the side before you move on to your next big conquest? Did you see my mother as easy pickings because she's older and a widow? Because if your intentions aren't what they should be Connor, you have to know you're going to be run out of town. My mother is not me. People don't give two hoots about my love life but if you jerk her around, you're going to receive death threats from most of the Bowls Club, not to mention the Repertory Society and the Tennis Club. Is it worth it?"

Connor grasped the bridge of his nose with his index finger and thumb. I could see him trying to squeeze the tension away. Clearly, he hadn't considered the ramifications of dating a woman old enough to be his mother. "Look. I know we didn't part on the best of terms—"

Something of an understatement.

"—But I truly like your mother. She makes me feel like I've never felt about women my own age. I want to do the right thing. I don't care that she's older than me. I mean, look at her. She's amazing."

Well, that was the truth.

I glanced at Mum. She had forgotten she was angry and was beaming like she was fifteen and Connor was her first boyfriend. Connor walked over and took her hand. He returned the gooey smile and ramped it up till it landed in a league that included beauty queens and very soppy people on daytime soaps.

Then he reached over and removed a lock of hair from where it had become stuck in a bit of spew trapped on the side of Mum's mouth. It was so sickening I almost felt the need to rush to the toilet myself.

He smiled again as he tucked the hair behind her ear. "That's better, honey pie."

"Thank you, snuggle bunny."

For Pete's sake. They had endearing names for each other too? This was the last straw, the absolute last straw. Were they doing drugs together or something? Because that would be preferable to the scenario they were expecting me to believe.

"In fact," Connor continued after a good two minutes of gazing into my mother's eyes, "I was going to ask your mother if she'd consider marrying me."

Pardon?

"Married?" The word that left my throat sounded more like a squeak than a single word sentence. It was one thing to have a bonk in the afternoons and a couple of wines at the pub or some companionship, but marriage? They'd only known each other a month tops. Nobody got married after that length of time unless they were absolutely insane. Then there was the little fact that she was old enough to be his mother. She was my mother for God's sake!

The idea seemed something of a shock for Mum, too. She'd begun to scramble in the bottom drawer of the kitchen cabinets for the stash of emergency cigarettes and lighter she kept there. She never smoked in front of me any more. In fact, I thought she'd given it up some time back.

Mum lit up and took a deep drag, releasing the smoke in tiny circlets that swirled above her head. She coughed and slapped at her chest. "You're kidding, right?"

"I'm more serious about this than I've been about anything in my life. Let's get married."

Mum sucked in another gulp of smoke. A thoughtful look came over her. But only after she took a large glug from the bottle of wine on the counter. "What the hell. Why not. You only live once."

"MUM!" Now I was grabbing for the wine. "You're not going to marry Connor."

"I think I might."

"Give me one good reason why."

Because I couldn't think of any.

"Well, he is quite good in bed."

"Which should never be the sole reason for a wedding." I was starting to sound like the parent. This could not be happening. How could it be that my mother, a widow of only six months had managed to hook herself a second husband — one who'd practically only started shaving —

when I couldn't even get a boyfriend? And Connor, of all people. Seriously, it wasn't fair. Not at all. Not to mention immoral. There had to be some sort of law against hooking up with your daughter's ex-boyfriend. I was positive of it.

"Your father did say he wanted me to move on if he departed this world before me," Mum added.

At that moment, the front door squeaked open.

"See! It's a sign. You're father is sending his approval."

"I've always believed in the spirit world. It's good to know Mr Merrifield has sent us a sign," Connor said.

I was not getting into some crazy conversation about my dead father and creaking doors. "Oh my God. That's it. I'm going home to the dog. You two are completely mad. Let me know what you're going to do about the nuptials etc etc. I'll have to save the day."

I turned on my one heel and began to hobble down the hall.

"Wait! Don't leave like this, darling. Please, stay for dinner. Family dinner."

Talk about rubbing salt into the wound. Connor was going to be my stepfather.

"I don't think so, Mum. I'm sure you've got lots to talk about and I'd be the third wheel. We can catch up tomorrow."

"But—"

"I need some time to process this development. Alone."

With my friend vodka.

*****

After declining a lift home, I began the slow walk along the street towards Blue Wren Cottage. Merrifield was a quiet country town. It was safe for a girl to be out in the streets alone at night, even if she only had one good leg. Besides, given the mood I was in at that current moment, I'd have had no trouble fending off a potential attacker — if one existed — with a wild swing of my crutch.

Walking home in the dark gave me plenty of time to think. Yes, I was upset about what had happened but my mother's life was her own. If she wanted to go out with a man half her age, who was I to stop her? I'd never have been able to anyway. Mum and I were a lot alike in that respect. We were both quite dogged when we put our minds to something.

Then something else occurred to me. If Mum could find a man, why couldn't I? There had to be a man somewhere that wasn't slimy or married or only after sex but if I didn't put myself out there, how would they ever know I was available? It was time to move on from the disasters of the last three years. A diet and a new body was not enough, though it was a pretty good start. It was time to man up or, girl up — if such a phrase existed — and get myself a boyfriend.

I reached the corner of Mum's street and feeling rather weary all of a sudden plonked down on the kerb, unhooking my crutches and resting my chin in my palms. I looked down the road to where the lights on Mum's house had been dimmed. Yes, I was pleased she'd found love, nobody would want to deny her happiness but why did it have to be Connor Bishop? And where did this relationship leave me? I couldn't face making chitchat with my new stepdad across the roast potatoes every Thursday night. It would probably take a good decade before I could bring myself to be polite after the things he'd said about me.

Worse though, Connor had seen me naked. No amount of roast beef and fine wine could gloss over the fact that it was practically incestuous. And if truth be told, I was also having a little trouble coping with the fact that Connor found my mother more attractive than he did me. She was almost twice my age. Why couldn't I have a boyfriend? I wanted a boyfriend. Someone who would love me the way I loved them. I wanted my own Connor.

Okay, not Connor — he was still a sleazebag — but a man. I wanted a man.

I sat in the gutter feeling forlorn until a four-wheel drive came speeding up the hill. It pulled to an abrupt halt, worthy of a stop in pit lane at the Melbourne Grand Prix, and swerved to my side of the road before coming to a stop along side me. A spray of gravel and mud flew in my direction, landing on my jeans. Fabulous.

The driver's side window wound down.

"Olivia."

It was Cole.

"Hey."

"What are you doing out here in the dark?"

I squinted into the car. Smells of something warm and sugary with hints of lemon wafted out the window. God. It was divine, like freshly baked lemon tarts or cake or something. Where did one get car freshener like that? My car invariably smelled of wet dog and dog hair. Sometimes dog shampoo if I were lucky.

"I was on my way home from Mum's place."

Cole glanced at the console of the car. "It's three degrees. Aren't you cold? And why are you sitting in the gutter?"

I glanced around. I'd been so consumed in my thoughts I hadn't even noticed the fog had settled early. And it was cold. Bloody cold. I must have looked utterly stupid sitting beside a foggy road with a pair of crutches.

"My mind was somewhere else, I guess."

"The Bahamas?"

"I wish."

"Hop in. I'll give you a lift."

I hesitated. Cole was nice. It was okay to be friends with him, no romance involved. People had friends of the opposite sex all the time. But being friends was pretty hard when you imagined the person naked whenever you looked at them. And Cole was the type of man you imagined naked a lot. And in many different positions.

"Uh, I only live about two hundred metres that way. The cottage on the left; I'm pretty sure I can make it there without freezing to death."

"Your lips are blue. You shouldn't be out without a coat as it is."

"I'll remember that next time, Dad."

Cole laughed. "Get in."

"You sure?"

"I won't be held responsible for you turning into an iceblock and being unable to clip Adelaide's dog. She'd have heart failure."

Why did he have to remind me he was married?

"Who? Adelaide or Lulu?"

"Both probably."

I opened the passenger side door and hopped into the car. Immediately, I felt the warmth from the heater on my toes. So nice.

"So, where to?" Cole asked.

"Oh. Back the way you come. On the left. The blue cottage."

Cole did a U turn and began the drive. "Did you enjoy the party the other night?"

"It was okay. You?"

"I felt a bit like Daniel in the lion's den, except the lions had turned into cougars. Some of those women were drooling and two of them pinched my bum when I went for a refill at the bar. Are they always that bad?"

"I wouldn't let it go to your head. Any new guy is fresh meat in their eyes."

"Thanks for bringing me down to earth. A bloke needs to know his place."

"And a town full of women are waiting to show you theirs."

"Can't wait." The fog had gotten thicker and Cole leant forward, squinting to see through it. "The doctor seems like an okay bloke."

"He's nice. Funny too."

"And that's high on your list of priorities in a man?"

"Not always. But it helps. I'm up for a laugh. Life can be so serious."

"I noticed you left the party early. Did you get home all right?"

"Ah, yeah. Sean gave me a lift." I glanced at Cole from the corner of my eye. His face, concentrating on seeing through the pea soup fog, gave nothing away. This line of questioning was quite odd. If I didn't know better, I'd have said he was checking on my status with Sean.

"So, how's the foot?"

Okay, so he wasn't engaging some sort of covert questioning about the state of my love life, he was just being friendly. A little bit nosy maybe, but friendly.

"Good until about two minutes ago."

Which it had been. But the combination of being in the cold, walking all day and now sitting in the warmth of the car was making it throb unmercifully. Either that or I was channelling the weirdness I was feeling being in a car with Cole into my foot. I was going to have to take a painkiller when I got home. And find something to eat that had sugar in it....

"You need to put your feet up. Get someone to give it a gentle massage."

"Are you offering?"

Images of Cole, sitting on the end of the couch with my foot perched on his knee, his fingers softly kneading my skin, travelling up my calves and tickling the skin behind my knee suddenly began to assault my brain. Crap. This was not good. I had to put a stop to it. Now.

"Stop the car!"

Cole slammed on the brakes, the force of which was so powerful I almost found myself as a dashboard ornament. He peered at me through the dark. "You okay?"

I would be as soon as I got out of the car and away from him. He was too close. Way too close.

"Um, uh, yes. We're here, that's all. I mean, home."

"And you felt the need to announce it by deafening me?"

"Sorry. Turn in there." I indicated the space behind a teeny latte coloured Fiat in the driveway.

Cole pulled into the drive. The headlights of the car lit up the lane, giving him a good view of my car and the garden behind it.

"That's your car?" Cole roared with laughter. "Jesus, it looks like a bread tin."

I let out a huff. "It's a Fiat. Thank you. A very stylish European car."

"Still looks like a bread tin. Typical girl car."

I opened the door, leaning my crutches on the side of it while I swivelled to get out. Hmph. The cheek of him taking the piss out of my car.

"Well, I am a girl, in case you hadn't noticed."

Behind me, I heard Cole mutter. "Oh, I noticed. Believe me."

"Pardon?"

A devilish twinkle glinted in his eye. "You heard."

Not the point.

The point was he was married. He couldn't be going around the town making comments like that and getting me hot under the collar for things that would never eventuate. It was disgraceful. Not to mention absolutely, categorically and totally unacceptable. He did have very nice eyes though. Rather dreamy.

"Um, er. Um."

"Would you like me to carry you in? For old time's sake?"

Oh yes.

"No! Of course not. I mean, I'm fine. But thanks." I knew I sounded anything but. I sounded like an utter lunatic.

"Okay. Well, good night Olivia."

"Night Cole."

"See you round."

"Not if I see you first."

"I hope not. I'm throwing those shorts out as soon as I get home." And he jumped back into his car.

Great, I thought as I fumbled with the gate and keys, dropping them twice into a bush before finally reaching the front door. If it wasn't enough my mother was marrying my ex-boyfriend, now I was being chatted up by the local married hunk. When would it ever end?

I opened the door to my darkened house, my house where I was alone, with nobody but the dog. I didn't want to be alone. I wanted a partner and a baby, damn it. I wanted a little life where I might learn to cook and I'd have someone to lean on when things got bad. I needed someone to cuddle me on cold nights and tell me they loved only me. I was tired of running to my friends and my mother for the solace that only a life partner could provide. I was so tired of fighting my life.

So I did what I knew best, I got in my bread tin car and drove to the convenience store — it was always open late. I bought packet Madeira cake and Mint Slice biscuits and some lemon slices that looked like they were closer to their use-by date than not. And then I sat at my kitchen table and cried while I ate the lot. Which wasn't very nice. The lemon slice in particular would have tasted far better without the added saltiness of my tears.

Chapter 15

The following week was not a good one for Cole. It seemed that the media of Perth had discovered his whereabouts and were intent on getting the latest update on his life. The phone had been ringing non-stop disrupting his schedule and Adelaide had refused to answer it anymore. It was only going to be for him anyway, so why waste the time she'd said.

A year or so before Phoebe had died, Cole had done a TV commercial for his renovation company. The concept, brainchild of his daughter, had featured him wearing a hard hat with a tiny crown painted on it, depicting him as the 'Reno King'. He'd also been wielding a sledgehammer at a wall whilst wearing a tight supposedly sweat-soaked t-shirt that showed off the rock hard body he'd honed over years of manual labour. The advertisement had finished with the line "I love nothing better than to make a client smile, let me do it for you" and though it was meant to be advertising his skills at renovating and decorating, Cole had been fully aware he was selling sex. He looked sexy. What he hadn't anticipated was the barrage of female clients it would bring. Or the paparazzi.

Suddenly he'd become public property. Reporters followed him everywhere. And women too. Some of them wouldn't take no for an answer. He and Phoebe had had to go into hiding for a while. He'd managed to stem the tide by doing regular interviews for the current affairs show *Today Tonight* and appearing in the lifestyle section of the paper — Phoebe had been the *Telethon* kid at the time so it was like an extension of their story — but with the move he'd been hoping they'd forgotten about him completely. How wrong had he been? It seemed he was destined to have them chase him forever.

On the second morning, having locked himself in the shop to check on the final decorating, Cole had decided to get up on a ladder and give the team a hand securing the shelves behind the counter. Everything had been fine until Lulu had gone bolting through, legs splaying in every direction like a cartoon character as she chased a soft rubber ball. She'd narrowly missed knocking over the open paint cans on the floor and as Cole twisted swiftly to chastise her he'd pulled a muscle in his neck.

He felt like the victim of a stabbing with a very blunt knife.

After stepping gingerly from the ladder, he'd spent the next hour locating a massage therapist who could fix the kink, which in Merrifield, was harder than trying to find taxi on a Saturday night. But there was no way he was going to walk around for the next week not being about to move his head.

Not only would he look like a right fool serving customers if he couldn't look them in the eye but he had things to do; decisions that could not be sensibly made when one was in so much pain a death by slow torture seemed appealing.

Having found a masseuse and taken two painkillers — the only ones Adelaide had handy were for period pain, but they seemed to be doing the trick — Cole now found himself sitting in the waiting room of a rather Zen space. He took in the room around him. He knew it was designed to make him felt at ease but Zen freaked him out. He had no idea why but the whole concept made him visualise zany, crazy women waving healing Reiki hands over his head and talking about chakras and heart healing and wanting to know the ins and outs of his life. Which he had no intention of sharing with a complete stranger. Jesus, he was barely able to open up to his family most of the time.

The door opened and a woman emerged. She was wearing loose, sage coloured hemp pants and top that look as if it should go to the same ragbag as his favourite shorts. Not that he was looking but her breasts appeared as if they hadn't seen a bra in a decade or so, possibly since she was a teenager. Cole swallowed reminding himself that looks weren't everything and that he had seen real paper qualifications on the wall. If she started that Reiki stuff though he was leaving. He'd massage himself if he had to.

"Cole? Come in."

Rising slowly and attempting to keep his head in one position, Cole followed the woman through the door.

"You've hurt your neck?" she began.

Blind Freddy could probably work that out, seeing that he was currently standing side on and his head was facing her.

"I'm pretty sure it's a pulled muscle but anything you could do would be great. I've got fairly limited movement, as you can see, plus a shop to open in the next week. I don't have time to be laid up." He demonstrated the slight movement from side to straight on.

"And you did it this morning?"

"Yep."

"Have you taken anything for it?"

Like hell he was going to tell her — or anyone — he'd taken period tablets. "A couple of Panadol. They've knocked the edge off but I still can't move it."

"Right. Well, I'll leave you to get undressed. Get on the table, face down and cover yourself with the towel. I'll be back in a minute. Oh, I'm Summer Merrifield, by the way. I forgot to introduce myself."

"Are you related to Olivia?"

"She's my cousin. She has this amazing deep red and lavender aura about her with tinges of green. Very creative. Bit lost at the moment. She's had a tough time of it."

Not exactly how Cole would have described Olivia. She was always so nervy and jumpy around him. Looked at him like he was the prime suspect from an episode of *Law & Order SVU* when she wasn't teasing him. He had no idea why. All he'd done was be nice.

Summer left the room and Cole undressed, getting onto the bed and placing the towel over his bum and legs. It was sheer agony trying to position his neck in the hole for his face, so he lay with his head to the side. Hopefully, Summer could work with that.

A gentle knock at the door interrupted his thoughts.

"You decent, Cole?"

"Ready."

Well, as ready as he could be lying in the most uncomfortable position ever. If this was what yoga was like, he no intention of trying it.

Cole heard a squirting noise above him. "I'm just going to pop a few blobs of this sports rub on your back. It might be a bit cold."

Cole exhaled. That sounded like a vaguely normal thing to do. Like a traditional massage therapist.

Two hands began to rub the area around his shoulder blades. *Ahhhhh.* Relief and release began to surge through his body.

Had he died and gone to heaven? Because Summer should change her name to Angel and have her fingers certified as a national treasure. It was pure bliss and not just for his sore neck. His entire body was beginning to sing.

"Are you able to turn your head into the space for it, Cole?"

"I don't think so."

"Okay. I'll work along this spot first. I should be able to loosen you up enough to give you most of your movement back. Then we can finish with the rest of your back and shoulders. If your neck muscles have seized there's probably some heavy duty tension further down."

Cole nodded. On the inside. That sounded feasible. He hoped she was able to fix him. This was hurting like mad.

Summer began to knead the muscles along the left side of Cole's neck and shoulder. Her hands, warm and firm, felt good on his aching body and he felt himself relaxing further. He closed his eyes, feeling the way her hands moved. Even when it hurt it felt good which was rather sadistic when you thought about it.

After a while Cole's mind drifted to thoughts of Olivia. He liked her a lot. She had the ability to make his heart palpitate in a way it hadn't since he was in his early twenties. But the feeling he got when he was with her wasn't only one of pure animal attraction — though he couldn't deny he had a serious desire to find out what exactly it was she kept under her exercise gear — it was deeper.

He wanted to know her as a person... and then rip her clothes off.

The problem was, for some reason she didn't seem to be interested in anything other than friendship. Every time he got closer to her than friendly conversation, she leaped away like a wounded animal. And to add insult to injury, she appeared to have no trouble with that doctor bloke. She'd been flirting with him so much at the hospital Cole had almost felt embarrassed watching. But why? Cole knew Olivia was attracted to *him*. He could feel it. So why was she attempting to behave otherwise? She didn't seem like one of those gold digger girls, she was genuine and sweet. Clearly, something else about him bothered her.

Cole felt the towel move down, exposing a corner of his bum. He shivered a little, suddenly feeling the cold as Summer squirted more sports rub on the area and began to knead the muscles of his buttocks. Then without warning, she pressed hard in the middle of his arse, almost sending him flying off the massage bed.

"Shit!" Cole's eyes sprang open. He wanted to squeal but it wasn't exactly a manly thing to do.

"Big knot there," Summer said, by way of explanation.

Like he didn't know that.

She increased the pressure. Cole thought he was going to cry. Wincing only made it worse.

"How do you know Olivia?" she asked, her hands continuing to punish him.

"We met at Zumba. When she ... Ouch! Damn! ... When she hurt her ankle."

"I guessed that was you."

What in God's name was she... Ouch! Bugger! ... on about?

While Cole wondered how one tiny body could do it, Summer pressed harder. It felt like she was using her elbow now and giving it the whole weight of that skinny underfed body, which obviously hid quite a few muscles beneath its bony physique. Eyes to the floor, he saw her feet seemed to have disappeared. She was balancing on her knees and elbows on his body. Shit, but it was excruciating.

"You've got a cheek," she added. Her soothing voice barely disguised the veil of annoyance.

"Pardon?" He let out a yelp of anguish.

"Trying it on with my cousin when you're married. Only the lowest of the lowest would do something like that." Summer pressed at the spot again before sending her knee back in to complete the torture. It was as if she were hurting him on purpose. In fact, as she squeezed again, sending shooting pains radiating through his body, Cole was utterly convinced she *was* doing it on purpose.

"I'm not married," he replied, his voice little more than a petrified squeak.

Summer stilled.

Thank bloody God.

"You're not? But I thought, we thought..."

Obviously, the town's focus had moved to things other than the gaping hole in his shorts. Honestly, did these people have nothing more to do with their time than to speculate on the facets of his physical and personal life? He wasn't that interesting.

"Nope. Not married. Not since 2011, unless you know something I don't know."

"But that girl... Adelaide."

"My sister."

"Oh."

"I moved to Merrifield a couple of months back. I'm starting a business. Adelaide's a trained chef. She offered to help me out for a bit while she's on holiday."

Summer's hands began to knead again, this time lowering the scale of pain from somewhere in the stratosphere to something more manageable. And as she pushed and pummelled it occurred to Cole that he'd hit on the problem. Olivia thought he was married. Totally understandable, if you didn't know him, he supposed. And being the girl he thought she was, Cole assumed Olivia hadn't wanted to involve herself with someone who was otherwise spoken for. Which was an admirable quality. He liked a girl with standards. It was something that was sadly lacking in society today.

His mind went back to the day on the stairs and the appalled look on her face. She must have thought he was some dirty pervert who played around on his wife or in one of those 'open marriages' or something. Well. As soon as he could walk again, he'd be rectifying that assumption.

Chapter 16

The following Tuesday, after being declared fit and well and separated from my crutches, I arrived at work to a very unusual sight. A long, red velvet rope was stretched in front of the shop across the road and a rather podgy man, who looked deceptively like Jim the Butcher in a security man's outfit, was guarding the door. A queue — unheard of in Merrifield, unless it was Seniors Day at the Shire and there was free morning tea — was forming outside Death by Cupcake. A queue. At a quarter to ten in the morning. Merrifield didn't have enough residents to form a queue. Anyone would think they'd heard Bruno Mars was stopping by for a latte or something. Either that or those cakes were the most divine in the universe.

Pushing the thought from my mind, I slid my key into the lock and swung the front door open, holding it back with the metal piggy doorstop I'd bought at Mrs Tanner's garage sale. It was a hideous thing and I'd pondered the idea of chucking it out on more than one occasion but how could I when Mrs Tanner commented on it every time she came into the shop? I flipped the light switch, went to the counter, booted up the computer and then, while it was loading popped out the back to fetch the float for the till.

Most people flashed plastic to pay these days, but Merrifield folk preferred cash, so I had to be prepared. Which was more than I could say for that shop over the way. I'd have bet the owners didn't know a jot about the Merrifield crowd. From the look of the exterior, that shop was about making a quick buck with flashy coffee machines and recipes that contained exotic ingredients only found in expensive restaurants in the city. I bet all they knew about was making mouth-watering cupcakes to tempt weak-willed girls into breaking their diets. Well, not me. I was on the path to success and feeling rather pleased with myself. I had no intention of ever stepping foot in that pit of sin across the road.

Things organised for the day, I spent a few minutes contemplating whether it was worth digging into my savings for a new pair of trainers. The budget was healthy this month and now that I'd decided to take up jogging, investing in a good pair of shoes would be an extra incentive to get out there. Plus, if I had cute sandshoes, people were less likely to notice that my body wobbled in the wrong places when I ran.

By the time I managed to do a few mental calculations and plug my Weight Watchers points into my phone, the queue outside Death By Cupcake had doubled. It was snaking its way past Jim's Butchery and towards the chemist. I frowned as I looked out the window and across the road. What on earth was going on in there? The shop had only been open for a day. Yes, the façade had been something of a talking point but even Mrs Tanner and my mother couldn't gossip enough to get a line that long outside a shop.

I hadn't noticed anything but a small ad in the paper the previous Wednesday so where were these people appearing from and why were the majority of them women? Well, obviously women liked cake more than men but what the hell?

Mystified by this turn of events, I watched as the clock ticked over, registering ten o'clock. A figure reached up to unbolt the lock and the doors to Death by Cupcake opened. A steady stream of women began to enter and leave the building carrying the most divine boxes filled with cake. They were chattering to each other in an excited fashion and giggling as if Bruno Mars himself had indeed served them.

Then, as I was about to log on to the Internet and order a new pair of runners, the freshly baked scent of cake began to waft across the road and in the open door. I felt a pull of longing like I hadn't felt since I'd begged Graeme to buy me that boxer puppy with its gorgeous velvety ears and big chocolate coloured eyes. My heart began to pound. My mouth went dry. If this kept up I'd be across the road with my purse in hand buying dozens of those cupcakes and I couldn't allow that to happen. Since the cake binging disaster of the other night, I was more determined than ever. I had a problem with sweet things. I couldn't be near them or even smell them, not if I wanted to achieve my goal. My only hope was that diverting myself with new runners would crush the craving.

I searched for a while and then, unable to concentrate, returned to gazing across the road. Every single person leaving the shop had an enormous pink and black box filled with cupcakes and decorated with sparkly silver ribbon. Maybe I could sneak a peek through the window? See the cakes but not buy anything? Adore from afar?

Yeah. Right. Maybe Queen Elizabeth would take up Ice Hockey.

If there was one thing I knew about myself, it was my weaknesses. And my biggest one was my ability to consume my bodyweight in cake within ten minutes. If I went within twenty metres of the shop, my diet would be lost forever and the self-confidence that I was slowly rebuilding would be gone for good. No. What I needed was a bigger distraction and what better distraction was there than Christmas? Beside cake, Christmas was like my second biggest obsession. Okay, so it was only September but that was beside the point.

Racing into the back of the shop, I grabbed two boxes of decorations from the shelf and began to lay them out on the floor, deciding on what to put where. That was the thing about Christmas decorations. You put them out of sight when Christmas was over and got on with life. Then, when you got them out again you found things you'd completely forgotten you had. It was like, well, Christmas. You got excited over cute sparkly things that you'd never have in your house at any other time in case people would think you insane. At Christmas it was acceptable for wadding filled angels to be flying over your front door and weird looking elves to be sitting on your shelf.

It was the one time of year you could be utterly over the top and nobody would say a thing.

As I took a fluffy strand of red tinsel from the box and hopped up onto the ladder, attaching it in a scalloped effect along the cornice, the doorbell tinkled. I turned from the window to greet my first client of the day, Mrs Di Marco and her grossly overfed schnauzer.

"Morning Olivia."

"Morning Mrs Di Marco."

Mrs Di Marco stared up the ladder towards me. Her eyes travelled along the trail of tinsel towards the huge red poinsettias I'd already hung and stopped at the six-foot tall nutcrackers on either side of the front door. "What on earth are you doing?"

I would have thought it would have been obvious.

"Putting up Christmas decorations."

"Why?"

And I would have thought that was obvious too but when I thought about it, I guess it was only September. A little early for decorating, even if the big shops in Perth had theirs up. They seemed to do it straight after Easter these days.

"Ah. Um, I thought I might have an Ausmas special, so I'm decorating the shop."

"A what?"

"You know, Christmas in July, Ausmas?"

"Oh, yes. Of course. But its not July."

"Minor detail."

"What sort of specials will you be running? I might book Dippy in for something."

"Not sure yet." Possibly because I only came up with the idea to cover up the fact that I am a complete nutcase. "I'll send out an email later in the week with the details. You're on the list, aren't you?"

"I am."

I got down from the ladder and walked over to take Dippy's lead from his owner.

"Lovely day, isn't it?" she said, looking out the window. "Pity it's being spoilt by that kerfuffle over the road."

"My thoughts exactly."

"What're they doing over there, anyway?"

"It's a cupcake shop."

"And that's brought every woman within a fifty kilometre radius into town? You've got to be kidding."

"Nope."

"Are they iced with twenty-four carat gold?"

I smiled. "Not that I know of. I think they're plain old cupcakes."

Muttering something about never seeing the likes, Mrs Di Marco opened the door with a pronouncement that she'd be back in a couple of hours.

I led Dippy to the grooming area and lifted him onto the table. I clipped his leash to a fastener so he'd stay put and reached over to switch on the electric shears. Again my thoughts went back to the cupcakes over the road. How was I ever going to survive the temptation? The decorations had been a quick fix, but only a Band-Aid and now I was stuck with having to come up with a Christmas themed promotion, when I'd only recently had one in the newspaper. If I kept giving my services away I was going to end up broke. Broke and still wanting a cake.

From the way I saw it, there were only two choices. I either had to black out the windows of my shop or have my lips stapled together, and neither seemed like a viable option.

*****

The morning passed quickly and at half past eleven, after Dippy had been returned to his owner, Alice and Ethan arrived. A cardboard tray containing two take-away cappuccinos balanced on the hood of Ethan's pram as Alice pushed her way through what could only be described as the flurry of photographers that had set up camp outside the door of Doggie Divas.

Alice paused, her eyes bulging at the Christmas tree I'd now put in the corner and decorated with doggie treats and pet-shaped baubles. "Looking for a distraction, are we?"

She knew me too well.

I nodded. "It's not working. Those paparazzi outside the door aren't helping either. They keep taking photos of people going in and out of the cupcake shop."

"What's with them?"

I closed the door to shut out the noise from out on the street. I'd managed to dull the cake craving by finishing the decorations and singing loudly to the radio whilst clipping Dippy. Oh, and drinking four litres of water — which had had the adverse effect of sending me to the toilet every fifteen minutes for the past hour. Understandably, I wasn't keen to have the cravings return because of stray wafting smells.

"They're reporters from the city. They've come to do stories on the cupcake shop."

"What? Real reporters? *Sixty Minutes* type reporters?" Alice grabbed a brush from her Mummy bag and ran it through her hair, following up with a quick swipe of lip-gloss.

"Yep."

"You'd think they'd be over the road then. You know, like at the shop."

"Have you seen the crowd over there? The guys outside are the second wave. They got here too late so they've set up camp in front of my shop. They're in for the long haul. One of them even has an Esky filled with food and drink."

The footpath opposite was stacked so full of near hysterical women it was bordering on being a health hazard. It had to be a publicity stunt to drum up business. No cake in the world could be that good.

"I've never seen so many people," Alice said.

"I know. And the reporters are blocking my doorway. I've asked them to move twice already but they just shrug and eat more cake. It's bad for business if my customers can't get past the mountain of men eating cupcakes to get in the door. They might go down the road to Pet Pals to get their worm tablets."

"It doesn't look like its affecting business to me," Alice whispered, indicating the women who were scattered in twos and threes around the display window of the shop.

"They're not here to buy anything," I hissed back. "They're waiting for the line to get short enough so they can hop on the end. I wish they'd go away so we can get back to normal."

"You think having a stuffed Santa sitting behind your counter in the middle of the year is normal?"

"It's Christmas in July."

"Yeah. Right. Instead of wasting time making the shop pretty you should be using this to your advantage."

I would have been offended if I hadn't known Alice was right. Again. "How?"

"Give the reporters an interview. It's a golden opportunity, Livvy. Free publicity. If you get your shop mentioned on TV who knows where it could lead. You might need your own velvet rope and security guard."

"I can't do that."

"Why? You used to be on TV. You look super on camera."

"Because I only just came in from yelling at them to leave. I can't go back out there and suck up to them."

"Sure you can. It's a woman's prerogative to change her mind. Blame it on hormones or something. I'll mind the fort for a couple of minutes. Here, pop a bit of lip-gloss on and run the comb through your hair."

I dutifully did as I was told.

"Now, scoot."

"I don't know why I'm bothering," I threw over my shoulder as I pushed my way out the door from one throng into another. "They don't want to talk to me. They want the owner of Death by Cupcake."

"Bat your eyelashes at them and titter. I'm sure they'll change their minds. You know what reporters are like."

I did. That was why I gave it up.

As I talked to the reporters, giving my opinion from everything beginning with the interesting façade and ending with the menace the women in the line were causing to traffic, it occurred to me that there must be someone very special behind the counter of that shop. Like Mrs Di Marco said, it couldn't be some old Nanna in a checked apron or a gay man with cute hair that was drawing every woman in the shire like stray cats to a feed. It had to be a hot guy. Women didn't line up like that for cake — well, not unless the owner had invented a cake that made you lose weight without trying. Now that would be worth the wait.

Chapter 17

Cole stood behind the old-fashioned glass fronted counter surveying the — at last — empty space in front of him. Screwed up patty pans overflowed from the rubbish bin near the door and cake crumbs littered the counter where customers had been taking advantage of the free samples. Inside the display cases, a few lonely cupcakes decorated the paper-lined shelves. Only a few. Unbelievably, they'd sold out of nearly every single cake in the shop. A week's worth of baking had disappeared quicker than you could say 'frosting.' Cole supposed he should be happy about this but he was so knackered all he wanted to do was sit down with a beer and fall asleep in front of the telly. Opening the shop was meant to be a new start, a pulling back on the pressures of life, but right at that moment, the only thing he felt was an overwhelming tiredness. Oh, and a massive urge to tell those reporters who'd set up sleeping bags across the road to bugger off. Jesus, he wished they'd go back to the city and leave him in peace.

It was 6.25pm and Cole and Adelaide were supposed to shut up shop an hour and a half before but Cole, never one to turn down money when it was being thrown in his face, had been unable to turn the customers away.

The hands on his watch had ticked over, announcing 5pm but the footpath outside had still been three rows deep with women wanting cupcakes. And when he'd calmly made his way though the sea of perfume and hair products to close the doors, he'd been met with a type of abuse he'd never before witnessed from a lady. Those women not only wanted cupcakes, they were not leaving until they got them. One slightly irate customer had gone so far as to wedge her wedge heel into the door so he couldn't lock it. For a cake.

He'd created a nightmare.

But now they were gone and he and Adelaide were left to tidy the mess they'd left behind.

They worked in a sort of stunned silence for a while, both unable to believe what had happened on only their second day of trading. Then Adelaide, who'd been wiping down the counters, stopped mid swipe and looked over to Cole, who was staring out the window with a goofy look on his face.

"Reliving your day of glory?"

"I don't understand, Addie," Cole said. "Those women were feral today. It's like they've never seen a cupcake before."

Adelaide finished wiping the counter and put the spray back in the cupboard. She tossed the dirty cloth into a plastic tub to be washed later on and delved into the fridge, rummaging in the tubs of fondant and butter cream icing Cole had premade.

"You have no idea, do you? Today wasn't about cupcakes."

What the devil was she on about?

"I know you make the most stupendously delicious cupcakes in the world and the new flavours you've been working on sold faster than I could unpack them from the trays. But those women didn't come to sample your cakes, Cole. They were after a lot more than that. One look at their lust-crazed eyes was enough to confirm it. The word's gotten out about the hunky guy in the cake shop and every single woman in the district came to check you out. The cupcakes were an added bonus."

"Adelaide!" She had to be joking.

"It's a small town, Cole. News travels fast. I mean look at what happened with those shorts of yours," she said, producing a bottle of champagne and two chilled glasses. "Want one?"

Cole hoisted his bum onto the counter. It felt good to be off his feet at last. Even if it was only a brief rest before they finished the last of the cleaning for the day.

"But the reporters? Where the hell did they appear from? Not that I'm knocking a bit of free publicity, but I don't understand. I thought we were rid of them."

"I overheard one of them saying it was something to do with Phoebe being the *Telethon* child. They were following up on her story. I guess you being a good looking, manly man adds another dimension to the fact that you're making cake for a living and fulfilling your daughter's dying wish."

Cole nodded. She was probably right. Not about the good-looking part but the bloke baking cakes in honour of his daughter's memory was a twist on a story. If people were still thinking of Phoebe that was a good thing.

It had started after Phoebe's diagnosis at age nine. Being a gorgeous looking kid with a great smile and intelligence to boot, she'd caught the eye of the people who ran the *Telethon* foundation and in the year she went into remission was asked to be their special 'kid' for the season of fundraising. Phoebe had become the subject of ads, she'd been interviewed on TV, had her photo taken at fundraising events where she spoke about how *Telethon* helped kids like her who were ill and their families. Cole had never expected that her flippant comment about wanting her dad to start a cupcake shop would ever be remembered. But it seemed Western Australia hadn't forgotten Phoebe and now they were coming to see if Cole had granted his daughter's wish.

"So they didn't remember me from the ad, then?"

"Oh, they remembered. You Tube is a powerful medium."

Shit. Cole wondered if he could contact them and have that video taken down. It was practically pornography.

"Mum said she overheard them discussing it when she went out to the bank. They'd been wondering what happened to the Reno King."

Jesus. This was a nightmare. Was there no place he would be able to have a nice quiet life?

Adelaide handed Cole a glass of champagne and he took a rather large gulp. It wasn't a beer but it'd do. It was cold and wet and alcoholic.

"What's this in aid of, then?"

"I was going to give it to you yesterday, seeing as how it was the grand opening, but I figured we should get our heads around things first. I wanted you to enjoy the moment." She handed him a card. On the front red cartoon letters jumped around the page reading, "CONGRATULATIONS."

Cole regarded Adelaide quizzically. She wasn't the card type. He leant over and placed a tender kiss on her forehead. "Thanks. But you did a fair amount of work too."

"It's not from me."

Curious, Cole opened the card. "You're simply the best, better than all the rest" sang a group of chipmunks from somewhere hidden inside it. When he'd finished laughing Cole began to read.

Dear Daddy,

By the time you get this I'll be no more than a star winking at you in the sky so I wanted to say a big 'WELL DONE' on making our dream come true. I wish I was there. I would give you the biggest hug ever. But I'm watching you from Heaven and eating cake, too. I love you more than the universe.

Your best daughter ever,

Phoebe xoxoxo

PS: If the reporters come back give them an interview and tell them to go away.

"She got it ready a month or so before she died," Adelaide said. "She threw a tantrum until I drove her to the bottle shop. I helped her pick out the champagne but she paid for it with pocket money she'd saved. She made me promise not to give it to you until today. Apparently, we're now meant to toast her for giving you the idea."

Cole sniffed back a tear. "That'd be like her. Cheeky little minx."

They raised their glasses to the small-framed photo that Cole had mounted on the back wall of the shop. It was in an inconspicuous spot, because even though he knew Phoebe would have hated it and would have wanted to be the talking point of the place, he didn't want his deceased daughter on show. It was bad enough that he'd called the shop by the name she'd chosen before her death. Bloody macabre, when you thought about it — a tribute to his dead daughter having the word 'death' in the title. But that had been Phoebe. She was probably laughing at it up there in Heaven.

"Here's to you, Phoebs. I'm sure you're up there giggling at the antics that have gone on today and I'm only going to say this once. You were right. To the best daughter in the world." He drank the champagne down.

"To Phoebe," Adelaide echoed.

Cole put the glass down and turned to the small commercial kitchen out the back. "Right. Enough of that. If we're going to open up again tomorrow, I've got a shitload of cake to bake."

"I'll go and get us some takeaways from the pub," Adelaide said as she grabbed her handbag from under the counter and pulled out her wallet. "You can't work on an empty stomach and you're not having cupcakes for dinner."

Like he'd want them. Right about then, Cole was wishing he'd never opened a cupcake shop.

"Should I give the reporters one last interview?"

"It might get rid of them. Do you want me to send them over on my way to the pub?"

"I guess. If I do it, it'll be done for another year. Then we might be able to have a bit of normality around here."

"I doubt that will ever happen. The women aren't going anywhere in a hurry."

As Cole stood for a moment, leaning against the doorjamb and mulling over the day, his eyes went out the window and over the road to Olivia's shop. Phoebe would have loved Olivia and he was positive Olivia would have loved Phoebe. Now that the shop was open and things were less hectic, maybe it was time to tell her how he felt. Olivia, that was. He loved his daughter but he wasn't in the habit of talking to dead people.

Chapter 18

Scrubbing mud and cow poo from the floor was not exactly my idea of a fun way to spend my after work hours, but there I was, at half past six at night, doing that very thing. Other than my interview with the reporters — it turned out I knew one of them and boy did he have some gossip about Graeme — it had been a crappy day. Mr Evans' cocker spaniel had been uncooperative resulting in one of his ears being trimmed considerably shorter than the other and a rather unhappy Mr Evans. The women who'd come in to shelter from the rain while they waited to get into Death By Cupcake had left crap all over shop. Anyone would think they'd never heard of a rubbish bin. But the most tiring part had been resisting the urge to join that line; the urge to go and see what the fuss was about. That had been absolute torture. So, rightfully, I was feeling a teensy bit peeved at the new shop owners over the road.

At last, I switched off the lights and prepared to lock up for the day and as I was doing so I looked up to see that the shop across the road had cleared. There was a lone light shining from the back and two figures were behind the counter. One of them was waving at me.

Oh, what of it, I thought, deciding to do the neighbourly thing. In hindsight, and after I'd checked the takings for the day, I'd concluded it wasn't their fault the shop was a huge success. And the extra people in my own shop had resulted in a few sales and bookings, despite the fact that people had to climb over the reporters outside the door and had left mess everywhere. I raised my arm and returned the wave. I couldn't behave like a right bitch forever. That shop wasn't going anywhere, so I supposed I'd have to find a way to live with it.

Then a second figure raised a champagne glass in my direction. Male. That one was definitely male.

Now, who would be waving to me like that? And who could that man be?

*****

"So, next Friday night's fine, then?" Mum asked, as she handed me a serving of low fat chicken curry with basmati rice that was small even by my new eating standards.

"Is that it? I'm on a diet not a hunger strike."

"You're beginning to look so trim, it'd be a pity to spoil it now."

I ignored the comment and concentrated on making every last bite — which amounted to about three — of my miniscule dinner enjoyable. And enjoyable it was, until my mother dropped the bombshell.

"So next Friday's okay?" she repeated.

I swallowed the mouthful as slowly as I could, letting the taste linger on my tongue. God it was nice. Since I'd gotten over the whole Mum and Connor fiasco, my tastebuds seemed to have taken a turn for the better. They'd begun to long to vegetables, of all things, and savouries. I hadn't wanted a cake for days. It was like that binge had been the final one.

"For what?"

"For the date."

Date?

"Did I agree to this? When did I agree to this?" I know I'd been preoccupied but I had no recollection of any engagements the following Friday night.

"Yes. I asked you the other afternoon."

I cast my mind back to the last time I'd seen Mum. Thursday. The shop had been chockers with people and I'd caught one of those cupcake women trying to make off with a dog lead and collar by sticking them down the back of her jeans. I hadn't exactly been on top of my game. I remembered Mum muttering something about a man or a date but I hadn't paid a great deal of attention. Seemed like that had been an error of judgement.

"So who is this date with?"

"Gerry. He's a lovely boy. I know you'll adore him. He's an accountant."

Bring on the party.

I gave myself an internal slap remembering I was trying to be positive in my love life as well as my diet. "And I agreed?"

"I double checked on the phone yesterday."

Where the hell had my head been yesterday?

"You said it would be fine. I think you'll like Gerry. He's very handsome. Pecs like rock... At least, that's how they looked when we met in the free weights."

God, if my mother had met this Gerry at the gym he'd more than likely have 'roid rage or something. Mum's taste, before Connor, had notoriously run to men with hairpieces and hideous orange tans. There was little hope he'd be below the pension age.

"You don't have to do this, Mum. I'm fine with you and Connor. Really I am. You don't have to set me up with every Tom, Dick and Gerry that lobs into town. I won't throw myself into a vat of cake mix if you have a man and I don't."

"But I confirmed it with you. You said it was fine so I told Gerry. You can't back out now. It'd be very rude."

I could feel a migraine coming on. "When and where?"

"Friday next. I told you. Six o'clock at Tom's Tavern."

"You told him I'd meet him at Tom's? *Mum.*"

Nobody was ever seen at Tom's unless they'd been barred from the other two pubs in town. Tom's bar staff were under the illusion that spirits were something that went bump in the night. The only drinks they knew how to mix came in a can, laced with mountains of sugar and were popular with underage drinkers. I couldn't have a date there. Gerry would have formed some preconceived idea about me before we even met. If my mother hadn't already supplied him with one.

"Can't you ring him and tell him I'll meet him at The Merrifield Hotel? At least they have carpet from this century and wine that comes in a bottle."

Mum gave me a look. "I don't know when you got to be so picky. You're going on thirty, possum. You don't want to be left on the shelf. You should be grateful you even have a date on a Friday night."

"Yes. I'd be more grateful if the venue was changed, though."

Mum forked a chunk of chicken and began to furiously chop it into even smaller pieces. "I'll see what I can do."

"And I won't be eating dinner with him. One drink. That's it. I don't want to waste my food points on alcohol."

Besides, if it were only a drink, I could beg off if we weren't suited saying I had a prior engagement. There had to be contingencies for this sort of silliness.

"Any other conditions, Your Highness?"

"Nope. I think we're done. Now tell what me you're planning for this wedding. Am I going to be a bridesmaid because if I am you have to wait until I can fit into a size 12 again."

Which hopefully would be sometime in the next few months.

*****

After dinner, I helped Mum to rinse the dishes and pack the dishwasher. As was the usual routine, I went to switch on the coffee machine to warm up but before I had a chance Mum's thin spidery hand flew out of nowhere to stop me.

"Ah, no. No coffee tonight," Mum said, hurriedly.

"What? Why?"

"Um, I'm tired. I'm having an early night." Her eyes darted about the room like balls in a pinball machine unable to meet mine.

"But it's only quarter to eight. You can't be going to bed now."

"Yes. Yes, I am. I'm super tired and I have to be up at five to go to Boot Camp." As if to prove the point, Mum began to wilt. It was as if someone had let the wind out of a balloon in front of me.

"So Connor's coming over for a booty call and you're too afraid to tell me."

"No."

I shook my head. "You're a worse liar than he is."

Having hung the tea towel over the handle of the oven, Mum went to gather my things. Dumping them in my arms, she raced me down the hall.

"I mean, it's not like I don't know he's coming over," I said. "I'm quite capable of having a conversation with him without ripping his head off, you know."

I wouldn't enjoy it but I was capable of it.

"I know, darling, but Connor's feeling self-conscious about the whole thing. I'm sure you understand. Now, pop off home and think about what to wear for that date. Don't forget to wash the Spanx before you wear them. I'll talk to you tomorrow."

With that, I was bustled out the door and the door slammed promptly behind me. My family was weird. Utterly weird.

Chapter 19

Happy hour on a Friday night at the pub was not typically a rip-roaring affair. Usually, a few of the local business owners pulled a couple of tables together in front of the open fire and drank for an hour or so before going home to a night in front of the telly. Some would sit at the bar and chat to the barman until they'd eaten the free bar snacks and analysed the weekend's upcoming football games. And Beth always had her 'girls' table, as she liked to call it. The group consisted of Beth, Shannon-down-from-Perth, Maggie and Jane. Sometimes I sat with them too but mostly I enjoyed mingling with whoever was available. By six o'clock the drinks crowd usually thinned out and families from around the town began to trickle in for a counter meal in the dining area. But there was always plenty of room. You could swing a tiger safely in the space. As long as you didn't let it loose. Tonight however, the pub was a different place. There were faces crowding the bar I hadn't been in contact with for a good three years. Footy jumpers stretched across bellies that were decidedly bigger than the last time I'd seen them. Even old Bangers, who I was positive had died in 2011 was there, plain as day, ordering a schooner of beer. The dining room was full too, the excitement level higher than a rock concert. It was like the town had won the lottery and nobody had told me.

Either that, or Mum had informed them I was on a blind date and they'd come to spy. Probably the more likely scenario.

I jostled my way to the bar and stopped to order a glass of wine. I swapped a cheery 'hello' with Jane and Maggie and turned to survey the crowd, looking for my date. It was pretty hard to see when every tall man in Merrifield was suddenly standing in the way but I cocked my head this way that, in vain hope I'd spot Gerry without the spectacle of everyone making a fuss.

Which was totally likely. The folk of Merrifield loved to be involved. In fact, they'd probably want to come on the date with us if they could.

"You look nice tonight, lovey. That top's very flattering," Maggie said, surveying me as I took some change from my purse to pay for my drink. "I can see how thin you're getting. It was a pity to hide yourself away under those baggy outfits. You're so pretty."

"Thanks Maggie. It's a bit of a struggle at times but I'm happy with my progress."

"How long has it been now?"

"Two months and twelve kilos."

"Twelve kilos! Lord. You never needed to lose that much did you?"

"Apparently."

"You look amazing."

"Hopefully I'll look even more amazing when I reach my goal."

"That's the spirit. Think positive."

"On a blind date, are you?" Jane enquired.

There were no secrets in this town.

"Only a drink. Have you been talking to Mum?"

"Jim told me."

I threw a glare towards Jim, who was by the pool table playing eight ball with Beth. He gave me what I supposed was meant to be an innocent head nod in return and went on with his shot. Old bugger.

"How did he know?" I asked. Honestly, the speed with which my mother could spread gossip was second only to Mrs Tanner.

"From the gym, I think."

I shook my head and taking my drink from the bar continued around the corner towards the tables.

"I reckon that's him over there, mate. In the yellow," Jim called after me. "He looks bloody nervous, poor bloke."

And who wouldn't, with their entire personal life on show for the town?

As I reached the other side of the bar I passed Fern, the yoga instructor. She was demonstrating seated yoga poses on a barstool. A group of lads from the Merrifield Bulldogs had gathered and were egging her on as she contorted her body into more and more complex positions.

"Oi, Jim!" one of the lads yelled, pointing to Fern, "Is this how you did your back in a while back?"

"Have you got a pair of these yoga pants like Fern's, Jim?" asked another. "Red is *so* your colour."

"Don't you get smart with me, young Jonesey," Jim retorted. "A bit of stretching wouldn't hurt your footy game any. You looked worse in that last game than my ex does when she's out for a jog. And everyone knows she can't run to save herself."

As the bar erupted in laughter, I spotted a man sitting alone at a table in the corner. Though how I hadn't seen him through the crowd was beyond me given he was wearing a bright mustard shirt and a thin red tie that coordinated perfectly with the colour exploding over his cheeks. He also wore a rather thick pair of black plastic spectacles that he clearly needed to have checked by an optometrist because even though the menu was centimetres from his nose he was peering at it as if he were unable to read. Then there was his hair — a full crop of rather tight tangerine curls.

He looked like a male version of the lead in the musical, *Annie*.

Gerry. It had to be him.

A sudden urge to kill my mother flooded through me. She'd mentioned nothing about Gerry being quite so challenged in the looks department. Probably because she'd known that no one on this earth would be attracted to a man who dressed like an oversized hot dog. And physical attraction of some sort was a prerequisite in a relationship. I couldn't kiss a man who looked like I should be putting him in a pot of boiling water before dousing him with mustard.

I considered leaving but decided instead to slip back to the bar for a second drink. If Gerry had made an effort on my behalf the least I could do was smile and have a drink with him. Who knew? He might be charming beneath the... mustard. If there was one thing I'd learnt as an adult it was that you never judged a book by its cover. Taking up my second drink and a deep breath, I headed in his direction, plastering my friendliest smile on my face.

"Gerry?"

The man looked up. Bright green eyes twinkled in a friendly looking face. He smiled nervously, his perfect teeth giving him a strangely handsome air. Mum hadn't exaggerated about the pecs, either. From the way that shirt was moulding to his body, Gerry had the physique of a Greek god underneath.

Well, this was a turn up. He was a bit cute when you saw him front on. In a geeky 'I've-escaped-from-the-set-of-a-high-school-movie' kind of way.

"Olivia?" Gerry stood and pulled out the chair opposite him, gesturing for me to sit.

Very gentlemanly. And not the norm for Merrifield where chivalry was an art form dying faster than an un-watered pot plant.

Surreptitiously, he slipped a travel bottle of hand sanitiser from his pocket and squirted a blob between his palms. He looked at me. "I was beginning to think I'd been stood up."

I glanced at my watch. "It's five past six. I'm not exactly late."

"Is it? Feels like I've been here for hours."

"When did you arrive?" Poor guy. He seemed overwhelmed by the whole situation.

"About two minutes before six. I like to be punctual." He withdrew a particularly white handkerchief from his pocket and proceeded to wipe down the space along the edge of the table.

Right.

"Oh well, I'm here now. And it's lovely to meet you. Have you ordered a drink? Would you like me to get you one?"

Gerry coughed into the hanky. "I don't drink. Issues with alcohol."

And Mum had suggested we meet in a bar? Talk about awkward. Though she most likely didn't know.

"Would you rather go somewhere else? The bistro across the road has great coffee. We could have a chat there. It's dreadfully noisy in here tonight."

"It's fine, Olivia. Part of my disease is learning to cope with other people's use of alcohol. I can't expect people to change their behaviour to accommodate me. I'm the one with the problem. Besides, I'm quite comfortable being here. With you. We could go to the bistro later." He gave me a second enormous grin that was rather disconcerting and also slightly creepy. I shifted in my seat. I was beginning to think my first impression of Gerry had been correct.

"You're mother tells me you're a failed weather girl? That you gave up your journalism degree to run a dog grooming shop?" Gerry said.

"I own the shop. But yes, I was a weather girl and a journalist. It wasn't for me." Neither was being called a whoring home wrecker on morning television and I knew all about that. I turned my attention back to Gerry. I knew he was only making conversation, but I didn't like his tone. And I didn't like talking about my past with people I didn't know.

"No ambitions to return? I hate to see an education go to waste."

"It's nicer being away from the pressures of city life. And journalism jobs in the country don't exactly fall from trees. But what about you, Gerry? You're an accountant? That must be an interesting job."

Personally, I'd rather have watched ice melt than sit behind a desk adding up numbers for a living. It sounded hideously boring. But each to their own. And accountants got paid quite well and were good with budgeting and taxes. If worst came to worst, I might at least acquire a new person to look over my books once a year. Gerry looked like he'd be adept in that area.

"It is. The thrill of balancing large sets of numbers is quite exhilarating. I know other people hate it but tax time is one of my favourite times of year. The crunching of numbers revs me up."

Okay, so that was a little left of centre. The average person would describe Christmas or a certain season or birthday as their favourite.

"I went to UWA, graduated with honours and worked for a big firm for a few years building up a good client base," Gerry continued, "Then I began my own practise in Perth. Two other partners are running it at the moment. We deal with big corporate companies. Mergers, acquisitions, financial advice and, of course, taxes."

I wondered if it would be rude to yawn. What on earth had possessed my mother to ever think Gerry and I would be compatible? We were as likely to become a couple as a footballer would be to take up ballet. "And how do you come to be here in Merrifield?" I asked.

"Lifestyle change."

Thank God he hadn't said 'tree change.' I abhorred those people who moved from the city thinking they were going to keep their city ways in the country. They wanted double decaf long macs at all hours of the day and were forever moaning about the lack of shops and bars and the constant smell of sheep poo and horses. Which was sort of the point when one moved to the country.

"I guess you'd say it's a tree change." Gerry gave a cross between a snort and a chuckle. "I have a lot of trees on my property."

I smiled politely. "And where's that?"

"Out Donnelly way. The old Truman place. Do you know it?"

"I do. It's very picturesque. Lovely rambling old farmhouse. Do you have any animals yet?"

"I'm allergic to sheep and cows."

"Oh." Couldn't say I'd heard of that before.

"But I'm thinking about getting a horse or two. My therapist thinks it'd be good for me. And being in a new environment with new interests will keep me away from temptation. After the whole rehab disaster and my wife leaving and the bogus fraud and gambling charges, Merrifield seemed like a great idea. Of course, I was hesitant at first about having to leave my social connections but now I've met you, I can see I've made the correct decision."

"Horse riding can be a lot of fun. There's a good club in town. You could join."

"Are *you* a member?"

"No. I don't have room for a horse at my place."

"I've been having lessons. I'm feeling fairly confident about tackling a trail ride. Would you like to come with me? We could rent you a horse."

I hadn't ridden a horse since I was twelve and Alice and I were going through our pony club phase. I loved animals but I'd never had the inclination to own a horse. Way too much work and expense. I couldn't be unkind though. He was only trying to be nice.

"That'd be lovely. I'm not very good though. I haven't ridden for a long time. I'd probably slow you down or fall off or something."

"My life coach could come with us to help you out. She's the one teaching me to ride. She's also my AA sponsor."

"She sounds like a talented lady."

Maybe Gerry should go out with her?

"She is. She's been encouraging me to set new goals for myself. One of them was going on a date, beginning a new relationship. You're so pretty Olivia. So vibrant. I feel we could make a go of this." His cheeks became tinged with pink as he said it.

"Er, ah, thanks Gerry."

The only thing I wanted to make a go of was getting out the door and fast. I didn't mean to be unkind, really I didn't, but Gerry was either a roo short in the top paddock or extremely desperate. Why else would you say that to someone you'd only known five minutes? It was good to have goals, I had some myself but surely his life coach hadn't rehearsed this with him?

I picked up my wine and took a large gulp. If only I'd had the sense to order a third glass. This whole thing would be so much easier if I were a little tipsy. At least I'd have an excuse for laughing at the things he was saying.

"Shall we swap numbers?" Gerry enquired.

Oh God.

"Sure. Why not."

We typed each other's numbers into our phones after which Gerry suggested that perhaps we *should* retire to the restaurant across the road for dinner. He was feeling rather peckish and had to eat on time so that his insulin levels wouldn't drop. Low insulin made him very susceptible to the lure of alcohol. And dessert. Apparently he had issues with dessert of any kind as well. It made him fat.

Like duh!

"I've taken the liberty of reserving us a table," he added, looking rather pleased with himself for taking such a responsible life step.

"Ummmmm—"

I didn't have the heart to tell him I wasn't interested in him. It'd been a long time since I'd feigned illness on a date. Maybe I could go to the toilet and call Alice who could then call me back and say there was some type of emergency. I looked around the pub, my eyes frantically searching for someone, anyone, to come and save me.

I didn't want Gerry taking me to dinner, no matter what goals he'd set with his life coach or his therapist, or whoever that weird looking lady two tables down was; the one who was staring at us.

"Olivia! Jesus, I'm so sorry I'm late. I thought you'd gone home."

Like a vision from heaven, Cole was standing beside the table, smiling and looking rather gorgeous in a pair of dark denim jeans and a navy t-shirt. His hair was mussed and a white powder, that looked vaguely like flour was dusted along his hairline above his ear.

I felt my body physically sagging with relief. How many times in one life was it possible to be rescued by such a handsome specimen?

"I got held up," he continued. "Are you ready to come up to the house now? I'm not interrupting, am I?"

Luckily, I'd always been a quick thinker. "The secret room, of course. I'd completely forgotten we agreed to do that after you finished work tonight. Gosh, I'm so embarrassed. I'm already here with Gerry. We were about to go across to the bistro. It's our *first date*."

I gave Gerry a quick rundown of the history of Cole's house and how I was possibly the only living person in Merrifield apart from Alice who knew the location of the secret room. With great emphasis on 'living' to add weight.

Cole looked at me expectantly. A small crinkle formed in the space between his brows and I had to stop myself from smirking at his faked earnestness.

"But this the only night I have free for the next two weeks."

"Yes, yes. I know. I'm so sorry, Cole. I can't leave my date. That would *soooo* be rude."

Then Gerry jumped from his chair. "What a fabulous idea! I'd love to tag along and see your secret room and your house, if I might. I love old houses. I've already begun a study of the history of properties in the area. It's been a thing of mine for quite some time. In fact, it's one of the reasons I decided to move to Merrifield in the first place. Did you know it's the only heritage listed town in the South West? So many interesting historical buildings! I'm hoping to write a history of it at some stage. It would be sure to be a bestseller."

The look Cole gave Gerry was similar, I'm sure, to the shocked bemusement I'd had on my face earlier but to Cole's credit he hid it under a grave-looking mask. "Yeah. Much as I'd like to, mate — any friend of Olivia's is a friend of mine — we can't do that. My wife, Adelaide, is at home. Very nervy since the accident. Has anthropophobia."

Gerry frowned.

"Pathological fear of people," Cole explained, completely straight faced. "Really bad. If I introduce her to anyone new without warning, she totally freaks out. Last time she had to be hospitalised. Olivia's okay. She's known Addie for ages. So sorry."

Gerry's face collapsed in something like extreme disappointment. "Sure. Of course. I completely understand. I've suffered from anxiety my entire life though I never knew until I began treatment for my alcoholism.

You go, Olivia. I'll text you later on and we can set up the horse riding outing."

I grabbed my bag and drained my drink before Gerry could change his mind. "Okay. Cool. And thanks, Gerry, we'll catch up soon. I enjoyed our chat."

About as much as I enjoyed sitting through action movies that featured Sylvester Stallone.

*****

By the time we reached the place where Cole had parked his car, we were both in fits. Cole bent double, his shoulders shaking as he held on to the side of the car trying to rein in his laughter. I grasped my stomach, sucking in breaths of air in an attempt to stop the giggles. I couldn't look at him. If I did, I knew I'd start over again and my stomach was clenched tight as it was. Plus, I'd laughed so hard snot had spurted from my nose. If only I'd had one of Gerry's hankies I would have been fine but as it was I'd had to settle for a screwed up tissue I found in the bottom of my handbag.

"What a weirdo," I spluttered, finally able to form a sentence.

"I could see that, and I wasn't even sitting with the guy. What were you thinking?"

"It must be the diet. The lack of sugar must have done something to my brain."

I clapped a hand over my mouth. Damn. I hadn't wanted Cole to know I was on a diet. I hadn't wanted anyone to know. Until this minute the ladies at Weight Watchers, Alice and my mother were the only people I'd shared the information with and I'd been reluctant to even tell them. I think it was a failure thing. My confidence had been at such a low ebb over the past few years, I'd often sabotaged myself into failure. It didn't matter that other people said I was determined and stubborn when I put my mind to a task. Most of the time I felt like a big, fat failure.

"I thought you looked thinner but what do I know, I'm only a bloke. Most of us are oblivious to the minor details. Why do you need to be on a diet, anyway?"

Awww. That was sweet.

"Um, because I weighed enough to have to buy an extra seat if I went on the plane."

"Really?"

Either Cole was a good actor, or that response was the most genuine thing I'd heard in years.

"Yep."

"Wow. I wouldn't have picked it. I thought your curves were pretty nice. I like curves on a woman. Those skinny chicks with bones poking out can be off putting for a guy. Soft and cuddly is a much greater turn on."

Was he flirting again or simply stating a fact from the man's point of view?

I'd had so many bad experiences with men I didn't trust myself to make a sensible decision anymore. To think I'd even been considering Gerry to begin with left me with serious doubts about my radar. At least I'd come to my senses when he'd started to talk taxes.

"Well, I'm sure I'll be as cuddly when I'm less curvy," I commented.

"I expect so. And the curves you have left will be more accentuated. That's a good thing, right?" A hint of a smile played on Cole's lips.

Okay, so he *was* flirting. Despite the fact that I knew it was wrong, I felt that flutter of excitement in my chest, again. I had to say something. He couldn't torture me like this; it wasn't fair.

"Cole."

Cole made a step towards me. He was openly grinning now, teasing me with his eyes. "Yes, Olivia?"

The flutter spread into a full-blown quiver.

"You can't keep flirting like this. It's not right."

How unconvincing had that sounded? I loved that Cole was playing with me and he totally knew it. It was right there, in his eyes.

"I think I can."

He stepped closer. His hand reached across to the hood of the car, backing me into the closed door. His breath was warm against my cheek. My heart began to pound. It was wrong on every level and yet, there I was practically begging him to continue. At least, I hadn't known Graeme was married. I'd been an innocent victim. This time though, I was letting Cole do it when I knew full well he was a married man. Even worse, I didn't want him to stop.

God, I wanted him to push himself against me and kiss me till I couldn't breathe.

Crap and shit and crap.

"In fact, I'm positive," he whispered, lifting a finger to gently caress the skin along my jaw.

Okay, so if he didn't give two hoots, one of us was going to have to be sensible. I sucked in a breath, torn between the fact that I was thinking about Cole's lips, so deliciously close to mine, and the fact that they belonged to Adelaide, who was without a doubt one of the nicest girls I'd ever met.

"Cole, please."

Cole looked into my eyes. His finger looped a hair behind my ear. His body pressed into mine. I could feel his heart pounding too.

"I'm not married Olivia."

"Pardon?" I stiffened. The blood pumping in my ears may have been the catalyst for some type of instant hearing loss but I could have sworn Cole had said he was single.

He leant into my ear. His finger traced the skin around the lobe. His breath was hot. "Adelaide's my sister. She's on leave from her job and offered to give me a hand moving house."

I felt a rush of shock, a tingle of recognition, a mushy smile making its way to my lips. A fissure of excitement was building in my stomach, though that could have been because Cole was stroking one of my most sensitive spots. What else was a girl to do if a guy touched her behind her ear?

Trying to gain some sort of clarity, I shifted, my hand on the latch of the car. "Are you positive? I mean you look pretty married and you certainly talk like you're married. You're forever bickering."

"Positive. I've seen Adelaide wearing nappies. I fought with her over who was the best band — Nirvana or Pearl Jam — for the whole of 2003, I think it was. Plus, I know she stood in line to meet Jamie Oliver for five hours only to find out she'd rocked up on the wrong day. Her tickets were for the next day. If we'd been married I'd never have been able to take the piss about a faux pas like that."

"She's your sister?"

"Only DNA could disprove it."

"So Phoebe is—"

"—Adelaide's niece. My daughter. Her diagnosis was too much for Jenny. She was my wife. She crumbled watching Phoebe waste away before our eyes.

She was never that strong. I never wanted her to leave but I couldn't make our marriage work and give Phoebe the support she needed to fight her cancer. I couldn't. It was better for us to separate. So Jenny left. And I was alone."

"Do you still love her?"

"Jenny? No. Shit happened. Lots of it. Words were said that can never be unsaid. The hardest thing was that she didn't have the strength to cope, so she left me to do it. She ran away."

"Gosh."

"She hurt me, Olivia. More than I can put into words."

I looked up into Cole's eyes. No wonder the poor guy seemed had so sad behind those twinkling eyes. It was dreadful what had happened to him. Fancy losing your *entire* family to cancer. I'd been devastated when my father had died so suddenly but to have no one to lean on at a time like that... how had Cole coped?

Then, a sudden thought — utterly unrelated to death — popped into my head. Cole stepped away, watching as I began to smile and then laugh. "Oh. My. God. Wait till I tell Adelaide what you said about her being anthropophobic."

"It wasn't *that* bad."

"No, but she'll be pegged as utterly bonkers by dinner tomorrow. Everyone heard you and people talk in this town. They love nothing more than to make a small story bigger."

"You can't tell her it was me. If you say one word, I swear, I'll never save you again."

I put a finger to my lips. "Hmm. Weighing up if it's worth it. Might be more fun to see you suffer. I mean, you must have known I thought you were married and you said nothing."

"I didn't know. I thought you were nervy. You kept jumping around. I wondered if you had some sort of emotional thing going on." He gave me another look. "That didn't come out exactly how I meant it to either, did it?"

"Not exactly. You seem to be as good at putting your foot in it as I am at tripping over mine. And I'm still telling Adelaide."

Walking around to the driver's side of the car, Cole pulled the keys from his pocket and flicked the remote to unlock the door. "So much for friendship. Next time I'll leave you to Gerry."

"Us girls have to stick together."

He opened the door. "Need a lift?"

"I was intending to walk, now I can, but that'd be nice. Thanks."

It would have been nicer, too, if he'd kissed me but there was no point getting ahead of myself. He'd only just become un-married, after all. I hopped into the car beside him, pulling the seatbelt across my chest and clipping it in. As I did so, my phone chirruped, announcing a text.

I slid it from my pocket, glancing at the screen.

"Crap."

"What?"

I waggled the phone in Cole's direction. "Gerry."

"Already? He's keen. You only left him ten minutes ago."

I opened the message. I felt my eyes bulging, reaching the dangerous level where they might pop from my head. "And clearly, that was enough time for him to — Oh my God. I can't look. I'm seriously traumatised."

Yet despite myself, that was what I was doing because there in all its glory was a close up picture of Gerry's erection above a caption that read,

<Can't wait to see you again>

"That is possibly the most disgusting thing I've ever seen at close range."

Cole leant over to look at the photo. "Man. That's one lovesick dude. I'd say you're in there."

"Cole!"

"It's not every day a bloke sends a dick pic to a girl. You should feel honoured."

"I'm not honoured, I'm appalled. And if I'd ever had any intention of going on an actual date with that fool — which I didn't — it wouldn't be happening now, let alone sleeping with him."

"Which is good."

Apart from the obvious I had to ask why.

"If you slept with him, I'd never be able to have sex with you because I'm pretty sure you'd be forever comparing us and finding me not up to it."

Before I could register the thought that we might even be having sex some day the phone chirruped again. I looked at the screen. A groan of disgust escaped my lips.

<Did you get my message?>

"Allow me." Cole grabbed the phone and began to type.

<Yes and truly penis is SO BIG have no idea how to respond>

Quickly, he pressed send, shooting the message into cyber space.

"Cole." I squealed again, snatching the phone back. "You can't say that. He'll think I'm interested."

Chirrup.

<You could send photo of breasts. I'd love to see them>

"See. Now what am I going to do?"

Cole began to laugh. He laughed so hard tears welled in the corners of his eyes. "I'll fix it."

"Like you did a minute ago? No, thank you."

"Trust me." He took the phone from my hand.

<Look Gerry. Am dreadfully sorry but could never show you my breasts. Am in secret relationship with Cole who does not have wife called Adelaide but does have secret room filled with bondage gear. PS: I don't like horses. Am more into whips>

Swoosh. The message was sent.

"There. Problem solved."

"Yes, but now we have a bigger one. Well, apart from the fact that the entire town is going to think you're some sort of sadistic sexual deviant after Gerry starts spreading the word."

"Which is?"

"Now I'm not sleeping with Gerry, I have to sleep with you."

Sometimes I even astounded myself with my verbal dementia. Why would I have said that? Well, other than that I wanted to sleep with him.

Cole nodded slowly as if taking it in. "You're absolutely right. Should we go straight to my place and get it over with?"

"I guess so. Are you hairless like Gerry? I don't know if I can go there if you haven't kept up with your manscaping."

"Hmm. You could close your eyes and pretend."

Our banter was interrupted by another chirrup.

<I don't suppose you and Cole would be up for a threesome? He's quite attractive>

"Oh no. No, no and no." I read the message out loud.

"Enough." Cole grabbed the phone.

<Dear Gerry, the only person Olivia is having sex with, debauched or otherwise, is me. Bugger Off. Cole>

I smirked. Right. Well, that was sorted then.

*****

By the time Cole got home somewhere around 2am, he was knackered, but not because of the hard week of work he'd done. He'd spent the remainder of the evening on the couch next to Olivia, trying to keep his hands to himself — God knows why. That damn tinkling laugh of hers, the one that made parts of him spring to life like he was a bloody thirteen year old hadn't helped his cause. Neither had the couple of glasses of red wine nor three episodes of *Game of Thrones* she'd made him watch. Geez, if he'd known that show had so many naked women in it he would have started watching it sooner, just not when Olivia was present. He had to admit it was a weird feeling sitting there with her watching those women cavorting across the screen when all he wanted to do was to touch the girl beside him. Everywhere. And a lot. But the weirder thing was the fact that he hadn't acted on the impulse. His hands had stayed firmly in his pockets or glued to his glass. Because for some reason Cole decided he should behave like a perfect gentleman, sensing that maybe Olivia might appreciate that more. He had the feeling her love life hadn't been all that great in recent times and she needed a little TLC. It had been hard though. Damn hard.

The evening had ended with them swapping numbers and making a date to go jogging on Sunday morning followed by breakfast at the bistro. It wasn't the usual way Cole began relationships — not that he'd had a great deal of practice over the past fifteen years — but then Olivia wasn't your usual type of girl. She didn't seem to care that she'd be sitting opposite him looking sweaty whilst eating poached eggs. And he liked that idea.

As Cole stepped out of his jeans and kicked them into the corner of the room he used as a laundry basket, his phone, lying on top of the bed, lit up. He picked it up and flopped onto the bed to read the message.

<Hi>

So she was initiating contact after he'd made the first move was she? He liked that sort of confidence in a woman. He couldn't abide those chicks that sat about waiting for the bloke to call. This was the twenty first century.

He began to type.

<Hi>

<Watcha doin'?>

He thought about the answer for a second and decided the truth was a good thing. Why beat around the bush?

<Thinkin' bout you. And getting undressed>

There was a brief pause before his phone pinged again.

\<Me too\>

This was promising. She wasn't balking at his attempts at intimacy now, though being able to admit such a thing to his face was another matter. It might be that she'd give him the run around, make him do the chasing. Cole didn't mind if she did. Chasing was part of the fun.

His phone pinged again.

\<To clarify - not thinking about self, thinking about U not being married to Adelaide. R U sure you're not married?\>

Cole chuckled as he typed his reply and sent it off with a whoosh.

\<Sure as I am that I'll never see Michael Jackson live in concert\>

\<Or Patrick Swayze doing real *Ghost*\>

\<Haha. Liked *Dirty Dancing*. One of my favourite movies\>

\<Are you taking the piss?????\>

\<No. Always wanted to be able to dance like that\>

\<From what I've witnessed, lessons might be required. Lots\>

\<Maybe you could give me a hand????\>

Cole put down his phone and waited for a reply. This texting thing made conversation so much easier. Plus, he could do it while wearing nothing but his boxers. It was a win-win situation. After a bit, his phone announced another message.

\<You've seen me dance. You really wanna go there again?\>

<Oh. Yeah. Forgot about that. Hey, had fun tonight. Thanks for introducing me to GOT. Never realised how awesome it was >

<U mean u never realised GOT had so much nudity and violence>

<That too. Gerry probably loves it>

<Don't mention that name. Was fully expecting him to be waiting on doorstep when I got home>

<You wish>

<Thanks for being knight in shining armour>

<Anytime. See you tmw?>

The screen went dark for a minute.

<Not if I see you first>

<Bye>

<Bye>

<Bye>

<Bye>

<Stop texting now or I'm calling Gerry to tell him you're available for horseback riding with whips>

<LOL. NOT. FUNNY>

As Cole put the phone down on the bed and stood to go into the bathroom, he caught a glimpse of himself in the mirror. The reflection that looked back at him was grinning like a girl, something he hadn't seen a long time. And Cole decided he liked it.

Chapter 20

Alice's eyes were blazing with an anger that was almost scary. A whirling dervish, rivalling the Tasmanian Devil cartoon character, she was flinging items of clothing into an open suitcase on the bed without stopping to see what it was she was tossing or where it was landing. The frenzy meant, of course, that I was doing a fair amount of ducking and weaving to avoid trainers, underwear, a bikini — though why one would need that in September was beyond me — plus various other articles of clothing. I was also folding. Fast. Alice would have kittens in the morning after she calmed down and opened that bag, discovering everything in a higgledy-piggledy mess. And my best friend didn't need to be having kittens. Not now or ever.

It was four days before Alice and Jed's anniversary and for the second night in a row, I had been comforting an increasingly distressed Alice while Jed was M.I.A. This time was way worse than any of the others in the last month or so, though. On a scale of one to insane, Alice had reached manic, which was only slightly below murderous from where I stood. One more flying shoe and I was going out to the kitchen to hide the knives.

The evening had taken a turn for the worse after Alice had received a phone call from a woman asking for Jed. Not recognising the voice, Alice had enquired who was calling at which the woman had hung up, leaving Alice so distraught she'd almost dropped the phone into the bath where Ethan was merrily splashing away. Luckily, I'd been on hand to catch it.

Or maybe not so luckily. The ranting that had ensued was approaching epic and though I loved Alice, it was hurting my ears. Even her cat had made an escape through the cat flap to escape the din.

"I'm going to kill him. Dirty, stinking, cheating arsehole. I'm going to cut off his balls with a steak knife and then I'm going to kill him." Alice raced out the door into Ethan's room returning with her arms filled with nappies and baby clothes which she shoved into a shopping tote beside the suitcase. "If he thinks his skanky girlfriend can ring the house and ask for him, he has another thing coming. Who does he think he is? Hugh Hefner? And more to the point what sort of cheek does *she* have?"

I pulled a balled jumper from the suitcase, folded it and put it back in. "It could be a mistake. Please don't jump the gun, Al."

The look I was given in return was one that could freeze water.

"And you're so totally qualified to give marriage advice, are you? You can't even keep a boyfriend."

Okay. So this was serious. Alice and I never traded anything other than positiveness in regard to each other's problems. Even when Alice broke her leg before the Miss Bulldogs finale, I had managed to spin it so she could ham up the disaster in the talent portion of the competition. Not an easy thing when your talent is tap dancing. Alice had won the pageant, of course. She would have won whilst wearing a full body cast.

I moved from the side of the bed, taking the remaining baby clothes from Alice's arms and putting them on the doona. Wrapping my arms around my friend, I felt Alice's body sag, then the shuddering as she began to cry.

"I'm sorry, Livvy. I didn't mean to say that. Truly I didn't."

I squeezed her tighter. "I know. We always take our pain out on the ones we love, don't we?"

We hugged for a moment more, until Alice pulled away, wiping her eyes and giving a loud sniff. "And the one I love the most isn't even here. Which could be a good thing. I have a lot of pain I'd like to inflict." She began to wail again. "I hate him. I hate him more than Brussels' Sprouts."

"I think that's highly unlikely. Don't you remember that time at camp when you threw up in your jumper because Mr Simons said you couldn't leave the table until you'd eaten every single one on your plate?"

"He was such an old bastard. Bit like Jed."

"Jed's not a bastard. There's a perfectly good explanation for this. I know there is."

"Yes. My husband is bonking another woman, that's the explanation." Alice yanked the zip on the suitcase so hard it almost broke. "Where am I going to go? Mum's already told me there's no room for us at her place. She thinks I'm overreacting. You expect she'd be more supportive at a time like this but the only person she cares about is Lisa. She's always been the favourite."

There'd always been a degree of tension between the siblings in Alice's family. Alice, being the oldest, had often felt her younger sister was treated differently. Her parents never gushed over her the way they did with Lisa, no matter what Alice did.

"Stay at my place in the spare room. It's big enough for both of you. We can set up the port-a-cot for Ethan."

"Can I?"

"That's what guest rooms are for, right? And if you stay for a few days, we'll be able to watch the rest of *Grey's Anatomy* without interruption. I'll get the DVDs from the lounge on our way out."

Alice gave a small smile. "Thanks."

I hoisted the suitcase from the bed, my knees almost buckling under the weight. Starting for the door, Alice following behind me, Ethan in one arm and the massive bag of nappies — and lord knows what else — in the other.

"There is one condition though," I said.

Alice stopped. "What?"

"If that crazy Gerry turns up, you have to hit him over the head with the frying pan."

"It'll be my pleasure. Might as well get some use out of it."

"Very funny."

Alice switched off the bedroom light. "Anything else?"

"Yes. If Jed comes round, I don't want any blood on my carpet. It's a bugger to get out."

"Fine. I'll stab him in the hallway, then."

*****

After Ethan had been settled for the night in his temporary bedroom and Alice had opened her suitcase to find everything neatly folded and packed, she and I had sat on the couch with a bottle of vodka and a block of chocolate.

"I know, I know," I said, holding up a hand to silence Alice before she could comment. "This is going to break every diet rule I've set for myself but extenuating circumstances are at play here. Emotional binge eating and drinking is absolutely necessary."

"You won't get any argument from me." Alice leant forward filling our glasses with vodka and lemonade, though it looked more like straight vodka to me. Her hand was shaking as she poured. "I think you're doing marvellously well, by the way."

"I can fit into my old jeans again. The ones I used to wear when I left Perth. And I went jogging this morning for the third time this week. I haven't done that in years."

"I'm so proud of you. I told you, you could do it."

"I was sceptical though. I guess it's hard to see the forest for the trees. Now I can see the changes happening, I'm more motivated than ever to stick with it."

"Good for you. Imagine how good you're going to look by Christmas." Alice's lip began to wobble. She picked up her drink, downing it in one go and refilling the glass.

"You okay?" I asked.

"Christmas. What am I going to do about Christmas?"

"Christmas isn't for a couple of months. It'll be forgotten by then."

"You don't know that." A tear slid down her cheek.

I picked up the tissue box, which I'd grabbed on way from the bathroom in case, and handed it to Alice. I hated tears in any form but when Alice, always perky, fun-loving Alice cried, it made me want to cry too.

The entire world knew what a big deal she made of Christmas — the family at her house, the traditional dinner, even if it was forty-two degrees outside, the colour co-ordinated outfits that looked perfect in photos, the obligatory uncle dressed as Santa. If Jed weren't around her perfect Christmas would be ruined.

"My strategy's always been to worry about it when it happens. There's no point getting het up over something that might not come to pass."

A snort came from Alice's nose as she blew. "I suppose so. But I'm not sharing my child at Christmas. I won't. Jed can get stuffed if he thinks I'm letting Ethan go off with him and his floozy for the day and be spoilt rotten. He's my baby."

"Like I said, let's cross that bridge when we come to it."

"Keep telling me that, will you? If you keep saying it, I might start to believe it."

"I've no intention of doing anything other than that."

And I definitely would not be getting in the middle of any argument between her and Jed or even taking a side if she wanted me to. Because if truth be told I agreed with Alice's mum. Until Alice knew exactly what was going on, she had to give Jed the benefit of the doubt. He'd never given her cause to treat him any other way.

Alice seemed to rally after that. We ate some chocolate, had a couple of drinks and ogled McDreamy for a while.

Then she turned to me. "Tell me what's happening with that delicious, Cole. The last I heard he was playing Sir Lancelot and saving you from the evil dragon Gerry."

I couldn't help smiling at the memory of Gerry's face when Cole told him Adelaide was anthropophobic. "We've done a bit of text flirting and he's been into the shop a few times. We went jogging and had breakfast after."

"And you managed that without breaking a bone? Well, done you."

"Don't be a cow."

Alice snickered. "You like him, I take it."

"A lot."

"There's no deep dark secrets to put a damper on things? No extra wives or girlfriends? No Mafia contacts?"

"This time I think I may actually have found a normal man. A lovely, normal man. He said he was jealous when he saw me with Sean at Shannon's party."

"And has he put the moves on you yet?"

"We almost kissed the other night but that's as far as it's gone. Having you staying here is going to cramp my style."

"There's always his place."

"Like I said, let's cross that bridge when we come to it."

I meant it too. For the first time in years, things were going my way and if that meant I had to take it so slowly even a snail would get laid before I did, then that's what I'd do. I liked Cole, and in my experience, that only meant that I was well on track to muck things up somehow. Not this time. This time there would be no bad karma ruining my chances because everything was out in the open.

Chapter 21

Cole sauntered down the stairs of the beer garden towards me, two glasses and a bag of nuts in his hand. The muscles in his arms flexed as he carried them and his jeans sat loosely on his hips in a certain way that made you want to rip them off. A nice thought, now that I was legitimately allowed to have it.

Pausing at the edge of the grass, he stopped to look around. Above him, the setting sun shone through the silver birch trees casting a dappled light over his face and jaw. I shifted slightly in my seat, letting my eyes roam over his body. Yes, I knew it was rude to stare but gosh, he was pretty. Possibly not an adjective a guy like him would appreciate but it was true. Cole was pretty, not to mention pretty damn hot.

Stopping in front of me, he put the glasses on the table. A swarthy grin spread over his face. "Whatcha lookin' at?"

Crap. He'd totally sussed me out. I tried to look as if I hadn't been checking him out. "Nothin'."

A dark eyebrow rose behind his glasses. "Well, it couldn't have been my bum, seeing as I was facing you."

More's the pity. After jogging behind him along the river track I was well aware of how nice Cole's bottom was. I didn't need an invitation to look at it.

"If you must know, I was looking at a bird in the tree behind you." I pointed to the silver birch where a parrot perched, cursing myself for not being able to come up with a remotely less lame excuse.

"Yeah and I'm Prince Harry."

"If you were, I wouldn't have been looking at the bird."

Cole released a chuckle. "Smart mouth." He tossed a bag of nuts in my direction. "Cashews. As requested."

"Cool. Ta."

Ripping the bag open, I took two nuts, popped them into my mouth and slowly sucked the salt off. They were such a treat for me now and I wanted to savour each and every one. At least it would give me something to concentrate on other than how cute Cole looked standing there in front of me or the disaster zone that was my house right at that moment. Alice still wasn't talking to Jed. If anything, the big freeze had turned into an iceberg of titanic proportions. If only they'd get over it.

"I thought a picnic at the falls might be nice. I've never been there. Do you want to go after work on Saturday?" Cole slid onto the bench beside me. His knee brushed against mine as he leant across to pick up his drink and a shot of something fizzy burst through my veins.

I hated and loved how he could do that to me — that we could be so attracted that I felt it physically.

"Olivia?" A hand waved in front of my face.

"Sorry?"

I'd been miles away then.

"Am I boring you?" Cole attempted to look offended but all it did was make him appear even more smoulderingly sexy than he did on a regular basis.

I gave him a slight shove with my shoulder. Cole could never be boring. He was, well... he was plain yummy. "Don't be silly."

"But something else is on your mind? Other than my manly good looks, of course."

God, what sort of a man was he? Everyone knew the dangers of asking what was on a girl's mind.

"That does go without saying. But no. I was thinking about Alice and Jed on this occasion."

"Gutted."

"Don't be. I spend a lot of time thinking about you. Well, your bum at any rate."

"And so you should. I think about your body way more than is respectable." Cole took a handful of nuts and pointed the open bag in my direction. "Alice is the pretty blonde one, right?"

"Yeah. Her husband Jed is the bank manager. Neat brown hair, quite tall, rather gangly."

"Do I know him?"

"Not sure. I don't think you've ever been introduced. Anyway, Alice is convinced he's playing up on her. Unfortunately, the signs seem to be pointing in that direction. Even though I find it hard to believe."

Yesterday, Alice had come blaring into the shop and announced she'd seen Jed and some unknown girl in the alley between the supermarket and Jim's. They'd been whispering and coordinating something on their phones. Most likely phone numbers. I stopped short of pointing out that was what most people did with phones — and who knew why Jed would need the girl's number — I hadn't wanted to start another crying fit or at the very least an argument. I also didn't want to know how Alice knew this because I was fairly sure Alice had taken up stalking in her spare time. She'd appeared wearing a trench coat, dark glasses and a beret when it was a beautiful day outside and warm enough for a t-shirt and shorts.

"And this affects you, how?"

"Alice is staying at my place. She's refusing to speak to him."

"Ahhh. Right. And you'd like her to leave?"

"No. I love having her around but it's so much drama. With Jed practically camped out on the doorstep, I feel as if my life has been invaded. Maybe I'm too old to be sharing a place. I haven't done it since I was at Uni. I'm too set in my ways to have other people's crap cluttering up my floor. I have enough problems keeping my own crap in order."

"You crotchety old woman. Remind me never to stay over."

He wanted to stay over? Luckily, he hadn't seen the state of my house. It looked like a scene from that *Hoarders* show at the moment. No man would want to stay over in that mess.

"She's driving me bonkers, Cole. She never washes the pots — apparently that's what dishwashers are for — and there's gym gear strewn over the laundry floor. Plus, the undies have to be hung on the line in a specific way or she has an aneurism. Who'd have thought I'd been doing it wrong all these years."

I knew most of these quirks were probably stress related but it didn't make it any easier. Having to re-peg my smalls had almost been the last straw.

Looking at Cole, I could see his lips pressed together.

"Don't laugh," I chided. "It's not funny!"

He made a serious face then began to waggle his eyebrows.

"Don't do that either. You'll make *me* laugh," I cried.

"If I'm not allowed to make you laugh, how about I take you away from this and we go on that picnic? Have a bottle of bubbly? Lie on the grass in the sun and feed each other tasty titbits from the basket like other people do when they like each other? That'll take your mind off Alice."

A good point, though lying anywhere with Cole would probably guarantee my mind was elsewhere. There was only one snag in the scenario.

"Uh, I don't cook. The only tasty titbit coming from a basket I own will be pate on a cracker from the supermarket."

"And you struck me as the domestic type."

"Maybe in a past life. Muffins from a packet are the extent of my culinary greatness."

Cole looked serious. "I don't know if this relationship can continue to blossom if you can't be chained to the sink where you belong."

I liked the idea that we were in a relationship that was blossoming. It sounded sort of sweet.

"I can make quiche," I added, hastily. "I haven't done it since high school, though, so it might be a bit of a fizzer."

"Desserts?"

"My prowess with mousse and pudding are renowned only for their failures."

"So basically you're a kitchen calamity."

"Basically."

Cole hooked a leg over each side of the bench, swivelling to face me. His voice was a soft rumble. A rasping, sexy rumble. "So what exactly are you good at?"

Apart from eating mountains of cake?

"Guess that's for me to know and you to find out."

"An event I look forward to."

He wound his arm about my waist, pulling me against him as he slid my sunglasses onto the top of my head with his free hand. His eyes locked on mine. I'd never noticed before — possibly because I'd never been that close to him — but he had the most interesting streaks of smoky grey in his eyes. They were beautiful.

"Olivia?"

"Yes?"

Was he going to kiss me? I certainly hoped so.

"You have salt on your top lip."

"Do I?" Reaching up, I put a finger to my lip.

"I'll get it." Cole reached forward, cupping my chin with his hand. His lips closed tenderly over mine. They were warm and soft and absolutely perfect. The kiss was absolutely perfect. Like no kiss I'd ever experienced before.

At last, he drew away.

"Did I really have salt on my lip?" I whispered, somewhat shaken by the emotion of the kiss.

Cole chuckled and gave my knee a squeeze. "Guess that's for me to know and you to find out."

*****

I arrived home to find Jed on sitting the doorstep looking like an orphan puppy.

Again.

His shirt was creased, as if he hadn't changed it in days and there was a faint trace of stubble on his normally smooth shaven skin. He looked defeated and the closer I got to the front door the more forlorn his demeanour became.

"This is starting to become a habit," I said, as I stepped over him. "If I didn't know better I'd think I'd you were auditioning to join my garden gnome collection."

His face remained inexpressive, like a spell had been cast on him freezing his features into a sad scowl. "You don't own any garden gnomes. You detest garden gnomes."

"Which makes it kind of lucky you're not a gnome then, doesn't it?" I slid my key in to the lock of the front door. "Is there any special reason for this visit or have you taken up full time guarding of my garden?" Between him and Alice there seemed to be an awful lot of covert operations going on.

Jed stood up. His face looked even graver but that could have been due to the fact that we were standing in the dark because Alice hadn't turned on the porch light. Or she'd turned it off, hoping he'd go away.

"You have to let me in, Livvy. I've tried everything. She won't talk to me, she won't let me explain."

"I'm aware of that Jed. She's been living with me for the past week, remember? And between us, I don't know how you put up with her. Alice is my best friend but she has some rather unusual habits."

"The undies?"

"One of many."

I turned the doorknob.

"Can I come in?" Jed begged. "Please. I have to see her. It's our anniversary tomorrow. I have to convince her to come to dinner with me. If I can get her there, everything will fall into place. She'll understand then."

I sighed. "All right. But I'm warning you, there was mention of cutting your testicles off with a steak knife earlier in the week."

"Probably the least of my worries right now."

I led the way down the hall to the lounge and poked my head around the door. Alice was sitting in the dark by the fire, nursing a glass of wine. What was it with these two and darkness? They took power conservation to a whole new level.

"Hey, Al."

Alice looked up. Her face was streaked with dried up tears. She had a crusty stain on the left shoulder of her top and her hairclip was askew making her look as if she'd sprouted a third ear. Marital troubles were doing absolutely nothing for her usually flawless appearance.

"I have someone here who wants to see you."

"Tell him to go away. Unless it's Patrick Dempsey. He can come in."

Jed moved into the space of the door. "Just me. Sorry. Mind if I join you?"

I wondered if they were going to turn the lights on.

"Well, I'll leave you to it, shall I? I'll be in the kitchen whipping up a gourmet dinner if you need me."

At least they cracked a smile.

"And Alice, remember what I said about my carpet. Okay?"

"If I kill him, I'll do it in the hall."

After checking baby Ethan, who was sound asleep and blissfully ignorant of the domestic disharmony between his parents in the next room, I turned on the kitchen light and began to rattle around in the fridge. I hoped Alice and Jed were okay in the lounge alone. Maybe I should have stayed to mediate. It was awfully quiet in there, which could mean only one of two things. Alice had indeed killed him or they were perched on the couch, like a couple of possums staring into the dark, both too stubborn to begin a conversation.

Chapter 22

Pacing the hall whilst jiggling a crying baby was not my first choice of Saturday evening entertainment and given my limited experience with babies, not the wisest life move I had ever made. Well, apart from wearing those teeny tiny shorts to The Killers concert that time. In hindsight, they were a bad choice, mostly because I looked like I was wearing underpants in the photos. How was I to know that being the local weather girl had meant I was going to be photographed on my day off? Or that the resulting social media furore over my bum crack would have caused a stir that was bigger than the bloody concert itself. I'd been so innocent before Graeme had taught me the ways of the media world.

And now here I was, at nine o'clock on a Saturday night, pacing the floorboards and wondering where to turn. Ethan was wailing at the top of his lungs. I'd fed him, I'd changed his nappy; I'd even played a lame version of peek-a-boo that only made him cry more. Nothing had worked. It was almost enough to put me off ever wanting a child myself.

Yeah. Who was I kidding? It didn't even come close.

After twenty minutes of pacing I reached the front door for what seemed like the hundredth time and began to pace in the opposite direction. My mind raced in time with my pacing and jiggling. There had to be someone I could contact for help but who? Mum gone on a mini-break with Connor — I was convinced she thought she was an older version of Bridget Jones or something — and I certainly wasn't calling Mrs Tanner, even if she was a retired midwife. Alice was off the list too. I had no intention of calling her. Not after it had taken every ounce of persuasive skills I'd had in me to convince her to go out for dinner in the first place. Besides, she'd never trust me with Ethan again if I couldn't cope on the first occasion she'd asked me to sit for more than an hour. And I didn't want to be the incompetent baby-minder. I wanted to be able to have Ethan stay over any time he wanted when he was older. I wanted to be like a cool auntie.

Until two hours ago, Alice had been set on staying home, standing Jed up. But after I'd pointed out she'd never be able to do that because I'd die of curiosity if I didn't find out what Jed had been up to, she'd agreed to go for my sake. I wasn't sure if she was doing a good job of pretending she didn't care less or if she really didn't but it wasn't every day your best friend, who adored children but had absolutely no experience with them agreed to babysit at the last minute. There was no way Alice could turn down an offer like that.

The louder Ethan squawked the faster I paced, my mind in a whirling frenzy. Who the devil knew anything about babies and would come at the drop of a hat to offer assistance? I'd mentally gone through every person in living memory and then some when the idea hit me. It hit me so hard I stopped dead in the middle of the hall causing Ethan to lurch in my arms and let out a gurgle of mirth. Then he began to scream even louder.

Cole.

I would call Cole. He'd had a baby once. He was bound to know what I should do. Now that we were in a 'blossoming relationship', there was no reason why I couldn't give him a call. Balancing Ethan, who was now squawking in my ear whilst trying to take out my left earring, I went into the kitchen and picked up the phone.

"Olivia?"

"Cole. Um, are you busy?" I know I was probably yelling into the phone but it was the only way I was going to be heard over the baby.

"What's that bloody awful noise? It sounds like someone's strangling a cat."

I didn't have time for this.

"I'm in a bit of a pickle."

"Does it involve a cat?"

If he made one more joke I was going to cry. This was beyond desperate. Ethan's cheeks had turned from red blotches to huge purple welts.

"No, it involves a baby. He won't stop crying. I've fed him and changed him. I've done everything I can think of but he won't stop."

"I gather this is Alice's baby we're talking about. Does he have a fever?"

I looked at Ethan.

"Feel his forehead, Olivia."

Wow, could Cole see through the phone or what? I put my palm to the baby's forehead. "It's warm but normal warm."

"Well, that's a good sign. But I'd best come over to be on the safe side. See you in five minutes."

"I don't know how to thank you for this." An audible sigh of relief escaped my lips. Not that Cole would have heard it over the wailing of the baby.

"I'm sure you'll think of something." He chuckled.

*****

Thirty minutes later, Cole and I were sitting on the couch in the living room, a very drowsy Ethan cuddled in Cole's large arms. The fingers of one tiny hand played at the fabric of Cole's shirt as Ethan's eyelids grew heavier and heavier. His other hand held a cooled teething ring, which he was sucking on furiously. Nobody would have believed it was the same child who'd been howling the place down half an hour before. He looked like a happy little angel, positively cherubic.

"I can't believe you fixed him," I whispered. "I thought I was going to have to take him to the hospital. I could kiss you Cole."

Cole's eyes twinkled. "I might let you do that a bit later. After we get this little one into bed."

Cole's arrival had been like a visit from the male version of *Supernanny*. Scooping the crying baby from my arms as I opened the front door, he'd stuck a finger in Ethan's mouth identifying a number of small bumps on his gum.

"Teething," he'd pronounced. There was something sexy about a man who took charge I'd thought, as he disappeared to the kitchen with me following along behind trying not to look utterly bewildered. Even the way he rifled through the contents of my fridge sent little shivers of excitement up my spine. Though it could have been because the freezer door was open. That always made me shiver. After a minute or so, Cole had produced a squishy blue ring, which he had given to the baby who stuck it in his mouth and begun to suck on it. The crying had ceased, enabling Cole to administer a dose of baby paracetamol, which he'd gotten from Mrs Tanner *and* somehow managed to clear with Alice on his way to my place.

I watched the entire episode with what must have been a look of stunned admiration on my face. "I wondered what that thing was. I thought it was some kind of toy."

Cole had shaken his head in dismay.

Back in the lounge, Cole had rocked and cooed at Ethan until he settled. He was like a baby whisperer the way he'd done it. The only other male I'd seen behaving in such a paternal fashion was Jed and though I thought it was sweet when he did it, Cole's fatherly touch definitely tugged at my heart strings. Images of babies, wedding dresses and big sandstone houses on the edge of town drifted into my head.

"I suppose we should get the little fella into bed before his parents get back. He must be knackered from the crying," Cole said, after a bit.

"Um, yeah."

I got up from the couch and led the way to the spare room where Cole settled Ethan for the night. The baby wasn't the only one who was knackered. This parenting business was very exhausting. I switched off the light and left the door ajar in case Ethan stirred.

"Phew. I'm glad that's over. I had no idea what I was doing before. Thanks again for helping." I leant against the wall for a second, my ear tuned to the soft rhythmical sound of Ethan's breathing.

Leaning forward, Cole pressed his body into mine. His arms wound around to cup my bottom and he gave me a cheeky grin that made a different sort of shiver run down my spine. "Anytime. Now, how about that kiss you owe me?"

*****

Alice and Jed arrived home to find Cole and I snuggled on the couch and the TV playing the second season of *Game of Thrones*. Naked women cavorted across the screen in front of us and on the coffee table, a bottle of red wine stood empty beside two bowls that had clearly held ice cream. I might not have been able to cook to save myself but I was a demon at making a banana split — and my new low fat version had met with Cole's approval. So much so, he'd had two helpings.

"Well, isn't this a cosy sight," Alice remarked, flopping onto the opposite sofa and patting the space beside her for Jed who'd sat close. Very close, indeed.

I eyed the couple across the coffee table. Something was definitely up. Alice was smiling so hard her face had to be hurting and Jed looked like the proverbial cat who'd got the cream or a good seeing to, at least. I pushed myself upright. "Have you two made up?"

Linking her arm through Jed's, Alice placed a tender kiss on her husband's nose before answering. "Why didn't you tell me I was acting like an idiot? Running about town in a trench coat and packing suitcases. It's a wonder I wasn't committed."

I had been concerned for her sanity at one point. And I hadn't been the only one. After Alice had been spotted lurking behind a stop sign wearing an Afro wig as a disguise — a remnant from a seventies costume party — there had been distressed murmurs in the shops up and down the main street. The fact that she'd taken to wearing ten centimetre heels and popping into the bank at random times of the day hadn't helped either.

"Mrs Tanner *was* a little worried. The words 'marital psychosis' were being bandied around in the supermarket earlier today. She questioned whether or not you might require medication."

"Great. I'll never live it down, will I?"

"I'm pretty sure nobody noticed you skulking near the newsagent last week," Cole said. "Not too sure about that wig the other day, though. You looked like Groucho Marx." Clearly he was finding the whole episode very amusing.

"Or you were doing research for that *Cheaters* show," I added.

"Okay. Enough taking the piss you two. I get the fact that I've behaved like a dick."

"I'm gathering you're in possession of a full set of facts now?" I asked.

Jed cuddled Alice closer. "It took a couple of slow dances before Al grasped the idea."

"Jed's been having ballroom dancing lessons as a surprise for our anniversary. The woman who rang the house was his instructor, Vicki, checking if she'd gotten her days mixed up because he was meant to be having a lesson and hadn't arrived."

"For real?"

Everyone in Merrifield knew Jed was as uncoordinated as polar bear on ice skates and how he truly abhorred dancing. It had been like car crash TV witnessing Alice and Jed's first dance as a married couple. He'd shuffled and clomped his way around the dance floor, out of time with the music. He'd trodden on Alice's gown and they'd both ended up sitting on Great Aunt Muriel's knee. Alice had been so mortified she'd wanted to sink into the wedding cake. I'd been mortified for her.

"He's been learning to waltz and we even did a salsa. Can you believe it? It's like I have my own personal Channing Tatum." Alice was obviously enamoured with the gesture and had completely forgotten that she wanted to fry Jed's nether regions in a pan of hot oil.

"Uh, don't think so, babe," Jed replied. "It was a gift for you. Don't expect me to get up and start any of that hip-hop stuff. The blokes at the cricket club would laugh their heads off."

"I hope you captured it on video," I said. "There's a lot of people in this town who wouldn't believe you know how to do anything more intricate than the Chicken Dance."

"You think I'd let anyone forget this?" Jed replied. "I reckon I've earned enough brownie points to last me until at least the next decade and after the torture I've gone through, I wasn't gonna to let it be forgotten in a hurry. I've got a copy preserved for posterity, or if Al decides to get into me about my lack of dancing or sensitivity in the future. Jim did the honours. He's got this new mini recorder and he wanted to break it in before his holiday to Brazil."

I hadn't even known Jim was going to Brazil.

Alice turned to Cole. "How's Ethan? Did the paracetamol do the trick?"

"As we suspected, it was teething. I sorted it though. He's tucked up for the night. Sleeping like a baby, excuse the pun."

"Thanks ever so much. I don't know what we'd have done without you."

I wanted to feel affronted that the babysitting rug had been pulled from under me but how could I? Cole was entitled to take the credit. I'd been as useful as flippers on an elephant. "Ah, excuse me. I helped. I held the bottle of medicine. In fact, now he's sleeping, why don't you two head off home and continue your romantic evening without him? You can pick him up first thing."

Alice bit her lip. "You mean like a sleep over?"

"Exactly. A bit of alone time will be good for you. I'm sure I can cope for the rest of the evening. Besides, it's nearly Sunday. I don't have to work tomorrow."

"Will you be involved in this sleep over Cole?"

Now there was a thought I hadn't considered.

Cole rubbed his hand along my thigh. "I most definitely will. If Olivia makes me a bed on the couch, that is."

Ha. As if I'd be doing that.

*****

"Tell me about Phoebe," I said.

It was 3am. Neither Cole nor I had had a wink of sleep since Alice and Jed had collected Ethan earlier in the day. It was like time had stopped the moment we discovered we were allowed to like each other. I wasn't tired. I was running on sex-filled adrenalin. And it was way better than cake. In fact, I hadn't even thought about cake or slice or anything sweet for almost twenty-four hours. If Cole was the catalyst for that, he was a keeper.

"What was she like?" I asked again.

Cole cuddled me and I adjusted the covers around us, snuggling closer. His chest was smooth against my cheek. I liked the way his arm held me tight. I liked the way I could draw little circles around his bare chest and make him twitch.

It made me feel very contented and rather like I was up to something naughty.

"Phoebe had the most amazing green eyes. From the minute she was born, her eyes were what people commented on most. Her eyes and her wit. She was intelligent too, very intelligent, though who knows where she got that from. Neither Jenny nor I are Rhodes Scholars. I did pretty well at school but I was lazy and I could never make up my mind what I wanted to be. I had half a dozen jobs before I fell into property development. Phoebe wasn't like that. She wanted to be a doctor and help sick kids. She would have been too, if she hadn't got sick. I don't doubt it."

"She sounds like a pretty cool little girl."

"She was. She was also the most obnoxious kid on the planet. But not in that annoying spoilt sort of brat way, more in the always-get-everything-right way. Every idea she came up with was bizarre and outrageous but somehow they seemed to work. And she never let me forget it."

"Like what?"

"Once she convinced me I should use myself in an ad for the business, you know, like the big builders do to get you to buy their spec homes. I thought she was insane but within weeks I was inundated with clients wanting everything from makeovers to full scale property development."

"I bet most of them were women." If I'd seen Cole on TV I'd be clamouring to have him work on my house.

"Funnily enough. The ad was like a magnet for every desperate woman in Western Australia to turn up on my doorstep and ask me to take my shirt off."

"Oh my God — you're the Reno King."

"That's me."

"You were *really* hot in that ad. I wanted you to renovate my house and I didn't even have one."

"What do you mean 'were'? I'm haven't exactly lost my looks."

I leaned up on my elbow. "You are so full of yourself."

"Hey, not as full of myself as some people, Miss I-met-Kirsten-Dunst."

"I did!"

"Did you get her phone number while you were at it? Share a latte?"

The punch I gave him in the arm was so forceful he winced. Then he grinned and grabbed me. "So, it's a fight you want is it? Come on then, tough girl."

I wished I'd never told him I was ticklish. I didn't have a hope of winning that fight.

Later, we talked about how Cole had come to live in Merrifield, his desire for a change of scene after Phoebe had died and what he wanted from his future. It was as if we'd known each other for years, the way he talked. Like he wanted me to know the most intimate details of his life because I was important to him. It made me comfortable to share things with him too. Most things anyway. I wasn't quite ready to divulge my love for David Cassidy and *The Partridge Family*.

"It must have been hard for you when Phoebe died," I said.

"It was the worst time of my life. I felt so guilty."

"Why? It's not like you could have found a cure."

"I still felt bad. When your kid gets sick you want to make it right. I wanted so much for Phoebe to live but it wasn't meant to be. And after she died, it was like some gaping void opened up. I didn't know how to fill it. I had this empty hole in my chest. The days were a blur. I can't remember a lot of it but I know I spent most of the first few months sleeping. Or drunk. I almost lost the business in that time but the guys I had working for me were great. They kept the wheels turning as best they could." He expressed a grief-laden sigh. "I don't think anyone could understand how the death of a child makes you feel unless they've experienced it."

"But one day you'll have more kids, right? I mean, Phoebe will always hold a special place in your heart and I know you'll never replace her but don't you want more children. When the time comes?"

Cole lifted a questioning eyebrow. His eyes twinkled as he moved in to nuzzle at my neck. "Why, Merrifield? Are you offering to have my babies? Because I've been thinking I'd like at least another half a dozen. Depends how tired I get with the practising."

I hoped he didn't feel me flinch.

Chapter 23

For the remainder of the week I felt like was floating on air. I was so happy I would have tap danced into work, swinging around lampposts like Gene Kelly in *Singin' In the Rain*— if I'd known how, that was. The week could not have been any more perfect.

First, Alice and Jed had gotten back together and seemed even more in love than ever which was sort of sickening if you were in the same room as them for longer than twenty minutes. Especially when they started that cooing thing. *Eww*.

Second, I'd managed — finally — to score myself a boyfriend who wasn't a complete degenerate or only after one thing. Cole was real, honest, single AND manly — qualities that when combined were unheard of in any boyfriend I'd ever had and a feat I never thought I'd see in my lifetime.

Lastly, that morning, I'd hopped onto the scales to find I'd dropped another two kilos. I'd spent so much time in bed that I hadn't had time to eat and the added 'exertion' had literally melted the calories away. I was actually beginning to like my scales. They weren't causing me stress.

And because I could feel myself getting thinner, I didn't feel the need to obsessively jump on them every time I went to the toilet. It was like my brain had been cauterised in my sleep so that that part of me no longer existed.

It was all because of Cole, of course. It was the little things he did, the cute way he pushed the hair back from his forehead, the masculine line of his chin, the sweet things he said that made me understand how he felt. But mostly, it was the way he made me feel when he gazed into my eyes before he kissed me — like finally, I'd found that person I could lean on when things went bad, that someone I could share everything with like I'd always wanted.

*****

I'd finished the morning's clients and was about to eat my chicken salad lunch when the bell on the front door tinkled and Mum walked in. At least, I thought it was Mum; the face was obscured by a massive bunch of helium-filled balloons, which she was swiping aside with her hand in order to see where she was going. I put down the container in my hand and stood to greet her.

Mum stopped at the corner of the counter, kissing my cheek. "Hello sweetheart. How's tricks?" She looked relaxed and content after her mini break with Connor, a smile from ear to ear gracing her face.

"Hi, Mum. Great thanks. How was your break?"

"Glorious. I didn't want to leave. There was such a lot to see and do. We had a couple's pampering session followed a horse and carriage ride to a picnic Connor had organised by the lake. It was very romantic."

I was happy for her. It sounded nice.

"Then, on the Saturday night we went to a movie under the stars," she continued. "Watched *The Notebook*. That Ryan Gosling is a bit of a looker but I didn't go much on the beard. We had the most amazing sex that night. I'm so glad I enrolled in that *Kama Sutra* yoga class."

Okay. Maybe not so nice.

"Then on Sunday—"

I held up a hand. "I think I've heard enough, thanks."

Mum appeared bemused. "I was only going to say Connor had had personalised cupcakes made. Pity I couldn't eat them. He'd forgotten I'm allergic to egg."

Reaching out, Mum placed the bunch of balloons — weighted so they wouldn't float away obviously — on the counter. Her hands went to my shoulders and she turned me this way and that, her gaze intent as it swept over my body. I imagined it was rather how a contestant in Miss Universe might feel. "You're looking quite trim," she remarked. "Are you wearing the Spanx?"

"No. I've lost another two kilos."

"Oh well done. The diet's going well, then?"

"The extra exercise seems to be doing the trick."

Not to mention the sex.

"Keep it up. You look so much prettier when you're not carrying extra weight."

I knew this was meant to be a compliment but I couldn't help feeling like Mum was having a go at me. Again. I know she didn't mean to, that the things she said and did came from a place of love but sometimes I wished she'd think before she opened her mouth.

"I heard about you and that lovely Cole by the way," Mum continued.

"Mrs Tanner?"

"No. Shannon-down-from Perth. She heard about it at her job interview."

What job interview? And why were they talking about me?

"She got the job. Started yesterday, I think. Isn't he simply adorable?"

What job interview? Who was adorable? Honestly, you were off the radar for a couple of days and everyone was getting a new profession.

"Who?"

"Cole."

Oh okay. We were back to him.

"He is rather." I could feel my face breaking into an ecstatic grin. I'd been doing such a lot of that my cheek muscles were beginning to ache.

Mum gave a knowing nod. "You'll need to lift your game if you're going to swim in that pool, possum. But you can do it. I have very confidence."

She made it sound like I was about to shoot the winning goal in a netball grand final. Ignoring the comment, I turned my gaze to the bunch of balloons. I'd never seen anything quite so gaudy. That amount of pink and sparkles would have even given Barbie nightmares. It was a wonder Mum had been able to get them through the door. "Who are the balloons for?"

"Oh, I quite forgot. I'm such a ditz lately, my brain has completely left the building." She handed them to me. "They're for you. A little gift."

What would possess her to buy a bunch of balloons as a gift was beyond me but I thanked her and took the balloons, sliding the weight to the end of the counter, where they bobbed around merrily before righting themselves and becoming still. They were quite pretty, in an over the top sort of way.

"Is there any particular reason for this gift?"

"There is. I have some very exciting news."

I hoped this wasn't going to be like the last time Mum sprung a surprise. I was still trying to get my head around *that* turn of events.

"Well, go on."

"You're going to be a big sister."

Mum was buying another cat? A puppy? Surely not. The way she jaunted around the world these days, the poor thing would spend more time in a cattery than at home.

"There's going to be a baby," Mum explained.

I swallowed. A wave of sheer terror — or was it disbelief — gushed through my veins. It had to be a joke. But it couldn't be. My mother never played tricks on people. She didn't even understand jokes. I looked up at the swag of balloons, my eyes coming to rest on the one hidden in the centre that had '*it's a girl*' printed on it. Slowly, like the sunrise over town in winter, the concept grew wings and began to fly around my head, rather like the stork delivering a baby.

"A girl," Mum announced. "Well, I'm pretty sure it is—"

She wasn't serious, was she?

"—I haven't had a scan or anything. I'm not far enough along but I have all the symptoms I had with you."

It seemed she was.

"It was a bit of a surprise. I thought I was late. The change and everything. You know how it is."

Well, I didn't but I had an idea.

I began to cough, large gulping coughs that threatened to choke me. Mum leant over, slapping my back.

She'd lost the plot with this one. It was one thing to be missing Dad but compensating with a baby? A kitten was a far more sensible option.

"And then I did the test and the little blue line popped up," she continued. "And ... it's so exciting. Aren't you excited, sweetheart? You always wanted a sibling."

Maybe when I was eight but not when I was twenty-eight. The very thought was enough to make me feel ill. I stared at my mother, incapable of forming words. How could she do this? Well, clearly I knew *how* she did it, of course, but...God.... Surely she wasn't planning to go through with it. She was forty-eight years old. How was it even possible she could *be* pregnant?

"Aren't you pleased?" Mum looked slightly crestfallen that I wasn't cartwheeling with joy around the shop.

"Shocked might be a more apt description. I'm assuming—"

"— that Connor's the father, yes. I know I've been living it up since your father passed, darling, but I haven't been a complete hussy. Connor's the only man I've been with."

Which somehow — I don't know how — made it worse in my eyes. Connor wasn't father material. He wasn't even boyfriend material.

It was one thing for Mum to be having a fling, but marriage? Babies? She'd be sixty-eight when the baby was twenty. Grandmothers were sixty-eight, not mothers. God forbid, she might even be dead.

And what about my feelings in this? Had she no respect for the daughter she already had? No matter what view I took, I could find nothing good in this scenario. I couldn't feel excited when I felt slightly appalled, a bit hurt and a great big bit angry with my mother for being so selfish. She was putting me in a situation where I was expected to be over the moon, hand out the congratulatory champagne. But I didn't feel that way and I didn't know if I could hide it this time.

Picking up the balloons, I handed them back to her. "I don't want the gift, thank you."

"But darling."

"Don't 'but darling' me. You had to know I wouldn't be happy, Mum. Did you think buying me a bunch of balloons and making like we were going on a big adventure would help me to accept it? I'm not six. I know it sounds harsh but you're old enough to be a grandmother. You've had your turn. You had me, remember?"

Mum's face sank. I thought she might cry. "It's a lot to absorb."

"That's something of an understatement."

"I might leave you to it, then. Give you time to think. I'll call you later, all right?"

"Fine."

Which of course it wasn't.

I walked to the door, opening it for Mum, who stepped onto the street and strolled off up the road, a certain bounce in her step I hadn't noticed since Dad died. She was so happy about the baby, which made me feel awful for behaving the way I had — like the selfish only child. But she'd shocked me. If I'd had time to prepare maybe I would have approached the news in a different way.

"Mum!" I called up the street.

She stopped and turned and I ran down and wrapped her in the biggest hug. "It's great news about the baby."

"Are you sure?"

"Positive."

Mum smiled. "Thank you sweetheart. Here, have some balloons."

As I got back to the shop, happy that I'd made my mother's day in some small way — even if I hadn't meant a word of it — I pushed the massive bunch of baby balloons through the door and shut it behind them. I stood for a second, staring at the cupcake shop across the way. There was no queue today. The paparazzi seemed to have disappeared too.

If I turned the sign around, I could pop over the road, buy a cake and be back in time for my next client. I didn't have time to walk to Maggie's and back. And I really needed a cake. My thoughts always became clearer after cake.

*****

As I approached the front door of Death By Cupcake, my heart began to thump uncomfortably in my chest. The inside of my mouth was more parched than if I'd eaten a bucketful of sand. I felt faint with anticipation. I didn't want to do it, I didn't want to give in but I was being compelled by something I was powerless to control. I paused, the doorknob in my hand, as a tiny voice in my head began to tease. I knew I shouldn't listen, that I should go back to Doggie Divas, drink ten litres of water and put cake as far from my mind as it would go but the voice was fairly convincing. Especially when it manifested itself in the form of a pink, sparkly demon, which perched itself on my right shoulder and began to whisper in my ear.

It's been a long time since a cake's passed your lips, Olivia. Don't you deserve it?

No, I thought. One should never use cake as a reward. Or an emotional crutch. I took a step away from the door.

But you've worked soooo hard, lost a lot of weight. One teensy weensy cupcake won't do you any harm.

Which was a total lie because I knew I wouldn't stop at one. And *that* would do me heaps of harm. I'd be back where I started before I knew it. This wasn't just about my weight. It was my mental health too.

It'll make you feel better. You know it will.

Drugs make you feel better in the beginning but look where Heath Ledger ended up, I countered.

The voice was silent for a minute. I thought I was winning. I turned to head back across the road. Then it hit me with the argument I could never ignore and I stopped short.

It's only one cake. Buy one, ease that bubble of hurt inside you. Your mother was such a cow getting pregnant like that with no consideration of how it would make you feel. She was mean. Cake is never mean. Buy a cake. It will make you feel good. You can work it off by jogging.

Well, yes. I could. I turned toward the front door again.

One cake never hurt anyone.

I guess not.

Think of that icing, the decorations. You love the crunchy decorations. It's only one little cake.

Oh what the hell. My hand on the doorknob, I twisted it and stepped inside, pausing to savour the sweet aroma of cake. It was only one little piece.

One cake and my craving would be gone and I could get on with the remainder of my day.

I walked up to the glass fronted display case. My eyes — feeling as if a filter filled with glitter had been placed before them — took in the rows and rows of beautifully crafted cakes, each one prettier than the one beside it and every one calling my name. I swallowed, running my tongue over my lips. My fingertips quivered as they pressed against the glass. Velvety chocolate mousse cakes, tangy lemon meringue ones and miniature carrot cakes laden with cream cheese frosting. I'd been avoiding this place for months and now I knew why. I could taste the cakes already. There was not a hope in hell I was going to be able to leave with only *one* cupcake. I wouldn't be satisfied until I was in possession of one of every variety of cake in the place, lovingly placed into a glittery cake box and tied with pink ribbon.

I was a cake addict. Cake was my comfort food of choice. When things were at their worst others turned to alcohol or drugs. Some people were addicted to sex. For me it was cakes and slices. And at that very moment I needed a cake fix like a junkie needed heroin.

Closing my eyes, I attempted to squash the temptation one last time. One cake. That was what I'd come for. One cake that would not ruin my diet and cause me to sink into the cycle of eating and self-loathing I'd fought so hard to get out of.

"Oh, Olivia, hello. How lovely to see you."

A chirpy voice alerted me to the fact that I was, indeed, drooling over the counter. Adelaide had appeared from the kitchen and was wearing a t-shirt that looked remarkably like the one Cole quite often had on when he popped in to Doggie Divas. Over the top she wore a candy-striped apron. Behind her — through the confused fog that was descending over me — I was positive I could see Shannon-down-from-Perth, standing in the doorway, a piping bag in her hand.

What on earth were they doing here?

"Adelaide?"

"Is there something I can help you with? Or have you come to see Cole?" Adelaide had slid the glass door of the cabinet open and picked up a pair of serving tongs in readiness. The smell of the cupcakes drifted into my nostrils, rendering me incoherent. I couldn't process the fact that Adelaide and Shannon were standing behind the counter serving. The smell was overpowering my senses, turning my brain into a bowl of raw pudding.

Then suddenly Cole appeared. On seeing me, his face lit up and he rounded the counter and walked towards me, smoothing his candy-striped apron as he did so.

"This is a nice surprise. Have you come to test out the house special? Phoebe's Double Choc Fudge Delight." He pointed to the most heavenly looking cupcake I had ever seen. Lashings of chocolate icing were piped on the top of the cake forming a whipped dark coffee-coloured peak.

White chocolate had been drizzled over it and finished with tiny white chocolate love hearts layered with edible glitter. It looked utterly delectable, so delectable in fact that my knees began to tremble. The only upside was, I hadn't begun to whimper.

But now I was even more confused. Was Cole's business the cupcake shop? How could this be?

The three of them stood staring at me as if it were the most natural thing in the world and they couldn't understand why I was acting like such a fool, which was the precise moment my brain finally decided to slot the random pieces into place. Like the Cole constantly had in his hair, the references to getting fat from too much icing, the fact that he always seemed to know when I was in the shop and what I was doing. He'd seen me from across the bloody road. And of course, I'd been so wrapped up in my own problems and the diet and everything, I'd taken every clue and stuffed it in a pink sparkly box in my head and ignored it. Why? How?

I was such a fool.

I'd fallen for the one man in the world I could never date — with the exception of Gerry, of course — the man who owned a cake shop. It was the ultimate in karma paybacks — though what'd I'd done to deserve it escaped me.

I looked at Cole, who was smiling as if all his Christmases had come at once.

Crap.

All I'd wanted was a bit of cake to help me get over the dreadful sadness I was feeling. How I was expected to deal with this?

"Olivia?" Cole was staring at me now; a concerned look had replaced his pleased-to-see-you face.

"Um, I... er... um." I gazed at the cakes trying not to faint.

"Have you come to buy a cake?"

"NO! THIN GIRLS DON'T EAT CAKE! I don't eat cake! Oh crap. I have to get out of here now." And without a look back — the fact that I was blinded by the image of that chocolate Phoebe delight or whatever it was enough of a torture — I ran from the shop.

Tearing across the road as if my life depended on it, I threw open the door of Doggie Divas, shut it behind me and slid the bolt into place. My breath ragged, I turned the sign to 'back in ten minutes'. Bugger if Mrs Jones turned up in the meantime, I needed to get my head together and, clearly, I was not going to be doing so with the benefit of the sugary fixings of a nice piece of cake or a slice. I could hardly leave my own shop now either and trot up to Maggie's. She wouldn't serve me. She'd made a promise not to give me one single peppermint slice until my goal weight had been achieved. I'd made her. Even though we both knew it meant a drop in income for her.

I pulled my mobile from my pocket. There was only one thing for it. I needed an emergency supply and I needed it now. My hands were trembling uncontrollably.

My breath was stuck in my lungs. It felt like I was having a heart attack or something. The tears welled. If I didn't do something to combat them, my next appointment wouldn't need the hydrobath.

I scrolled my recent calls and dialled. I felt ridiculous and silly that I was losing control but I couldn't help it. It was as if every problem in the world had suddenly taken root in my head and I had no idea which one to tackle first or even how I would tackle them.

I gave a sniff and took a deep breath. "A...A... Alice?"

"What's wrong?"

"Can you come to the shop? Now? And bring cake. I need cake."

Alice repeated her question.

"I... I can't talk about it. Can you come? Please?"

"Give me ten minutes."

*****

By the time Alice arrived, I'd pulled myself together enough to begin working on Miffy. Mrs Jones had arrived smack on time for her appointment and had almost thumped the door into next week to get it open. Which had only made me feel worse for being unprofessional. I should have been able to handle it. I should have been able to wait until I got home before I went into full meltdown mode.

"I think maybe you should turn the clippers off," Alice said, pulling a bite-sized Mars Bar from her pocket putting it on the bench in front of me.

I stared at it, inspecting it like it might be about to explode. That wasn't a cake.

"I know it's not a cake or a slice but I figure you've been so good you'd be very upset with yourself if you gave in now and started on a binge. The chocolate is sweeter than cake. It should get rid of your craving. And it won't ruin your points for the day. It's only little. I bought you a black coffee too. It's got five sugars in it."

She plonked the tray of coffees on the bench and went out to turn the sign on the door back to 'closed'.

I looked down at the chunks of hair I'd already taken from Miffy's back. It was probably a wise move to stop clipping. My hands were shaking so much the poor dog would go home with one ear and if I stuffed up the clip, Mrs Jones would have a convulsion — after she'd had a screaming fit first, that is. Mrs Jones was infamous about town for her screaming fits.

Making sure the dog was secured and couldn't leap from the grooming table, I reached over and turned off the clippers.

We sat down, me on the bench and Alice on the chair beside it.

"Eat your chocolate," Alice said.

I unwrapped the Mars Bar and slowly nibbled at the corner. I gave a ragged sigh as the chocolaty coating melted in my mouth. I felt better now Alice was here. And as usual she was right. I would have been angry with myself if I'd started on another binge — which was what I'd intended to do until I'd got into the cake shop and discovered my boyfriend was the owner. The combination of him knowing I was cheating on my diet and also being there had certainly stopped me in my tracks. Plus I felt stupid. How did I *not* know Cole owned Death by Cupcake? If I was any dopier they could have used me in a production of *Snow White*.

I took a bite of the gooey centre of the Mars Bar, letting the sweetness sit on my tongue before swallowing. My blood pressure began to level. Much better.

"Did you know Cole owned Death by Cupcake?" I said.

"I thought the whole town knew. It's not exactly a secret."

"I didn't."

"Are you serious?"

"I guess I was so caught up in myself I never paid that much attention. And we've never spoken about his work here. We don't have time for talking when all we do is have sex—"

Not that I was complaining about that.

"—I mean, I knew what he did in Perth. I just assumed he was running the business from here."

"Oh. I take it you just found out you were wrong?"

"I went over there to buy a cake."

"Why?" It was a logical question. I *had* sworn off cake.

"Mum's pregnant."

Alice looked as if I had announced I was joining The Spice Girls on a reunion tour and then, once her mouth had returned to its usual position, she sat quietly, absorbing the information. She shook her head a few times. She frowned at nothing in particular and looked about, almost as if she couldn't quite comprehend what I'd told her. Gradually, though, her expression became sadder and sadder, and her eyes filled with sympathy.

"Oh, Livvy. No wonder you wanted to eat a massive slab of cake. I'd down a bottle of vodka if my mother broke news like that to me. It must have been such a shock."

"It was. I've accepted that Mum and Connor are an item but I never expected this. I feel like I've been slighted by my own mother and it hurts. It really hurts. She gets to have a baby and a husband and I get nothing. Big fat nothing." I wanted to bang my head on the table. It seemed the only way the huge lump of pain in my chest would be relieved was if I replaced it with some other sort of pain. I wanted to scream and punch things and throw things at the unfairness of it all but I knew it would make no difference.

"To top it off, I find out Cole owns the bloody cake shop. I stormed in there ready to eat so much cake I'd never walk again and there he was. He was talking to me but I couldn't answer because his head had morphed into a giant cupcake. I can't take anymore. I just can't."

Alice leant over and gave me a hug. She held me tight and I felt some of the anxiety leave my body.

"I guess I could say it'll get better with time or not to worry about it but I'd be lying. Your mum being pregnant isn't something you can fix with cake. It's not going to go away. Cole owning the cake shop, however, is a minor blip if you want to be with him."

I knew that. I also knew I'd overreacted to finding him there but at that point I'd lost all control. Rational thinking wasn't exactly my first priority.

"I feel like such shit. Utterly useless. And idiotic."

"Your mum's pregnancy is a blow, for sure, and you've got every reason to feel like rubbish but you have to pick yourself up. Move on. You've done it before."

"Do I have to do it right now?"

"Nope. You have my full permission to wallow for the remainder of the day. Now, eat the rest of your Mars Bar."

That was another reason I loved Alice. Even though she wasn't trying to make me feel better with fluffy words, she still did.

"I thought you knew about Cole," she continued. "I was so proud of how you were managing to have a relationship with him and not going into his shop."

"Things might have been different if I'd known. I would never have gotten involved."

"I disagree. You make a lovely couple. You'd have got together eventually."

"Maybe, but I don't think I can be in a relationship with him now. Not yet. Every time I look at him, I'm going to think of that Phoebe cupcake. I can't get it out of my head. It's taking every ounce of willpower I have not to run across the road and eat every single cake in that shop."

"It's a response to the bomb your mother's dropped. You're trying to find comfort. Remind yourself that comfort eating is what got you into the weight pickle in the first place. Get your comfort from Cole. That's what boyfriends are for."

I tried to remind myself but all I could think of was cake or Cole feeding me cake like a drug dealer providing free samples. Somehow, his whole beautiful persona had suddenly become tainted and I didn't know what to do.

"Not helping."

"It's a double whammy of disasters, isn't it? You must feel like the man upstairs gave you a big kick down them."

"I don't think I even believe in God anymore," I replied, the tears beginning to come again. "If he did exist, he wouldn't let these terrible things keep wrecking my life, would he? Oh Al, it's so unfair."

"I know sweetie. I know. But we have to deal with life's blows, don't we?" She squeezed me tighter.

"Why is it always me? How come every time I think things are going well something bad happens? I try to be nice to everyone. I never say boo when people do me wrong."

Well, except Connor but he deserved it for being a prick.

"Maybe you're too trusting?"

Not anymore. "Graeme cured me of that."

"Too nice?"

I snorted. "I think Mrs Tanner would disagree. I gave her a massive serve when she started quizzing me about Cole the other day. I'm so tired of everyone poking their noses in my business."

Alice sat back on her stool and picked up her coffee. "So your Mum's going to have Connor's baby? That's a bit of a head spin."

"Sure is. Don't you find it slightly ironic that my mother, who already has a child, a.k.a me, and had no desire to procreate again, has become pregnant the first time she had sex in a year?

Yet I, who dreams about having a baby and feels an almost physical ache for one, is unable to conceive."

That had been one of the other knock-on effects from the affair with Graeme. Shortly after arriving back in Merrifield, I'd discovered I was carrying his child. Ecstatic at the news — though I was aware I'd never have any type of support from him — I'd started preparing for the baby's arrival, which had been a dreadful mistake. The pregnancy turned out to be ectopic and I found myself on the receiving end of an emergency surgery. One that had saved my life but terminated the pregnancy and most likely left me infertile because — oh yes — Graeme it seemed had also left me with another lasting reminder of his 'love'. The complications had been so intense the chances of me ever giving birth were about as slim as Australia topping the medal tally at a Winter Olympics. Not only that, but after it happened I'd had to return home alone to face the spare room I'd already begun to convert into a nursery. Those cute baby things I'd collected had become an evil presence in the house while I was gone. I couldn't bear to look at them, yet I couldn't get rid of them. So I'd locked the door, refusing to acknowledge their existence and hid behind a mountain of lovely peppermint slice and mud cake. As my hips had expanded and my self-confidence plummeted, my need had turned into something much bigger.

When Alice became pregnant with Ethan, I finally found the strength to enter that room. I cleared it out, handing the majority of the contents over to Alice to use for her baby.

The weakness for sweet things, though, was not as easily dealt with and now, every time I held Ethan and smelled his baby smell or saw someone in the street pushing a pram, I longed for a baby of my own. The only way I knew how to compensate for that loss had been to eat more cake.

"It does seem selfish of her," Alice replied. "I can understand why you're so upset."

Now, on top of it all, the man I was beginning to fall in love with — yes, I was willing to own that fact — turned out to be the owner of a fucking cake shop. No wonder I'd been so attracted to him. He probably had pheromones laced with cake.

Chapter 24

"What was that about?" Adelaide asked Cole as they watched Olivia fly out the door, slamming it with such a force the hundred-year-old glass in the windows threatened to fall onto the front step of the shop.

Cole shook his head. "No idea. But I s'pose I'd better go find out. She seemed pretty upset."

"Give her half an hour or so. She looked like she needed to calm down. I know I'd hate to be seen in a state like that."

Cole nodded. He knew Adelaide was right. Rushing across the road that instant might only make whatever it was worse. Maybe he'd do a tidy of the kitchen first. Shannon was great with a mixer but she had terrible aim when it came to the piping bag. The amount of icing she got on the cakes was nothing compared to what ended up on the bench and floor. He'd clean up the mess and then he'd pop over and see Olivia because he *wanted* to help. He wanted to cradle Olivia in his arms and make her feel better.

Twenty minutes later, Cole untied his apron and hung it on the hook behind the kitchen door before heading out the back and up the lane to the main road. He stopped at the kerb, glancing across the road at Olivia's shop. The sign on the door was turned to closed. Olivia obviously didn't want to be disturbed.

Cole stood for a moment, trying to formulate a course of action. He could leave her to it — a wise move when you were dealing with upset women. He knew from experience that trying to help his mother or Adelaide when they were in a tizz only made it worse. His brand of concern was apparently nothing a woman could fathom. On the other hand, if he didn't try to help, Olivia would most likely go on some rant about how he didn't care and if he was any sort of boyfriend he would have been over there like a shot to console her.

This was a no win situation.

Maybe he should knock on the door. Even if she told him to bugger off, at least she'd know he'd made an effort.

But what if she let him in? What if he had to sit and listen to her go on and on about women's stuff he had no understanding of, or interest in. Whatever her problem was, it must be big. He'd never seen her behave in that fashion before. He could be stuck there for hours. Not that he didn't care but, man, he had work to do.

The last option was a text but Cole discounted the idea as quickly as it popped into his head. A text would be viewed as a cop out. Even he knew that.

There was nothing for it. He'd have to knock on the door and hope he returned with his hair still attached to his scalp.

With a deep steeling breath, Cole stepped off the kerb and dodging a couple of cars, reached the footpath on the other side of the road. The sign on the door still said 'closed' but he knocked anyway.

A head emerged from the grooming area and disappeared. A rather dejected sounding dog began to bark. Cole knocked a second time with no response.

Oh well, at least he'd tried. He'd give her a call later to see if she was okay.

Just as he was turning go, Alice turned up at the door. She snipped the bolt. Her head jerked in the direction of the grooming room.

"She's through there," she whispered. "But be warned, she's not in the mood for any advice. She may not even talk to you. She's pretty upset."

What the devil had he done? He had no idea. The only thing he knew for certain was whatever it was, the smallest thing — so totally unimportant to him yet obviously huge for Olivia — could have set it off. Had he forgotten her birthday? Was it the anniversary of the day they'd met? Had he told her he'd drop by and then let it slip from his mind — easy enough, when the shop was as busy as it was.

Cole followed Alice to the space where a red-eyed Olivia was sniffing while attempting to trim the bouffant topknot on a poodle's head. She looked dreadful. So lost, so deflated, like the stuffing had been knocked out of her. But that paled in comparison to the job she was making of the poodle. The poor dog looked as if he'd been put through a car wash the wrong way.

Tentatively, Cole stepped up to the table. "Are you okay?"

Olivia's eyes were suddenly filled with fury, flashing like something from a seventies horror movie. The clippers were poised as if she were going to shave *him*. Or something worse. Was it too late to turn and run?

Not that he wanted to. What he wanted to do was to hold her and make this terrible hurt — whatever it was — disappear.

"Go away Cole."

Right. Not a good start to the conversation. He couldn't back down, though. He had a feeling she wouldn't forgive him if he did. If she ever spoke to him again, that was.

"Please tell me what's wrong."

Olivia swivelled back to the dog. Her body was rigid, her shoulders tense but at least she wasn't pointing the clippers in his direction anymore. And the anger he glimpsed in her eyes had been replaced by something like hurt as she turned.

"I don't want to talk about it. Just leave."

What was he going to do now? Pressing the case obviously wasn't going to have any effect, she wanted nothing to do with him. He walked towards her. He reached across her shoulder, took the clippers from her hand and turned them off, placing them on the bench. She still refused to look at him.

"I asked you to leave."

Cole ignored her. Instead, he stepped closer. God, she was beautiful. Even with big long stains of mascara trailing down her cheeks, she was still beautiful. Slowly, he lifted his arms and wrapped her in them. He could feel every muscle in her body tensing as he did so. She was wound so tight.

"What's wrong?" he whispered.

Olivia sniffed. Her body relaxed slightly and she nestled into his chest. "Nothing Cole. It's nothing."

She was a shit liar.

"Did I do something?"

"No. You're perfect. And I'm sorry I behaved like such a dick in the middle of your shop."

He held her for a minute longer, feeling her heartbeat returning to normal.

"So it's nothing I've done?"

"Not really. I can't talk about it. Not now. I can't. Just hold me."

Tears coursed down her cheeks and she clung to him, sobbing. Jesus, what did he do now? Nothing, he guessed. Just hold her.

After a while, Olivia pulled away. She took a tissue from a box on the shelf and blew her nose. "Sorry about that."

"Are you going to tell me the problem?"

She looked up into his face, her own a mixture of sadness and... was it embarrassment at her behaviour? "Not now."

"When?" Cole knew he was probably pressing the issue but he didn't know what else to do.

"I don't know."

"Will I see you later on?"

"Not tonight. I'll call you."

"Okay." Dejected and befuddled, Cole walked slowly towards the front door. Alice was standing near the SALE bin fiddling with the things inside and trying to look as if she hadn't been eavesdropping.

"Not too good then?" she asked.

"I think 'shit' would be the correct response," Cole whispered.

The worst thing that could happen now would be for Olivia to think he was talking behind her back, but he had to know. If it involved him, he had to find a way to fix it. "What the hell's going on? What have I done?"

Alice bit the corner of her lip. She opened the door and gestured to the footpath, looking furtively back in the direction of the shop as if the information she was about to impart required security clearance. "It's not you, as such. More a culmination of things. Olivia racing into a cake shop to discover her boyfriend was the owner was simply the icing on the cake. If you'll excuse the pun."

Cole frowned. Surely, having an unlimited supply of cake on tap was every chick's dream, wasn't it? Yeah, they moaned about their weight and all that guff but it never stopped them from hoeing into a cake. He'd seen girls in the shop recently who looked like they'd commit murder for that Phoebe cupcake. "I don't get it."

"Olivia's addicted to sweet things. Cakes, biscuits, slices. She's never been diagnosed or anything but she can't stop at one. It's not like she has to have a stint in rehab or anything but once she starts eating she can't stop. She knows that and she's working hard to overcome it."

"But how? Why?"

"It's an emotional thing. She hasn't had a cake for over three months now. Your shop has been a constant temptation but she's managed to fight the urge, even move past it. Until today, anyway."

"What was so bad about today?"

Alice sounded hesitant. "I don't know that it's my place to say. She should probably tell you herself."

"But she won't talk to me."

"Look, Cole. You have to give her time. She's had a lot of stuff happen over the past few years. The cake thing is a reaction to it and I'm sure she'll tell you about it in due course but right now she needs some time to process. She's going to have to work through this. Give her some space."

Not a phrase he liked to hear, that was for sure. Jenny — his ex — had 'needed space' and look where that had landed him. Olivia was a lovely girl but he wasn't overly happy about this turn of events. He'd moved to Merrifield to make a clean break, a fresh start. Did he want to be stuck with a girl with baggage when he was trying to get his own shit together?

"Right. Okay. Give her space. How much space should that be?"

"It'll only be for a day or so. Positive. She likes you, Cole. She does. But she needs to sort some stuff out."

Maybe so, but did he like Olivia enough to wait until she came around? That was the ten million dollar question. Maybe he needed to sort some stuff out too.

*****

The next few days were hell for Cole. As Alice had suggested, he gave Olivia space but all it did was make him lonely. Despite the fact that the shop was overflowing with people and the one or two reporters were still lurking he felt as if he'd been dropped onto a desert island. Now that he'd found Olivia, he wanted to remain part of her life. He didn't want to be without her. If only she'd call.

So what if she had issues? He wasn't exactly Mr Perfect. And he was positive they could overcome her issues if she'd let him in and what could be so bad, that she'd simply cut him from her life as soon as they'd become intimate? He didn't know about Olivia but it wasn't his way to have casual sex with anyone that walked. He may have been a bit of a lad when he was nineteen but his days of sowing wild oats were long over. He longed for stability, for a life with one girl who would make him happy.

As things had settled down in the shop, Cole had found himself spending way too much time thinking about things like relationships. He missed Phoebe and if truth were told, he missed Jenny too.

Okay, it wasn't her so much that he missed — she'd been a bitch at the end — it was the things she used to do when things had been great, the relationship things. That was what he missed, he decided — the passing caress of a hand, the look across the room, the feeling that someone in the world loved you for who you were.

No amount of casual sex could measure up to the way he'd felt when he'd been on the receiving end of acts such as those. He'd started to think he'd have that with Olivia. He liked the little things she did that made him feel special — the ridiculous banana splits she made him, the way she let him watch sport on TV when he knew she hated it, the fact that she bought him a new pair of shorts to replace his old torn ones. Had he been wrong about her?

The days turned into a week. Then two. So many times Cole had the phone in his hand or his foot out the door to cross the road but something always pulled him back. It was Alice's words that had done it.

Give her space.

He was doing that but it wasn't easy and he didn't know how long he could keep it up for. Merrifield was a small town, for Christ sake. They were bound to run into each other at some point in time. What was he meant to do then? Ignore her? Cole hated that he had no control over this situation or any idea when it was going to end but he supposed the only thing he could do was wait.

And he bloody well hated waiting.

Chapter 25

Cole's feet pounded the gravel track that wound along the river's edge. It was a beautiful morning and he was glad he'd opted to go for a run before he went into the shop. Running helped him to clear his head and when the weather was kind enough to allow him to partake, he enjoyed the feeling it gave him. Even though those Zumba classes had turned out to be a bit of fun and more of a workout than he'd ever admit to, the wriggling bottoms and high-energy antics had somehow lost their sheen. He didn't enjoy them as much as the quiet solitude of a run where his mind could wander without having to think about which leg went where. Plus, every time he set foot in the gym he instantly thought of Olivia and he was trying very hard not to do that. It only made him sad.

He'd been running for about twenty minutes when he rounded a sharp bend in the path, overhung by branches. It was quite a hazard, not that the Merrifield Shire saw it that way. He'd been told to get over it, in no uncertain terms, when he'd rung to complain. Huh, wait till someone broke an ankle. Then they'd listen.

He hoped Olivia never ran this way. If someone were bound to fall, it'd be her. And knowing her, it'd be in spectacular fashion that would begin with an ambulance and end with stitches.

Cole slowed his steps. The track had narrowed and there were more fallen trees than last time. He had to be careful. More than once when he'd first run here he'd ended up arse over tit on the ground without even trying, so concentration was key. Especially on the slippery parts. Well, it was until...

Smack!

"Crap! Watch where you're going."

Standing — or trying to — in front of him and looking thinner and more beautiful than ever with flushed cheeks and loose strands of hair falling from her ponytail, was Olivia.

Okay, there was blood dripping from her nose into her mouth and she looked slightly annoyed that he'd almost knocked her off the path and into the river but she was still beautiful. Did every time they crossed paths have to end with a trip to Emergency?

She righted herself. "Cole."

"Olivia."

"Hi."

"Hi. Are you all right?"

He wanted to reach out and touch her but he could see her guard had gone up the second she'd realised it was him under the cap.

Olivia pulled a tissue from her sleeve and scrunched it against her nose. A smear of blood stretched across her cheek towards her ear. "Fine. You?"

"Yeah, fine. How's things?"

"Apart from the fact that you've given me a home nose job, not too bad. You?"

"Been better."

Right. So this meeting wasn't going the way he'd planned it. Cole had been visualising it since the moment he'd left her shop and this definitely wasn't the version he'd imagined. In that one they hadn't been wearing clothes. A small smile crept onto his lips.

"Is something funny?" Olivia asked. "Have I got blood on my face or something?" She rubbed the back of her hand over her forehead as if to clean it.

"No, no. Nothing like that. I... It doesn't matter."

"Well, I'll be off then." She side stepped him and started back along the path in the opposite direction.

He couldn't let her go. He couldn't let it end without some sort of closure. Seeing her made him realise. He wasn't going to live in limbo. Either she dumped him properly or they got back together.

He needed resolution so he could move on. Jesus, had that thought come into his head unbidden? He sounded like a guest on a daytime talk show.

"Olivia!"

Olivia turned.

"We need to talk," he said.

"Yeah, I guess."

"Do you wanna walk? Please?" He knew he was putting himself out there by asking but the silliness had gone on long enough.

Olivia hesitated. "All right, for a bit. I have to be back soon."

"To fix up your nose?"

She hinted at a smile. "Yeah. Sort of."

They started along the path. The day suddenly seemed to have taken on a sombre tone; a large grey cloud had moved over the sun. Cole wondered if it were some type of sign. Not that he believed in stuff like that but you never knew. He sucked in a breath. He may as well come out and say it.

"Did I do something wrong? Is that why you haven't called me?"

The silence of the last couple of weeks had turned into outright avoidance. He knew because when he'd waved to Olivia across the road the other day, she'd put her head down and dashed into Your Dream Kitchen faster than if Gordon Ramsay was doing a demonstration inside and she needed to beat the rush. He'd then caught her peeking through the display in the window to see if he'd gone. When he'd waved again, she'd pretended to be inspecting a mincer.

Olivia up looked at him. Her eyes were filled with sadness. He wanted to wrap her in his arms again, hold her and make that sadness go away.

"It's not you Cole. It's me."

Great. The old 'it's-not-you' line. Everyone knew that was a cover. It didn't make breakups easier.

"Explain it, then. Please. Help me understand. I thought we had something going. The least you can do is tell me why you don't want to be with me."

Olivia's lips twisted. She pushed the stray hair behind her ear and gestured to a grassy knoll ahead. "Sit."

Right. They were making progress.

Cole stretched out on the grass, giving her his full attention. "I'm all ears."

Olivia wiped the blood from her nose with her sleeve and sighed heavily. Then she began to pace.

The monologue lasted a good twenty minutes. Cole was so flabbergasted he didn't so much as grunt the entire time. It started with some bloke called Graeme who'd broken Olivia's heart, travelled down a road to where she'd discovered she'd been given a dose of chlamydia, which had led to pelvic inflammatory disease and ended with a statement about her being a cake addict. That was a new development, or so she said, something she'd only owned up to in the last few months, but one she was convinced was as real as any other addiction. Sometimes, she used to eat so many sweet things in a day she actually threw up because of it.

Man, she had issues.

The last straw apparently, had been finding out he was the owner of Death By Cupcake, though how she couldn't have known was beyond him. After the publicity and the story on *Today Tonight*, Cole was convinced the whole bloody country knew. The tourist bus that did a weekly tour of the South West had added his shop to their itinerary. People came into the shop not only to buy cake but also to get his autograph for God's sake. How could she *not* have realised?

"So you're addicted to cake?"

"Yep. When things get tough my sweet tooth is the first thing I turn to. I can't stop at one either. I eat until I feel sick or throw up, which ever comes first. If it's extra bad I get into a cycle of guilt and eating to get over the guilt."

No wonder she'd freaked out when she'd seen him behind the counter.

"I dreamed about that Phoebe cupcake for a week after I went into your shop."

She had it bad. The only thing Cole had dreamed about lately was Olivia.

Olivia swallowed. Her lip was quivering. Her eyes were filling with tears. Damn. He hoped she didn't start crying. He couldn't stand to see a girl cry. It choked him up every time.

"I don't see how it can work between us when your head turns into a giant cupcake every time I see you." She gave him a weak smile and Cole wanted to say she was being ridiculous but he had a strange feeling she was deadly serious.

"There's nothing I can do to change your mind, is there?"

She shook her head. "I like you. A lot. I think I might even be in love with you a little, which makes this even harder. I can move on from the whole cake thing in time, but when you were joking about having kids the other week... you know, when we were in bed? Well, I've realised, it wouldn't be fair to get involved with you."

"Why?"

"There's a distinct possibility that I'll never be able to have children after the pregnancy and the P.I.D and everything. I love kids, Cole. So when Mum told me she was going to have a freakin' love child it was like she'd ripped the baby from my own stomach, the pain was so big. It wasn't so much about her as about me.

I was being selfish. And me, being with you, when I know you want more kids would be even more selfish. You should find another girl, one who can give you children. It's better for us to cut our losses before we both get hurt."

How did he tell her he was already hurting?

Cole pushed a hand through his hair. In his wildest dreams he could never have imagined such an insane scenario. It was like something from a soap opera. He had no idea what or how to think anymore he was so damned confused. And as for the kid thing... where the hell had that come from? He'd thought it to be some offhand comment meant as a joke but Olivia had taken it to heart. She wanted to dump him because she thought she'd be doing him a favour.

Reaching up, he tentatively took her hand. She stared at it but she didn't pull away.

"Look," he began. "I know I said I'd like more kids but that was a joke. I hadn't even considered the idea until you came along. I was satisfied wallowing in my own self-pity after Phoebe died. When you and I started to get close, those thoughts came back. It's a natural progression when you like someone, isn't it?"

"But I can never give you what you want. Well, it's unlikely."

"I don't care. I don't even want to think about what's around the corner. I want to spend time with you. We can worry about the future if it happens."

The desperation in his voice was a shock. Did he care so much about Olivia that he was reduced to begging? If it got any worse, people would start to think he'd been taking lessons from that stalker, Gerry.

"But you need to be with someone who can make you happy and fulfilled."

"You make me happy."

"And... you make me happy."

"So apart from cake, I don't see a problem."

Olivia flopped onto the grass beside him. She sat for a minute gazing out at the fast flowing current of the river. Then she sidled closer, giving him a gentle shove in the side. Her finger traced the space between his knuckles. "You're not going to take no for an answer, are you, Anderson?"

"I can be pretty stubborn when I want to, Merrifield."

Though he had a feeling Olivia could be, too.

She leaned a little closer, looking up into his eyes. Her hand moved slowly onto his knee. A charge of electricity bolted up his leg and into—

Yeah, he probably shouldn't be thinking about her hand when she was being serious like.

"Can we make a deal?" she asked.

"Depends."

"We need to take this slow. I'm not saying we're back together or anything. I'm saying let's see. 'Cause I'm not convinced I can do it and I don't want to let you down."

"You're not convinced how much you like me?"

"Oh, I'm pretty convinced about that." She squeezed his thigh and giggled when he winced.

Damn, but she was infuriating.

"I'm saying, I need time to get my head sorted."

Right. More bloody time. At this rate he'd be seventy before he got laid again. Maybe he should engage the services of a shrink? He might need one by the time she made up her mind. Unless, he could do a little subtle convincing himself, of course.

*****

Cole fell through the back door panting and stopped in front of the fridge. Having stopped to talk to Olivia, he'd tortured himself by running home at double speed, surprising himself with the spring that was in his step now there was some hope for a relationship between them. It wasn't that he was frantic about it or anything. Any other time he probably would have cut his losses and moved on but Olivia was special. Everything about her made him feel alive — her walk (or limp), the cute wrinkle she got in the top right of her forehead when she was being serious, even the cake addiction. Some blokes would find baggage like the stuff she'd shared a turn off but, hey, he had skeletons. Didn't everyone?

He reached into the fridge and pulled out a large bottle filled with water. Not bothering with a glass he tilted the bottle and took a few hefty gulps.

"You were gone a while."

Adelaide came into the kitchen, Lulu trailing behind her.

His heart rate beginning to return to normal, Cole took another swig of water and wiped his hand over his mouth.

"That's totally disgusting you know. If Mum catches you, you'll be for it."

Cole wiped the 'germs' from the neck of the bottle with his shirt. "There. All fixed."

"Oh my God, you're revolting." Adelaide snatched the bottle from Cole's hands and took it to the sink. She tipped out the water and rinsed the bottle under the hot tap before refilling it.

"I saw Olivia," Cole said.

"What, then?"

"She was out for a run too. She's so thin. How is it that women can get so thin so quickly?"

Adelaide stopped, her hand on the fridge door. "Maybe she's been upset. Worry can tend to make a girl go one of two ways — either you comfort eat or you stop eating entirely. Did you speak to her?"

"Yeah. We had a good chat. She did seem sad."

"I'd be sad if I had to deal with the stuff she's been through lately. It's all over town. Imagine if Mum waltzed in and told us she was having a baby with one of my exes. The mind boggles."

"Mum's way past child-bearing age. And you don't have any exes."

"Very funny. And not the point. Did Olivia say anything about the two of you?"

"It was mentioned."

"But you're not going to tell me?"

"Not right now. Let's say we came to an understanding. But she wants to take it slow."

Adelaide's eyes lit up. "*Ohhh*. She wants you to woo her. This is so up your alley, Cole. You can do wooing. Let's make a list right now."

"Of what?"

"Ways to win Olivia's heart. You could start with a personalised cupcake."

Not the wisest move considering what Olivia had told him. Even a low fat one would probably end up as pie on his face.

"I was thinking of a more subtle approach...."

He wasn't, but if it would stop Adelaide from going gung ho into matchmaker mode then that's how he'd do it.

Adelaide went to the dresser and pulled out a pad and pen. Returning to the table, she sat next to her brother at the kitchen table, her pen poised to write.

"This is perfect timing, too. With Mum and I off back to Perth in a couple of weeks you'll have the house to yourself. This can be like a project."

"Are you thinking Olivia and I may need alone time?" Despite himself, he grinned.

"Well, of course. So, number one...." Adelaide wrapped her arm around the pad so he couldn't see and began to scribble furiously. She stopped every now and then to nod or titter to herself. It was as if every girlish fantasy she'd ever read in those silly romance books she adored was being brought to life in her list. God knows what he was in for.

After ten minutes, Cole took the pad and began to read.

"No. No and no. Definitely not."

He was not going to be seen carrying swags of red roses and spouting love poetry outside the door of Doggie Divas. The townsfolk would start talking about him for reasons other than his shorts if he did that. Nor would he be dressing up in some monkey suit and taking her dancing in the city. Neither Olivia nor he could dance. Her crutches were testament to that.

"What about the picnic idea?" Adelaide asked. "Every girl loves a picnic."

"We were going to go to the falls but it never eventuated."

Cole's eyes scanned the rest of the list. There were a couple of possibilities and one of them, he was almost certain would make Olivia change her mind.

Chapter 26

I was right in the middle of this amazing dream where someone — I don't know who but they were nice — was about to tell me something of extreme importance, when my phone chirruped. It was Sunday. My only day to sleep in. I was trying to make the most of it. Unfortunately, I'd already been interrupted by Alice who'd come to collect a few things she'd left behind, then Mrs Tanner playing Neil Diamond at full volume with the window open and, finally, a group of Seventh Day Adventists who were desperate for me to convert.

Chirrup.

There it went again.

With a groan, I opened one eye and leaned over to pick it up. Okay, so it was 11.30am, probably a respectable time for someone to message me but seriously... I flicked to the messages.

Mum.

<Are you at home?>

<Yeah. Why?>

<Are you sure?>

I looked around the crumpled bed sheets. Yep, definitely at home. Alone.

<Pretty sure. Why?>

<Have you been hypnotising yourself again? You know it can only lead to disaster>

<I haven't been hypnotising myself. Why?>

I stopped short at adding maybe she could do with some hypnosis. Or medication.

<I've been knocking on the door for five minutes>

Ah. That explained it. Pulling on my dressing gown, I ran down the hall. Whatever it was, it had better be good.

I opened the door. Mum was standing on the doorstep wearing exercise gear consisting of purple sandshoes, a pair of turquoise coloured three-quarter leggings and a singlet top that emphasised her baby bump. And in case I didn't know she was pregnant, the top bore the slogan 'Baby On Board'.

Which sort of rhymed with 'Oh my lord'.

It was almost as bad as the 'My Family' stickers she on the back of her car — the ones that showed cartoon versions of me, her and dad... leaning on his gravestone.

Without waiting for an invitation, Mum pushed past me, wailing. A waft of her favourite Jennifer Lopez perfume hung in the air as I followed her to the kitchen where she sat at the table and threw her head into her hands. The sobs got louder.

"My life is over."

I sat down beside her, offering her a tissue from the box on the corner before getting up to put the kettle on. Looked like I wasn't getting back to my dream anytime soon.

"And good morning to you too, Mum."

Mum snatched a tissue from the box and dabbed it to her eyes. Her makeup usually always so carefully applied, even early in the morning, showed streaks of tears. Her eyes were puffy.

"Didn't you hear me?"

Well, of course I had. Her histrionics could probably be heard in Perth she was carrying on so.

"I did. I thought you might like a cup of tea before you die."

"Sometimes I wonder if you were switched at birth, you're so callous."

She wasn't the only one who had wondered that. I was certainly not a chip off the old block. I never wailed as loud as she did. Well, I hoped I didn't.

I put two teabags in mugs, added extra sugar — clearly, I was going to need the energy — and took the tea to the table. Mum was still crying. I reached over and squeezed her arm. I gave it a little rub and a sympathetic sort of smile. Hugs were not our thing. Never had been.

"Tell me about it."

"Connor's left me."

I stopped, mid-sip, nearly choking on the scalding tea. He'd done it again. I knew this would happen. I knew it all along. Slimy, sleazy piece of work.

"The absolute bastard. When did this happen?"

Mum fished her mobile from her handbag and slid it across the table to me. Surely, even Connor couldn't be so low as to dump her via text. She was pregnant.

I opened up the message sent forty minutes previously.

<My darling Bettina>

Yeah right. In a minute he was going to say she was too wrinkly.

<I hate to do this but I'm breaking up with you. I've simply realised I'm not ready to be a father>

As I'd predicted. Worm.

<Also the age gap between us is too noticeable for me to get past>

Huh! He hadn't had much trouble getting past it when they'd been in bed together.

There was a text from Mum then.

\<Is this some kind of a joke?\>

\<No\>

\<What about the baby?\>

\<I'll sign my parental rights over to you. I don't want a baby\>

\<The wedding?\>

\<You haven't paid a deposit for the venue have you? Should be easy enough to cancel\>

\<But I've ordered the cake\>

\<Keep it for your 50°. Fruit cake never goes off\>

There was a final cutting blow.

\<By the way, can I have the ring back? I met this great girl on Instagram. SexyKelly19. I leave for Singapore tomorrow\>

There was no need to look up SexyKelly19's Instagram account to know she was probably nineteen with massive boobs or rich. Or both. Mum had been another notch in the bedpost that was Connor's. It was a wonder his bed could keep standing with the amount of wood that must have been carved out of it by now.

I handed the phone to Mum. She looked as if she were torn between throwing it against the wall and doing the sensible thing. I was glad when she tossed it back in her bag.

"Oh Mum—"

"You don't have to say 'I told you so'."

"I wasn't going to. I was going to say how sorry I am. I know I didn't approve of yours and Connor's relationship but I was willing to accept it if it made you happy."

"You won't have to worry about that now."

"Guess not. But look on the bright side; you're going to have a gorgeous baby in a few months time. I'd love to help you. You know I would."

It only hit me in that moment that I *did* want to help. I was going to have a little brother or sister. Being with my family and being happy was the most important thing. Yes, it was unconventional and people would talk to begin with but I didn't care. If I couldn't have a baby of my own, I'd do everything I could to be a part of this new baby's life. Along with Ethan, it'd be like having two kids but without the hassle.

"Do you mean that, darling?"

Mum had sparked up. There was a twinkle in her eye.

"I can't wait for the baby to be born."

Now Mum started to cry again. Seriously, her emotions seemed to be swinging faster than a pendulum on a clock but I suppose that was hormones. I leaned over and we hugged — yes, even though we don't do hugs there was hugging and tears. Tears of joy, from both of us.

"And if Connor Bishop comes back to town and expects to see the baby," I said, pulling away at last, "I'll personally chase him away with the dog clippers."

The whole of Merrifield knew how anal Connor was about his hair. He'd run to Sydney if he thought someone was going to touch it.

Chapter 27

A couple of weekends later, Alice and Jed invited me to Karaoke Night at the footy club. It was to be a farewell of sorts for Adelaide and Ella who were going back to the city now that Death By Cupcake was up and running. The plan had always been for them to return and for Cole to hire a local girl to replace them. Shannon-down-from-Perth had settled into her new role as cupcake connoisseur nicely. She'd even begun to suggest new flavours for future cakes. What Cole would do now alone in the big house on the hill would be anyone's guess, though. You couldn't hire a family. He'd rattle around like a marble in an empty suitcase.

I adored anything to do with karaoke — the tacky songs, the movies made about it, but mostly the fact that seemingly sane people suddenly thought they'd developed the vocal chords of Celine Dion. It was fun watching Jim the Butcher do his version of Elvis complete with the suit. If Elvis ever heard it, I'm fairly positive he would have blocked his ears from the grave. Not that I was one to talk. I could keep a tune but I certainly wasn't going to be auditioning for *The Voice* any time soon.

Mum and I got to the club after 8pm. Now that I was on board with the whole baby thing, I was taking extra care of her. I was trying hard to get our relationship back to the way it used to be before Connor cocked it up. I'd made her an appointment with the best baby doctor in Perth and on the way home I'd bought her tonnes of pampering things and a few outfits. Though, I should say that selfishly, the outfits were more for my benefit. Mum had a great figure but I wasn't sure the world was ready for eighties maternity outfits to make a comeback. Pink fluorescent tunic tops with massive shoulder pads did not look good with bike shorts. No matter what her legs were like. For once, she didn't protest. I think she knew it was my way of making amends and she was trying to do the same.

We did a circle of the room, stopped to say a few hellos and at last, found Alice and Jed and sat at the table they'd reserved for us. Alice was back to her usual gorgeous self, now that the anniversary fiasco was over. She kept touching Jed's arm or leaning over to kiss his cheek like they'd only recently got together. It was nice to have my favourite couple back on track again. And my house felt much homelier when I didn't have to hang my underwear according to colour or nag about pots and pans.

Jed stood up and fished his wallet out of his pocket. "Drinks, ladies?"

Alice gave him her empty glass and asked for another of the same.

"Lemonade for me." It was cute how Mum rubbed her hand over her belly as she said it. She was looking forward to the birth.

"I'll have a vodka, thanks," I said.

Jed gave a chuckle as he headed for the bar. "I didn't need to ask, did I? Do you want them to water it down?"

So rude! It wasn't my fault I couldn't handle my liquor. And since I'd gotten thinner, the problem had only seemed to compound.

"I think I'll be fine thanks."

I turned to Alice. "Has Jim done his thing yet?"

"Nope. But Shannon-Down-From-Perth did a fabulous job of 'Holding Out For A Hero'. She even had moves this year. And Jane and Beth were hilarious singing 'I Will Survive'. It was like a nanna girl band."

I looked over to where Jane and Beth were standing at the bar in their matching sequinned, one-size-clearly-doesn't-fit all jumpsuits. I wished I'd been there early enough to see it. Beth was a mover and shaker in all the wrong ways. "At least they've moved on from Diana Ross." I giggled. "'Chain Reaction' was stuck in my head for over a week after last year."

Alice leant closer to us. "Cole's here."

Well, duh, of course he was. It was a farewell for his mother and sister.

She nodded towards a table where Cole was sitting with Ella, Adelaide and a couple who looked like they were from out of town. "He looks handsome tonight, I think he's spruced himself up for you."

He did indeed. My heart gave a flutter of approval.

"That boy doesn't need any sprucing," Mum said. "What he needs is a good root."

"Mum. Please."

The more pregnant she got the more unfiltered her mouth became.

"But he does. I thought you'd have seen to that by now. He won't stick around forever, you know. A man with looks like his can have any woman he wants. And the way those women traipse in and out of his shop there'd have to be temptation."

And what was I saying about being nice to my mother?

"We're taking it slow," I replied.

"Piffle. If you take it any slower, he'll be pushing up daisies."

"Right. Thanks. I'll remember that."

Was it too early to ask for a double vodka?

"It doesn't look like Cole's intending on taking it slow," Alice said, indicating the stage where the man in question had stepped up and was fiddling with the dials on the karaoke machine. "Look."

In the time we'd begun to talk about him, Cole had somehow managed to change into a costume. Okay, well he'd slipped on a leather biker jacket, a pair of retro shades and had slicked back his hair. The intro to the song he'd chosen had began to play. He walked up to the microphone and gripped it like he was about to make love to it.

"Oh my Lord, he's channelling Patrick Swayze." Mum's mouth fell to the table. Her lemonade glass tilted in her hand, the liquid spilling over her new top. I think she thought Cole *was* Johnny Castle. "Has he seen the stage show?"

"A long time back, I think."

Up on the stage, Cole had begun to sing the theme song from *Dirty Dancing*. He didn't move. He didn't blink an eyelid, not even when the netball girls began to squeal like they were front row at a One Direction concert. He kept warbling 'I've had the time of my liiiiife,' with his eyes trained on mine.

"No prizes for guessing who this is dedicated to," Alice whispered.

"Shut up."

Cole continued to sing as the crowd egged him on, whooping and hollering at every note that passed his lips. I wished it'd stop.

Not the whooping, but the singing.

Cole's singing was truly appalling. It was absolutely gorgeous and very flattering that he was doing it but so truly appalling I could feel myself cringing. Especially when he whisked the microphone from the stand and leapt ala Patrick Swayze into the crowd, dancing towards me. My eyes were glued to his gyrating body. My head was shouting 'no, make it stop'. I embarrassed for myself but I was even more embarrassed for him.

The crowd began to clap in time. They formed a circle. Someone pulled my chair —with me on it — away from my table so I had a better view, God help me. I don't know what they expected us to do when Cole reached me but if they thought he was going to hoist me into the air and hover me above his head like Baby, they had another thing coming.

The song changed. Cole upped the tempo. Now, he was singing The Black Keys, 'Lonely Boy' and the crowd were joining in on the chorus — the bit about having a love that kept him waiting. He sank to his knees crooning like he'd watched one too many Michael Bublé DVDs.

"Oh. My. God. This is better than Jed's dancing lessons," I heard Alice yell as she pumped her fist in time with the music. "It's like being at a live concert."

"So adorable," Mum added.

You mean, so humiliating. Every molecule of blood had left my body and taken up residence in my head. My ears were tingling. My temples were pounding. My cheeks felt like I'd stuck my head in a hot oven. And there was throbbing in parts of my body that should not be talked about in company. I was positive the entire town could see. Yet I couldn't avert my eyes and I couldn't get the goofy smile off my face.

Absolutely mortifying, yet strangely sweet.

"I think it's safe to say Cole likes you," Alice said, after the song was over and Cole had returned to the stage to hand the microphone over and take a bow.

"I can't believe he did that. He must have practised for weeks." Despite the fact that I wanted to slip under the table and die I was extremely flattered by what he'd done. Not to mention rather turned on.

Jed returned with the drinks. After handing them out he sat down next to Alice, his hand on her thigh. "Wow. Cole's not afraid to put it out there is he? Are you going to sing tonight too, Livvy?"

"That'd be a big NO."

"Why not? You've got a great voice. I could line a song up for you now. How about 'I Will Always Love You'?" He gave me an evil smirk.

"How about not." I took a gulp of my drink.

It was about then that Cole appeared beside me. His hair was still slicked back and he'd lost the biker jacket but, boy, he looked handsome. My very own Patrick Swayze.

Well, not exactly mine. Maybe one day.

He gave me a tentative grin. "Can I sit down?"

I shuffled over to share the seat of my chair with him.

"I liked the song."

"Songs. I've been learning the lyrics for over a month."

"What? You mean you didn't already know the *Dirty Dancing* song?"

"I'm more of a *Grease* man when it comes to songs."

"Please tell me you're not going to get up and do 'Greased Lightning' for an encore."

"I'm never singing in public again. I stink as a singer."

At least he knew. It would have been hard to break it to him.

"Why'd you do it then?"

In my chest, my heart did a little flip. I thought I knew why he'd done it but I still wanted to hear him say the words.

"I did it for you. I know you love that movie."

"Thank you. You made my night."

"That's not the only surprise I've got." He reached into his pocket and pulled out an envelope, which he handed to me. Inside it were two tickets to see the new stage show of *Dirty Dancing*. "I thought we could go together. If things don't work out you can always go with Alice. It's not till after Christmas."

"But why? It's not my birthday."

"I wanted to. You've had a rough time lately. It'll do you good to get out of town for a weekend. Chill out. Have fun."

"You're the nicest man ever." I reached across, taking his hand in mine. I'd never had a boyfriend who'd been as considerate as this. Cole had put so much thought into this gift.

"I know."

"Humble too."

"Can I have a kiss?"

My lips pressed together. He was tickling the palm of my hand and it was difficult to stifle the giggle. I leant into his ear. "Not here."

His fingers pressed into my palm again. "Later?"

"If you play your cards right."

"Can I give you a lift home?"

"I'd like that." I returned the squeeze on his hand. I liked this game we were playing. I wanted it to go on and on. I also wanted Cole to kiss me and that was the best feeling.

After a bit, Cole went to the bar to get the next round of drinks. It seemed like he'd had enough of being the man of the hour. With Mum and Alice *oohing* and *ahhing* over his thoughtfulness and practically setting the date for the wedding, I could understand why. It was the sort of pressure I felt at times.

"How's the pregnancy going, Bettina?" Alice asked, after the excitement had settled. "You look very well. Glowing."

Mum straightened in her chair. "Very well, thank you Alice. The baby has been kicking a lot."

"That's exciting. Do you know the sex?"

"I do but I'm not sharing it with anyone but Olivia. Imagine if I went around spouting about baby girls and buying clothes and it turned out to be a boy? It's been known to happen."

"Are you enjoying pregnancy the second time around?"

"Everything has changed so much since I carried Olivia, it's as if I'm a new mum again. There are so many rules these days about what you can eat and what you can do. Back in the day, you gave up smoking and drinking and everything was fine. Now I can't even have a coffee without a doctor's certificate."

"I s'pose the rules are even more stringent when you're at the age you are," Jed piped in.

Mum balked. I saw her eyes narrow. If there was one subject that was taboo with her, it was her age. "I'm not exactly over the hill."

"No, but you're not running up it either. Aren't you concerned what people are going to say? You'll forever be mistaken as the kid's grandmother."

"I'm aware of that."

"But you don't care? 'Cause if this is about being lonely since Mr. Merrifield passed over why don't you buy another cat?"

I smothered the gasp that had built in my throat. Jed had no right to give his opinion. It was none of his business.

"It has nothing to do with being lonely." Mum had a glint of a tear in her eye.

"It's everything to do with being lonely," he continued. "It's selfish to bring a kid into the world if you haven't considered any future but your own."

Oh my God. Where did he get off?

"I think it's time we changed the conversation." I threw Jed my stoniest, most disapproving glare. "After you apologise to my mother for being such a bastard, that is."

Mum raised a hand. "No, let him go on. I want to hear what he has to say."

Maybe so, but I didn't. Enough was enough.

Mum looked Jed straight in the eye. "Are you saying I should have an... an abortion?"

Jed's gaze fell to my mother's ever expanding stomach. "Even if I advocated abortion, I think it's a bit late for that, don't you? What I'm saying is, it's not you that's going to have to live with this decision. It's that baby. And if there's one sure way to screw up a little life it's to bring it into the world with a shitload of baggage around its little neck."

Tears were rolling down Mum's cheeks. She pulled a hanky from her handbag and dabbed them away. I put my arm around her shoulder and rubbed her arm. "I think it's time for you to go and see what the cricket guys are up to, Jed."

"Why? What did I do? I'm only saying what everyone else is afraid to. The whole town is talking behind your back."

"Now, Jed," Alice hissed.

He drained his drink and made for the corner mumbling away to himself about hormonal women and only making conversation as he went.

Alice turned back to us. "Sorry about him, he's such a moron sometimes."

"I understand," Mum said. She sniffed and wiped her eyes again. Then she took a sip of lemonade and a long slow breath.

"I'm going to have to face a lot more of that in the coming months and then after the baby's born. People have already stopped to stare when I go into the library. The other day I heard Elaine and Jane saying it was 'disgusting' to be doing such a thing at my age. And Judy Di Marco won't even speak to me. She deliberately crossed the road to avoid me. They're meant to be my friends."

This was awful. A thing that was meant to be joyous was dividing the community. And Mum had been keeping this knowledge inside, suffering in silence, pretending their actions weren't affecting her. I wanted to strangle each and every one of them. I did. Where was the support? The love? Were they so shallow that they couldn't rise above the narrow mindedness of others?

"Oh Mum. Forget about them. You have me."

"And me," Alice chimed in. "I can't wait for Ethan to have a playmate."

"And me." Cole had returned and was standing behind us. Clearly, he'd witnessed the conversation. "I think you're very brave to have the baby, Mrs Merrifield and more so to do it as a single parent."

"Bettina."

"Bettina. There's a reason why this baby has been sent to you at this time. You might not know it yet but I'm pretty sure fate has had a hand in this. Look at your family — you and Olivia. There's so much love there. Your baby will have the best life. Ignore those fools."

Mum gave him a coy smile. "Thank you, Cole."

"If there's any way I can be of help, let me know."

"He's pretty good with a nappy." I giggled. "Way better than me."

"That wouldn't be difficult, would it?" Cole let out a belly laugh and we joined in.

Chapter 28

It had been six long months since the night I stepped into the community hall to attend my first Weight Watcher's Meeting and as I stood in the line for my weigh in, I thought about how much had changed since then. The same women were there, still discussing points values and snacks and although they didn't seem a great deal thinner, they sounded happier. Mrs Tanner was still manning the scales. I remembered how scared I'd been to even step in the door, the humiliation I'd felt when I'd acknowledged the heifer I'd become, the sadness that had engulfed me and caused me to eat. Then eat more because I felt guilty for eating in the first place.

Not any more.

I was Olivia Merrifield, nicely curvy, yet thin girl, cake addict and soon to be Weight Watchers graduate.

"Hello, Olivia. You've got a spring in your step tonight," Mrs Tanner said as I stepped up to the scales.

I handed her my membership card but said nothing. Then I stepped on the scales. I watched the numbers tick over.

Mrs Tanner looked up. Her face changed from a look of concentration to a broad smile. She checked my membership card. "Well, young lady, it looks to me as if you've reached your goal weight. As a matter of fact," she checked the scales again and did a quick calculation, "I'd say you're six hundred grams under it."

"Really?"

"If I were you, I'd go out and buy yourself a couple of new pairs of jeans. The ones you're wearing now are at least two sizes too big."

They had been feeling baggy in the crotch area lately, I thought, feeling rather smug all of a sudden.

"And while you're at it, pick up some new knickers. With that lovely Cole sniffing around, you want to be at your best."

Did everyone in town know Cole and I had moved from the slow stroll to the brisk walk?

Mrs Tanner went to her trestle table and came back with a small blue book. She handed it over to me. "Congratulations. This is a milestone not everyone who begins the journey reaches. You are officially in the maintenance phase. You can come to meetings forever without having to pay, as long as you stay within two kilos of your goal weight."

I felt like I'd been presented with a gold medal. I'd done it. I'd really done it.

As I bent down to reach my shoes and slide into them, I felt a tapping on my shoulder. I looked up to see a woman — possibly one of the only people in Merrifield I didn't know — smiling at me. She had a round face and ruddy spend-all-day-outdoors cheeks that puffed up with her grin. Her eyes crinkled cheerfully.

"I don't mean to be rude but I couldn't help but overhear. Did Elaine say you've reached your goal weight?"

"I have." I felt very proud all of a sudden. "In fact, I'm half a kilo under."

"Wow. Do you mind if I ask how much you've lost? You look amazing."

Cue chest puffing a little more. At this rate, I was going to need to get those older, bigger bras out again.

"Twenty kilos."

A quiet buzz began to spread through the remainder of the queue. Clearly, my weight was something to be talked about. And for once, not in a negative way. Then the clapping started. Slow, deliberate clapping that increased in speed as I walked along the queue towards my seat in the meeting area. I felt like I'd won an Oscar. So much so, that if Patrick Dempsey had popped out of the loos to escort me through the door, I wouldn't have batted an eyelid.

Okay. I probably would have. I mean he is super hot.

"You go, girl," one woman said as I passed.

"If you can do it, so can I," said another.

And that's when I dawned on me. I was an inspiration to these women, a motivator. Oh. My. Gosh. I was the exact thing I never thought I'd be six months ago — the perfect poster girl for weight loss success.

I'd done it. *I'd actually done it.*

*****

"You should have seen them," I said, as I sat in Mum's lounge an hour later. "They made me a guard of honour as I left the building."

"I know." Mum dropped a kiss on my forehead and came to sit beside me.

"Mrs Tanner?"

"She sent me a text as soon as you weighed in."

I wondered what she'd been doing behind that trestle table for so long. Sneaky thing.

"I'm so proud of you, possum. You gave yourself a target and you didn't give up till you achieved it. Not many people can say they achieve their goals. You're very determined. That's one of the things I love about you."

I didn't know where this sudden attack of mush had come from but it'd certainly got Mum.

"Er, thanks."

She crossed her ankles and assumed a serious pose. "On that note, I'd like to talk to you about something. I've been mulling it over for a while now and I'd like to know your thoughts."

Oh Lord, she wasn't going to buy a motorbike with a sidecar for the baby, was she? She'd been on about it for weeks, ever since she'd seen a replay of that doco where Billy Connelly rides about the place on one. I bit my lip, praying she was going to ask whether the nursery should be lemon or mint green.

"I think I might adopt the baby out. I'm too old to be a mother again, especially a single one. If Connor had stayed it might have been different but the things Jed said were perfectly true. It's hard enough not looking like mutton dressed as lamb when you're my age but fancy that poor baby going to school and wondering why the other mothers are perky and young and his Mum looks like, well, a granny."

The mug of tea I'd been nursing fell to the carpet, soaking into the leg of my pants as it did. Crap. I raced for the kitchen and began to scrub furiously.

She couldn't be serious, could she? How could she give up her own child?

Mum had followed me into the room. "Are you all right?"

"What? With the burns or the fact that you're going to give my baby sister away?"

"You didn't let me finish explaining."

What the hell was there to explain? Of all the ridiculous ideas, this one took the cake. The motorbike idea would have been better.

"Well. Go on."

"I'd like to give the baby to you. You would adopt it officially."

I straightened, narrowly avoiding the corner of the benchtop as I did. I put my hand to my mouth. I could feel my face wrinkling into a frown but it wasn't one of disapproval, rather absolute and utter confusion.

"We both know the chances of you ever carrying a baby to term are slim, right?"

"*Yeeees.*"

"Well, I saw on *Guiliana & Bill* the other night about how they had another woman carry their baby for them and I figured that I could do the same. I could be your surrogate. This baby obviously isn't your baby, but it has half the same genes as you. The odds are it will have a lot of the same characteristics as you because you're so like me."

Now there was a concept I didn't want to consider.

"You want to... to give... me the baby?"

"Yes. I'll help you out, naturally, but in the role of grandmother. At my time of life, it makes so much more sense and it would make everyone happy. You'd have the baby you've always wanted, I'd be a granny instead of a mummy and the baby would have a vibrant young mum who can climb the slides and take her to ballet. It's the perfect solution."

"Are you sure?" I mean, giving up a baby had to be the hardest thing a mother could do.

"Positive. I've thought about this a lot over the past few days. I think this is the solution."

Flabbergasted. There was no other word to describe the way I felt at that moment. My mother was prepared to make the supreme sacrifice not only for the happiness of her unborn child but for my happiness too. It was so unbelievable. I looked down. The tea towel had fallen onto the floor. My hands were trembling. My whole body was trembling. Tears were streaming from my eyes but I had no idea when they had even started.

"Do you mean it?" I asked, again. I couldn't even fathom that my dream was coming true, well in a few months it would be.

Mum gathered me into her arms. Her hug was warm and comforting. "Of course I mean it, you silly billy. Do you think I'd make a joke of something as serious as this? Besides, your father always said my funny bone was invisible. I don't even get jokes."

I wept into the fabric of Mum's shirt for a long time after that. Then we sat and talked until we began to yawn. Plans were made. Futures were decided. And I was happier than I could ever remember being.

Chapter 29

When I woke up the following morning, the sun was streaming through the window. It was a glorious day. I leaped from bed and raced to the shower. While I lathered my body and washed my hair — three times because the first two had been with cream cleanser meant for my face — I considered the events of the last twenty-four hours. I'd never have believed anything could eclipse the happiness I'd felt at reaching my goal weight. But this, this surpassed my wildest dreams. I still found it hard to believe that it was going to happen.

As I stepped from the shower and dried myself, Cole's words came back to me. He'd said Mum's pregnancy was fate that it had happened for a reason. Maybe he'd been right? It certainly seemed that way.

But how would my decision affect him? He'd fallen in love with the single Olivia. Single, childless Olivia. I know he'd said he wanted more children but it wasn't fair to lumber him with a child that wasn't his, was it? Our relationship could never go further than dating if he didn't want to be a father to this child. That was a lot to ask. And I wasn't sure I could ask it of him.

But whatever became of Cole and I, I knew that the plan Mum and I had come up with was the right one for us. And I was so excited about it, I'd put my trousers on back to front and then caught my knickers in the zipper.

I stopped and pushed the pants and underwear to my ankles, trying to free myself of them without falling over. I was such a dipstick, I thought, how the hell was I going to manage a baby? My attempts with Ethan had been pathetic to say the least. It wouldn't be easy but I had Mum and Alice and I was confident I could make it work because as my weight had melted away, my confidence had returned. I felt like that girl again, the one who had graduated from Uni top of her class and landed a prestigious TV job at her first interview. If I could survive Graeme, Connor and the various other losers that had infiltrated my life at one point or another, I could take care of a child. Whether I'd be doing that as a single parent, well... I guess time would tell.

I arrived at Doggie Divas about twenty minutes later to find Cole leaning against the doorjamb. "Morning, baby."

Baby? That was a new development.

"Morning." I gave him a peck on the cheek and he pulled me closer stealing another kiss as his hand reached around and squeezed my bottom. "I s'pose you want me to call you Johnny now, do you? 'Cause you might look hot in leather, but your vocals need work."

"You cut me to the core."

"You'll get over it."

I laughed and stepped from his embrace to unlock the door. I was buzzing inside but I didn't think it was the right time to bring up the subject of the other 'baby'. Not yet. There was every chance he'd call quits to our relationship when he found out and I was getting used to the idea of him being around again.

Selfish? I guess so. But I did have every intention of telling him. Just not when he was standing there looking at me in that way that made me want to melt, though.

Cole followed me into the shop. "*Ooohh.* Who's full of herself this morning?"

"I'm allowed to be. I reached my goal weight yesterday. I am officially a weight loss success." I did a little happy dance around the SALE bins.

Cole grinned and moved closer again. He smelled of lemons and lemon icing. It was delicious. "Does that mean I'm allowed to see you naked with the light on?"

"Possibly."

I might have been thinner but there would probably always be lingering doubts about my body in my mind. It was something I'd have to work on.

"I have news too," Cole announced. "Well, more of a surprise."

"Another one? You do know spoiling me is totally the wrong way to go about winning my heart. Not."

"Have you got a couple of minutes to come across to the shop? I want to show you something."

I could feel my body tense. This was it. The test of how well I was going to maintain my weight probably relied on what happened when I got into that shop. I had to be strong in the face of those Phoebe cupcakes and not give in because what sort of a girlfriend would I be if I couldn't pop in and visit my own boyfriend? I pulled myself up tall and swivelled, heading for the door.

I checked the time on my phone. There was time.

I took a deep breath. I counted to ten in my head. I closed my eyes and recited the mantra I'd invented for myself.

It's only cake. Eggs, flour, milk. It's only cake. Eggs, flour, milk.

When I opened my eyes Cole was looking at me like I actually had lost my marbles. He'd definitely sensed my trepidation.

"I was preparing myself."

"It's only cake, Merrifield. It's not gonna jump up and eat you."

Not exactly what I'd been worried about.

"Right, let's go."

We walked across the street to Death by Cupcake and Cole pushed the door open allowing me to enter first. It was early, the usual busload of tourists hadn't arrived yet and Cole's new shop assistant, Shannon-down-from-Perth, had made herself scarce out the back. I paused for a second, taking in the smell of those delectable cakes and strangely, I didn't feel the need to scoff down every one in sight. That could change, of course. I was at least four arms' lengths away from them.

I took another calming breath, said my mantra a few more times and turned to Cole smiling, because despite my nerves at being within ten feet of cake, I was also rather excited. "So, what's the surprise?"

"This way, madam."

Cole led the way to the display case.

Oh, the cakes were calling me now. I could hear them but I wasn't going to answer because I knew they couldn't talk. They were little blobs of eggs and flour and milk. Very attractive little blobs, all the same.

Cole swept his hand towards to a lone piece of dark, muddy, chocolate cake sitting on a white porcelain plate. It had been garnished with a strawberry, sliced lengthways and fanned out. It was dusted in cocoa and bore a glittered label that read 'Olivia's Chocolate Cake' in silver writing.

Olivia's cake? What the hell was he thinking?

Instantly, my heart began to pump faster. I could literally feel the clamminess in my palms. I tried to swallow and smile but my tongue was a furry tennis ball in my mouth. How could he make me cake? He knew. He absolutely knew what it would do to me.

Cole must have sensed the change in my demeanour because he held up a hand, right as I was about to speak. "Before you go blowing a gasket, let me explain. This is a flourless, sugarless cake. There's nothing in it you can possibly become addicted to and one piece every now and then won't do any harm to your diet."

A flourless cake? Such things did not exist. How could cake be made without flour and sugar? It'd taste revolting. Those ingredients were the whole point of cake.

"What's in it?"

"Dates, some cocoa, that sort of stuff. The dates give it the sweetness without the sugar and they're a fruit so you're technically fulfilling a portion of your 'five and two' for the day. I've tried out a few different recipes but this one's the best. It's bloody delicious, and that's not me talking myself up either."

Dates in a chocolate cake? It was madness. But not as crazy as the fact that Cole had spent who knew how many hours scouring the 'net for recipes and then testing them before deciding on the one in front of us.

"How many is a few?"

"Eight at last count."

"And you tasted them all?"

"Shannon helped. Some of them were effing disgusting. Wouldn't feed them to Lulu. But a couple were okay and the one I've made for you has been tweaked to enhance the flavour and so the texture is extra muddy. I know you like mud cake. You up for it?"

I turned my eyes to the cake. I wanted to try a piece but the nerves were building in my stomach at the idea. "I guess so."

Cole went behind the counter and took the cake from the cabinet. He dipped a knife into hot water and carefully cut two slithers and plated them with a measured dollop of double cream, a strawberry and an extra dusting of cocoa. He handed the first plate to me. "For you."

"Thank you."

I considered the cake for a minute.

"It's fine, Olivia. It can't hurt you." He handed me a sheet of paper that contained the recipe. I glanced at the ingredients. He was right. As usual. There was nothing in that cake that was going to make me want more cake. It was made of disgusting things like coconut oil and almond meal. I didn't even like almonds. In fact, I wasn't so sure I even wanted to eat it.

It looked delicious though.

Taking the spoon, I cut off a portion and some cream and popped it in my mouth. Oh boy. It was heaven.

After months of denying myself, I felt like I'd been given free rein in a chocolate factory complete with a swimming pool filled with chocolate for me to dive into. The cake was moist and smooth and oh, so, chocolaty. I took another mouthful, savouring the flavours before I swallowed.

"Like it?"

I don't know why he had to ask. I was licking my lips in anticipation of the next bite. "I've never tasted cake like it before. Are you sure this is flour and sugar free?" Because no matter what Cole told me, I was sceptical. Something that tasted so good would have to have implications for my hips.

"You saw the ingredients. I wouldn't string you along. The only things in that cake are what's written on that page."

"Well, it's amazing."

"So you think I should add it to the product line? It's not strictly a cupcake but I'm going to try out a few on the weekend to see if the batter holds up when it's done as individual serves."

"Definitely. In fact, I'll even come and help you taste test if you want. As long as we can go for a run beforehand." I was about balance in this new life of mine. All I had to do was work out the points value of that cake and I was set.

"Sounds like a plan. Now I'd best get to work. By the way, I have a favour to ask." Cole stuffed the remainder of his slice into his mouth.

"Yeah?"

He swallowed his cake and put the plate on the cabinet top. His face took on a serious appearance. "It's Phoebe's birthday on Sunday. I know it sounds like I'm a head case but I've had her ashes sitting in a box in my bedroom since she passed away. I was wondering if you knew a pretty place we could scatter them? Somewhere she'd like. And… if you'd come with me to do it?"

There was nothing I'd like more than to provide some moral support after everything Cole had done for me. "I know the perfect place. We can discuss the logistics on Saturday."

"Great."

"Cool."

I handed Cole my empty plate and went up to my tippy-toes, kissing his mouth. "Time to get back to the shop. Fannying around here won't get Mrs Di Marco's dog clipped."

"Pity."

I quirked an eyebrow. "Why?"

"You do fannying so well."

Chapter 30

Olivia's car screeched into the driveway around eleven on Sunday morning and came to a halt millimetres from Cole's front veranda. From the sitting room window, he watched as she flung open the door and dashed up the front stairs like a blonde tornado.

Geez, she was only ten minutes late; it wasn't like the world was going to end. But knowing Olivia, she'd be having a stress attack about it. She was so anal about punctuality, he was finding. Not that he minded. He couldn't stand people who constantly turned up late either. It was one of a number of things he'd found out they had in common which had been something of a surprise to him given she was such a contradiction in terms. How was it even possible to adore troll dolls yet think garden gnomes were creepy? Those ones painted in football team colours were a bloody crack up.

Smiling to himself at the quirkiness of this wonderful girl he'd gotten himself involved with, Cole went to answer the door.

Olivia was panting but her face lit up when he bent to gently peck her lips.

"Sorry I'm late. The dog threw up on the rug. Again. Do you realise how hard it is to get spew from between the pile of a shag pile rug?" She flung her hands in the air as if to demonstrate the difficulty of the situation.

Cole didn't want to think about it. "Next time we have sex in front of the fire, you can be on the bottom."

"Next time? Who said anything about a next time? I have carpet burns on my knees from last night; I'll have you know. If there's to be any next times, it'll be in the comfort of a nice soft bed."

"Party pooper." Cole gave a chuckle.

"Weirdo," Olivia countered.

Cole turned to the hallstand, picking up his car keys, a picnic basket and a violet coloured glittered box that looked as if it had been decorated by a five year old in art class. A very reluctant five year old.

"Is that Phoebe's box?"

Cole could see the amusement in Olivia's eyes. "Don't take the piss. If I'd had my way, Phoebs would have been kept in one of those tasteful karri wood boxes with a brass lock but she wouldn't have it. So I made this one for her. I tried my best. Craft has never been my forte."

"Obviously. Did Phoebe see the box before she passed away?"

"Yes and her reaction was the same as yours. I was going to paint hearts on it but she said she'd rather die than be stuck in a box with love hearts over it. So she ended up supervising while I decorated this one."

"She had a sense of humour, then, that daughter of yours?"

"Crazy kid." He walked to the door. "Ready?"

"Yep. I thought we might take my car. I'm shocking at giving directions. It's better if I follow my own nose rather than pointing yours."

"Okay by me," Cole replied. He pulled the front door shut and they headed for the car.

Olivia flipped the rear door for Cole to dump his gear and ran around to the driver's side. By the time she reached it, Cole had already buckled himself into the passenger seat. She ducked her head and got into the car, swallowing a snort, which he was pretty sure, was because of him.

"You look like a giant sitting on a toadstool," she said.

"I feel like one. This is the smallest car I've ever been in. How the hell do you fit your groceries in?"

"Told you. I don't cook. Therefore, there is no need for groceries."

"Right. Is this place where we're going to far?" His knees were around his neck and his body was practically bent double. He didn't know if he could sit in that position for more than a couple of minutes. He was positive he'd be unable to get out of the car when they got there.

"Put the seat back if you like. It'll give you more leg room."

"I already did."

Olivia giggled. "Oh well. It's only a couple of minutes away. Think you can survive?"

"I hope so. But next time we're going in my car. This is like sitting inside a Legomobile."

Olivia turned the keys and the ignition began to purr. "Let's get going then."

*****

Two or three kilometres out of town, Olivia made a sharp left turn that threw Cole's head against the passenger window. She began to drive down a red gravel track.

Well, it was more of a bumping motion. The crown of Cole's head was so close to the roof of the car, he thought he was going to go flying through the sunroof at one point.

"Where are we going?" He was intrigued. He'd blithely driven up the highway passing the gravel road on numerous occasions but had never noticed it before. There were so many places in town he hadn't had a chance to explore yet, many of them he was sure only locals would know of. Hopefully, Olivia would agree to be his guide on another occasion. They were getting along pretty well. And despite her insistence that she wanted to take the relationship slow, Cole knew she was becoming attached to him, as he was to her. He could see it in her eyes every time they met. There was a certain brightness that hadn't been there before.

"Told you. It's a surprise. I was considering blindfolding you but I heard you were afraid of the dark." She suppressed a smirk. Damn girl seemed to be doing a lot of that today.

"Have you been talking to Adelaide?"

"Only via text."

"Which is plenty enough." Cole reached over and put a hand on Olivia's knee, squeezing it hard on the muscle. "What else did she say?"

"Ouch. I don't think that's any of your business. And torturing me isn't going to make any difference."

"I could withhold privileges."

Not that he would. A minute without his hands on her was like a lifetime. Didn't hurt to string her along, though.

Olivia swiped his hand away. "Two can play that game, Anderson."

She swung the car into a clearing and switched the ignition off. "We're here."

Cole looked around him. He assumed she knew what she was doing 'cause so far, this place was nothing to write home about. Pretty ordinary, in fact. A bunch of eucalypt trees, a few yellow bushy things and a signpost labelled 'Little Bangor Pool' that pointed to a track leading somewhere he couldn't see.

"I know it doesn't look much," Olivia said, "but our destination is a minute or so down that track. And as you can see, it's not exactly suited to cars."

Cole nodded. Didn't look like it was suited much to people either but he'd trust her. If Olivia said she knew the perfect spot to lay Phoebe to rest, then that's what he was going to see a minute or so down that track.

By the time Cole had unwound his body and reached the back of the car, Olivia had already unpacked. She had the picnic basket hooked over her arm and had tossed a red chequered blanket in on top of the food.

"Sure you don't want me to carry that?" Cole asked.

"I'm good. You look after that precious cargo." She indicated the box that held Phoebe's ashes.

As Cole followed Olivia down the narrow track, she chattered away telling him how much she thought he'd love this spot, how she used to come here with her parents when she was younger and about the spectacular scenery. She spent a good five minutes extolling its virtues, or she could have been trying to take his mind off things. Cheeky minx. She must have known this was like the final goodbye for him, that Phoebe was going to be gone forever after he cast her ashes to the wind. Which was a lot healthier than keeping them in a box on the bedside table like he'd been doing. That was bordering on weird; even he knew that.

The track turned a corner and opened into a clearing with trees framing a vista like Cole had never seen before. Holy cow.

Even with the incessant chatter, Olivia had managed to undersell the sheer beauty of the place. It took his breath away. Cole looked to where Olivia stood beside him, grinning.

"Great, huh?"

"I've never seen anything like it."

A sheer cliff face made entirely of boulders smooth from thousands of years of water running over them stretched as high as the eye could see. The water cascaded into a lake — of the brightest emerald green — surrounded by native bush on three sides and rocks where they now stood.

There was a viewing platform made of timber and someone had carved a set of steps into the rock to form seating areas at the side of the pool, so you could sit or dive or whatever. He could imagine Phoebe there, plunging into that water or crawling from it to lie like a mermaid on the rocks. She'd always loved water.

A hand came to rest on his arm. "What do you think?"

"I think it's perfect. Phoebe would have adored this place and I know she's going to love being here for eternity."

"I knew you'd like it. It was one of my favourite places as a kid. I still like it now, though I don't get the chance to come here often."

Cole knew how that felt. Life tended to get in the way. "We'll have to rectify that — once a year on Phoebe's birthday, at least."

Olivia gave him a gentle smile. It was like the whole world shone in her eyes, like she understood everything he'd gone through and was still going through. "I think at least twice a year. Half-birthdays are the best."

What the hell was she on about?

"You know, every six months you have a half birthday? Don't you do that?"

"Can't say I've heard of it."

"Hmph. Must be another one of those things Mum made up so we could have family time. She does that a lot."

"Might be a good tradition to continue." Cole picked up the box of ashes and began to scan the surroundings. "Right. Let's get this thing done then."

"Any ideas where?"

He pointed to the place where the waterfall cascaded into the pool. "There. That looks like the place."

"Great."

He opened the backpack he'd bought and pulled out a small portable CD player. It was old and covered in paint splatters but it would do the trick. And it was the only thing in his house that still ran on batteries. Essential if you were in the middle of nowhere.

"What's that for?"

"Mood music. Phoebs asked me to play it."

"Oh. Right. Well, you carry the ashes and I'll carry the 'boom box'." Olivia tittered, hoisting the thing onto her shoulder. "God, I feel like I should be wearing tiny underpants and prancing around in a rap video showing my bellybutton."

Cole gave a faint smile. "Interesting thought."

Leaving the picnic gear for later, they clambered over the rocks until they came to a large flat splay where Cole sat down. Olivia sat beside him, putting the CD player on the rock beside her. Cole gripped the box. This was it. The time was right, the setting was perfect but now that he was here, he didn't know if he was ready.

"Do you want to be alone?"

"No. I like it that you're here. Stay." He sat for a moment longer, staring at the box.

"Do you want me to do it?" Olivia's voice was soft, comforting.

"No. It's fine. Press play."

Olivia did as he asked. The air around them was filled with the sound of Norah Jones singing 'Somewhere Over the Rainbow.'

Cole stood. He lifted the lid of the box and walked as close to the water as he could go without actually being in the water. A lump, like a baseball, choked in his throat. He felt as if his heart would break in two but it was too late because it already had. Raising his arm, he threw the ashes to the breeze watching as they fluttered and landed in the emerald splashes of the waterfall.

He sank to the ground, his head collapsing on his knees, his hands gripping it as if it would explode. Then he wept.

He wept until there were no more tears.

Chapter 31

"How can I tell him now?"

Mum and I were standing in the pram section of Babies R Us. We were looking at prams — clearly — but we weren't getting very far towards purchasing one because Mum was insistent that it was bad luck to purchase a stroller before the baby was born. Along with not eating strawberries in case the baby was born with a birthmark and avoiding looking at animals in case the baby ended up looking like a monkey or some such, my mother had taken on every superstition in the book. She'd even stopped wearing heels for fear it would give the baby weak ankles. And as for not opening boxes... boy, she was taking it to the limit.

Mum picked up a cute pink grow suit and examined the stitching. "You have to tell him, darling. He's your boyfriend and this is your baby. He has a right to know that if he continues in a relationship with you, his life is going to change in a couple of months."

I knew she was right of course, but since the day at Little Bangor Pool, I'd been reluctant to tell Cole about my adoption agreement with Mum. He'd been so distraught over Phoebe.

How could I lump another baby girl on him? How would that make him feel? I know he'd said he wasn't fussed when I'd explained my childbearing situation and I loved him for the fact that he was able to accept me warts and all. But this was an entirely different kettle of fish. Being around a newly born baby and being asked to care for it would have to bring back memories he didn't want to have.

"I can't tell him. Not yet."

Mum had wandered further down the aisle and stopped in front of a display of beds. "Time's a running out. What do you think of that cot? Isn't it adorable?"

"It's sweet. I like the detailing on the ends. What if I tell Cole and he runs for the hills?"

"Then it wasn't meant to be. But if you don't tell him and he turns up at your house one day to find you changing the nappy of a child that looks remarkably like you, then what? He's going to be a lot more upset. Especially since he was willing to accept that you can't have children."

Another fair point.

"I s'pose I don't want to have to choose between him and the baby."

"It will never come to that."

"How do you know?"

"I know; that's all. Cole's not that sort of man. Tell him. I think you'll be pleasantly surprised."

Mum turned away, suddenly distracted by a display of snow globes, nightlights and other decorating items essential for a baby's bedroom but not before I saw a twinkle in her eye, the type of twinkle that usually got me worried.

She took a porcelain snow globe containing a merry-go-round from the shelf and wound it a couple of times. The tiny striped canopy inside the glass ball began to rotate. The tune of 'Somewhere Over the Rainbow' filtered through tiny holes in the base. "I might get this one. It would look lovely on that chest of drawers we bought."

Oh God. I couldn't listen. All I could think of was Cole sitting on the rocks, sobbing.

"Put it back, Mum."

"Why?"

"Put it back."

"It would be so soothing for the baby."

"No."

"But why?"

"Choose something else. Now."

It would be bad enough if Cole stepped into the house, found me with a baby and decided he wanted nothing to do with a child that wasn't his. He'd never speak to me again if I let my mother put that snow globe into the baby's room.

*****

Late the next afternoon, after I'd watched the final busload of tourists pull away from Death By Cupcake and Mrs Tanner had collected her dog, I stood with the keys to my shop poised against the lock. I'd been thinking about what Mum had said the entire night. I knew I had to tell Cole and that I was being a sook about owning up to it but it seemed to me that Mum knew something I didn't know. Either that or she was up to something. She'd burst through the door like the world was going to end earlier on in the day. Her face had been so twisted with tears, I'd thought she was having a miscarriage and made her sit on the stool out the back while I called the ambulance. It was only after they arrived she informed me — well, us — it was an attack of hormones and she was worried for my future if I didn't break the news to Cole ASAP. Apparently my stars were only aligned for news breaking of any kind for the rest of the week, so time was of the essence.

Honestly, she'd have been better off being worried about her future right about then. I wanted to strangle her for frightening me that way. I don't think the ambulance people were overly impressed either.

But that had been one in a string of crazy events that had me questioning my mother's sanity. She had also rung twice to ask if I'd spoken to Cole yet and became quite hysterical when I told her I hadn't plucked up the courage. I was taken aback by her abruptness, to tell the truth. Mum had been on about avoiding stress for weeks. She didn't want the baby to come out 'all angry'. Yet, there she was blasting me for not giving Cole the heads up about the baby.

So, when you thought about it, I had no choice but to take the bull by the horns. If I didn't, Mum was going to begin a fifteen-minute vigil and I couldn't handle that.

Digging up my courage, I stepped off the kerb and headed for Cole's.

"He's not here, love," Shannon-down-from-Perth told me as I opened the door. "Have you come for your cake?"

"Not today, thanks Shannon." And who'd have thought there'd ever be a day when I'd be turning down cake? The last six months had seen so many changes in my life but that one was the most amazing. "Is Cole coming back?"

"He said he had some stuff to take care of at home. Won't be in till the morning when that reporter's coming." The *Today Tonight* people liked to keep up with Cole's antics in his little cake shop. He could always be relied upon to provide a feel-good story between the sea of rising petrol prices or how to spot a meth lab in your neighbourhood. Plus, I think the fact that he was supremely hot was good for their ratings.

None of that was helping me though. I pulled my phone out of my pocket.

<Are you busy? >

It took a minute before my phone chirruped in reply.

<Just finished dance practice. What's up?>

Ever since the day at the pool Cole had changed too. It was only subtle and I'm fairly sure not everyone would have noticed but he was bursting with something. It was like he'd started on a new course, not taken up dancing — which he hadn't by the way. He was taking the piss again.

<Such a smart mouth>

<That's me. Wanna come over for a bit?>

This was perfect. I hadn't wanted to break the baby news in the middle of the shop. Being alone would make it easier. At least I hoped it would. Quickly I typed my answer.

<Sure. Now? I've finished for the day>

<Whenever you're ready. Not going anywhere>

Within five minutes — give or take, because I had to stop the car once because I was so nervy I almost ran Jane down as she crossed the road with Jim — I pulled into Cole's drive.

He was sitting on the front steps looking very pleased with himself and rather handsome. His hair was mussed the way I liked it and his shoulders filled out the checked shirt he was wearing that was just the right side of cool. He'd forgotten to do the last two buttons up, so I could see the faint trail of hair that led down his torso and into his jeans.

Oh Lord.

I couldn't look. I had to have my wits about me and that view was something of a distraction.

I walked up the steps and sat beside him. "Anderson."

"Merrifield. You look gorgeous today." I probably didn't — one of my earlier clients had cocked his leg on me and there was a large stain on the side of my trousers — but it was nice of him to say so.

"Thanks. You don't look too bad, yourself."

He reached over and squeezed my knee. Damn, I hated it when he did that.

"So are we going to sit here complimenting each other or are you going to tell me the reason for this impromptu visit — apart from wanting my body like crazy of course." He let out a chuckle.

"I do not want your body!"

He threw a disbelieving look at what was clearly a lie.

"All right, I do but that's not the reason I'm here."

"Pity." He moved closer, snaking his hand so it cupped my shoulder. He pulled me nearer. I could feel the warmth in his side and the firm muscles of his thigh. "Am I going to like this reason? Or is this one of *those* talks?"

"Oh shit no! God! I... I."

"*Yeeesss?*"

I had the distinct feeling he was enjoying my discomfort. His eyes were twinkling a tad more cheekily than normal. I swallowed and blurted it out. Everything. The baby, the adoption, the fact that I'd understand if he wanted to end our relationship and the reason I'd been too chicken to tell him sooner.

"I love you. And I'm not saying that to influence you in any way; I wanted you to know it's why I've found it so hard to tell you about the baby. I was afraid you'd break up with me and I love you and I don't want that to happen."

Cole went silent. He removed his arm from around my body and leant back against the heels of his hands. He looked off into the distance.

"Right."

Crap. This couldn't be happening again. He was going to dump me. I'd stuffed up the best thing I'd ever had because I was too weak to tell the truth. Shit. Bum and bugger.

Then he began to speak. "If we're being honest, I guess I should tell you I already knew."

"Pardon?"

"I already knew."

"Knew what? That I was in love with you?"

It figured. I'd never been good at keeping my emotions to myself. I probably had some sign written across my forehead.

"Yeah. That too."

Call me dim but I had no idea what he was on about. What was I missing?

"I knew you were in love with me because I'm in love with you. I have been for ages. It's been sneaking up on me slowly and I can't pinpoint the moment I realised but it's true. I love you and I don't want to be without you."

I could feel that goofy smile spreading across my face but it was tempered with worry. "So what's the rest? You said — 'that, too."

"I knew about the baby. The adoption, I mean."

"How?"

"Before I answer that — and risk you having a meltdown — I think you should come with me."

Cole got up, dusting the bum of his jeans. Then he held out his hand and helped me up. Then he led me into the house. I had no idea what was happening or where we were going. I was so confused but I followed along because I couldn't think of another way to get to the bottom of it. We took the stairs two at a time — great for him, not so easy for me with him grasping my hand like we'd been super-glued together in a prank — and came to a stop on the landing.

"I've found a use for the secret room." He was panting. But then so was I, we'd dashed up those stairs so fast; I'd nearly stripped the carpet from them.

"Go on. Go in." He indicated the door, open a crack.

Reaching across, I pulled the heavy timber door open. I stepped into the room, looking around me. Someone had been busy. Very busy, indeed.

The space I'd loved so much as a child had been redecorated in girlie hues of pink and mauve. The dollhouse had been revamped and the bookshelves painted and filled with every possible toy and book a little girl could want. Chequered and floral bunting swagged the picture rails. A clothes rack filled with dress ups stood under the window next to an old fashioned rocking horse with a chocolate brown mane and a pair of red leather reins. There was even a rocking chair.

The thing that brought tears to my eyes, though, was the oak writing desk. Cole had had it refurbished and painted crisp white.

A colourful blotter protected its surface and a tin of pencils and pens sat next to a writing pad as if they were waiting for someone to sit there.

What the hell was going on? Phoebe was gone. We'd thrown her ashes into Little Bangor Pool. Surely, Cole wasn't suffering from some delusion that she was going to walk through the door and sit at that desk to do her homework? Because he'd misplaced a few of the spanners from his toolshed if that were the case.

"It's beautiful... but... Phoebe's never going to come back. You do know that, don't you?"

Cole gave me a quizzical look. He looked around the room and began to laugh. A great, loud, guttural guffaw of a laugh. "Is there any other woman in the world who could see the signs and yet get it so totally wrong other than you?"

I didn't have to give him my baffled stare. I think he got it.

"Your mother told me about you adopting her baby."

"So?"

"She seems to be suffering from the misconception that you and I are meant for each other. Must be the pregnancy hormones but she thinks we should get married and then the baby will have two parents. I tried to set her straight but she wouldn't have it. She was pretty insistent."

It was official. I was going to kill my mother when I left here. That was after I killed Cole, of course. The cheek of him. Saying we weren't meant for each other.

"Not that it matters what she thinks," he continued, a smile tilting the corners of his mouth. "I agree with her. We're meant to be together, Merrifield — well, I think we are — and I couldn't think of another way to show you that I love you and support your decision to adopt the baby than to decorate this room for you both. My efforts at cooking and being Johnny Castle fell on deaf ears."

Okay, so I was in shock now. My mouth had begun to flap but no words came out. If the window had been open a few Willie Wagtails might have flown in though.

"I want to be a part of yours and the baby's lives." He said this extra slowly, like he was hoping I wasn't going to faint at the thought.

"If that means somewhere down the track we officially become a family, I want that too."

I could feel my brow tightening. "You're saying you want me *and* the baby? Even though you know I'll probably never be able to give you a house full of children."

"Sometimes you behave like a house full of children. I'll cope."

"You don't mind that cake will always be my enemy? That you'll never be able to road test in the house?"

"I thought we'd solved that problem."

"What about the singing? You know I run rings around you at karaoke. And dancing? Can you cope with being the second best entertainer in this relationship?"

He'd moved towards me, gathering me in his strong arms. He was laughing. "I'll give you the singing, but there's no way you're better at dancing than me. You can't even keep upright. Now, if you've run out of objections, I think you should shut up and let me kiss you."

So I did.

Chapter 32

KING OF CUPCAKES FINDS HIS QUEEN

By Barry Bloomsfeld

Over the past twelve months, this reporter has followed the story of Cole Anderson, owner of Death By Cupcake in Merrifield. Regular readers to this page will remember Cole as the father of Phoebe Anderson, delightful Telethon Child of 2011. Sadly, Phoebe passed away in 2012 but to fulfill his daughter's dying wish, Cole has opened a cupcake shop. This reporter is happy to announce that earlier this month Cole's Phoebe cupcake was awarded with Best Cake in Show at the prestigious Perth Cake Bake-Off. Judges from a number of major cooking shows proclaimed it the most exciting new flavour in cake and sources report Cole has been offered a guest spot on Masterchef Australia.

But Cole hasn't only been busy in the kitchen. It appears that, out of the women who've leant on his cake stand over the past year or so, he's fallen for capricious ex-weather girl Olivia Merrifield. Olivia caused a stir after photographs of her shorts — or lack thereof — at The Killers Perth concert were splashed across Twitter.

The photos trended on three continents with the hashtag #bootybabe, a ratings windfall for Channel Seven News who were set to promote her to The Morning Show before she then disappeared from the public eye.

The two celebrated an intimate wedding in the grounds of their renovated Georgian mansion, Oak Hill, last month. Olivia looked stunning in a custom designed gown by Wayne Cooper. Her headpiece was a vintage Chantilly lace veil worn by female members of the Merrifield family. Cole did not disappoint either, donning a Prada dinner suit for the occasion, despite calls for him to make one last appearance as the Reno King. Shortly after, the couple announced the birth of their first child, Anna Phoebe Anderson. The child was delivered via surrogate on June 30th.

Olivia now spends her days caring for their baby. She has returned to the world of journalism, via a blog on parenting which she writes from the small refurbished room Cole decorated for her as a pre-wedding gift. Cole Anderson is busy developing his newest cupcake flavour, to be named after his baby daughter.

THE END

Lindy Dale

Thin Girls Don't Eat Cake

Printed in Great Britain
by Amazon